Praise for

New York Times **and** *USA Today* **Bestselling Author**

Diane Capri

"Full of thrills and tension, but smart and human, too. Kim Otto is a great, great character. I love her."
Lee Child, *#1 World Wide Bestselling Author of Jack Reacher Thrillers*

"[A] welcome surprise... [W]orks from the first page to 'The End'."
Larry King

"Swift pacing and ongoing suspense are always present... [L]ikable protagonist who uses her political connections for a good cause...Readers should eagerly anticipate the next [book]."
Top Pick, Romantic Times

"...offers tense legal drama with courtroom overtones, twisty plot, and loads of Florida atmosphere. Recommended."
Library Journal

"[A] fast-paced legal thriller...energetic prose...an appealing heroine...clever and capable supporting cast...[that will] keep readers waiting for the next [book]."
Publishers Weekly

"Expertise shines on every page."
Margaret Maron, Edgar, Anthony, Agatha and Macavity Award-Winning MWA Grand Master

BULLETPROOF JACK

by DIANE CAPRI

Published by: AugustBooks
http://www.AugustBooks.com

ISBN: 978-1-942633-81-5

Original cover design by: Cory Clubb

Published in the United States of America.

Visit the author website:
http://www.DianeCapri.com

ALSO BY DIANE CAPRI

The Hunt for Jack Reacher Series
(in publication order with Lee Child source books in parentheses)

Don't Know Jack • (The Killing Floor)

Jack in a Box (*novella*)

Jack and Kill (*novella*)

Get Back Jack • (Bad Luck & Trouble)

Jack in the Green (*novella*)

Jack and Joe • (The Enemy)

Deep Cover Jack • (Persuader)

Jack the Reaper • (The Hard Way)

Black Jack • (Running Blind/The Visitor)

Ten Two Jack • (The Midnight Line)

Jack of Spades • (Past Tense)

Prepper Jack • (Die Trying)

Full Metal Jack • (The Affair)

Jack Frost • (61 Hours)

Jack of Hearts • (Worth Dying For)

Straight Jack • (A Wanted Man)

Jack Knife • (Never Go Back)

Lone Star Jack • (Echo Burning)

Bulletproof Jack • (Make Me)

Bet on Jack • (TBA)

The Michael Flint Series:
Blood Trails

Trace Evidence

Ground Truth

The Jess Kimball Thrillers Series

Fatal Distraction

Fatal Demand

Fatal Error

Fatal Fall

Fatal Game

Fatal Bond

Fatal Enemy (*novella*)

Fatal Edge (*novella*)

Fatal Past (*novella*)

Fatal Dawn

The Hunt for Justice Series Due Justice

Twisted Justice

Secret Justice

Wasted Justice

Raw Justice

Mistaken Justice (*novella*)

Cold Justice (*novella*)

False Justice (*novella*)

Fair Justice (*novella*)

True Justice (*novella*)

Night Justice

The Park Hotel Mysteries Series

Reservation with Death

Early Check Out

Room with a Clue

Late Arrival

Short Reads Collections

Hit the Road Jack

Justice Is Served

Fatal Action

CAST OF CHARACTERS

Kim Otto

Carlos Gaspar

Charles Cooper

Lamont Finlay

Travis Russell

Derrick Braxton

Nigel Morin

Lucas Stuart

Liam Stuart

Ace Fox

Ashley Westwood

Michelle Chang

Audrey Ruston

Ira Krause

and

Jack Reacher

Perpetually, for Lee Child, with unrelenting gratitude.

BULLETPROOF
JACK

MAKE ME
By Lee Child

"We can't fight thirty people," Chang said.

Reacher said nothing.

We can't fight thirty people.

To which Reacher's natural response was: *Why the hell not?*

It was in his DNA.

Like breathing.

He was an instinctive brawler.

His greatest strength, and his greatest weakness.

CHAPTER 1

Thursday, June 2
Detroit, Michigan

LUCAS STUART SAUNTERED ALONG Woodward Avenue toward the crowd leaving the Fox Theater. Dressed in charcoal gray silk blazer, slacks, and a silk polo shirt, he blended easily with the theatergoers. No one gave him a second glance as the crowd moved toward the Detroit Athletic Club where Kim Otto was dining tonight with a friend.

Lucas remained acutely aware of his surroundings during the seven-minute walk. Valets ran to the parking lots to collect vehicles. Limo drivers waited halfway down the block. Patrons entered and exited businesses along the route.

He paid close attention to faces, clothes, and especially, behavior.

Which convinced him that he wasn't being followed. No one seemed the least interested in him. Exactly as planned.

Lucas kept a steady pace until he completed the left turn onto East Adams Avenue. Two groups were walking behind him, chatting about the Broadway touring company's performance.

At Witherell Street, Lucas turned right. So did the theatergoers behind him, seeming never to stop for breath as they chatted endlessly, comparing one actor to another in this role and the last.

Lucas turned left onto Aretha Franklin Way, a short walkway named after the Detroit native and musical powerhouse.

Straight ahead, the classic Italianate Detroit Athletic Club welcomed members and guests under a royal blue awning, just as it had done for more than a century.

The new entrance on the side of the building had been added during a renovation a few years back. Most evenings, visitors were funneled through what was once called the side door. But Lucas had confirmed the main door was open for a special event inside tonight.

He noticed no one paying particular attention to him, but he took another quick look across the street toward Detroit's historic Music Hall to confirm.

No one was hiding in the shadows or sauntering nonchalantly out front.

Satisfied, he turned back and stepped inside with a group of others entering at the same time.

Lucas had never visited the Detroit Athletic Club building before, but he'd studied online images and read articles about the structure. He'd soaked up enough knowledge to pass as the guest of a legacy member.

Which should be good enough.

But he didn't need to test that theory.

No one questioned him as he sauntered inside past the grand old entry.

He rode the elevator to the fourth floor with another group of visitors and approached the open double doors leading to the Grill, one of the building's smaller dining rooms.

Lucas stopped at the entrance to scan the tables looking for Otto among the diners. The room was almost full.

No children present. Diners were adults only, males and females, mostly middle-aged, dressed casually but expensively.

Pricey baubles glittered from earlobes, wrists, and around slack-skinned throats. Had he been a thief, he could have lived several years on the proceeds from sale of the jewelry in the room.

He spotted Otto quickly. She was seated facing him. Another woman was seated on her left. A woman Lucas didn't recognize or concern himself with.

Reacher said to convey the information to Otto alone.

Lucas had hoped to do that here surrounded by people she wouldn't want to offend or alarm. Safety in numbers and all that.

But he couldn't approach Otto as long as the other woman was there.

The two had finished their meal and seemed to be wrapping things up. Otto should be available soon enough.

Lucas retreated into a booth at the end of the hallway to wait amid Detroit's glitterati. He'd barely settled into his seat when the burner phone began to vibrate.

He fished the phone from his jacket pocket and quietly murmured, "Yeah."

"Any luck?"

"On track, so far," Lucas replied. "You?"

"Your brother is still missing, if that's what you're asking."

Lucas heard the frustration in his voice. Nothing he could do about it. "Right."

"You haven't heard from him."

"Not yet." He saw Otto and her companion as they exited the dining room. "I'll need to call you back."

Lucas disconnected and dropped the phone into his pocket as they strolled casually past him.

Otto's eyes met his briefly. He stood and stepped into the light to give her a clear view of his face.

Lucas wanted her to recognize him when he approached her. His goal was to talk with her alone and gain her confidence. Reacher said she'd help him. Maybe she would. But not if he provoked her into defensive action.

Lucas smiled and nodded toward her.

Otto nodded in return, but she didn't stop to chat.

Lucas followed the two women discreetly all the way to the valet stand where the companion collected her car. Lucas overheard her.

"Are you sure I can't give you a lift home?"

The two chatted back and forth, briefly debating Otto's desire for a pleasant evening walk or a quick, safe ride.

Lucas held his breath awaiting Otto's decision. He crossed his fingers by his side, as if the childish gesture would make a difference.

If she rejected the ride, he could still approach her outside the club, where people socialized easily with strangers.

If she accepted the ride, he'd be required to risk approaching her at home. Her apartment building was a fortress. It would be more difficult to get in and get out.

All of which was why he'd chosen to meet her at the club.

Lucas preferred the easy way. Plan A was always easier than plan B.

"Dammit," he said, under his breath a moment later, when his crossed fingers failed to produce the desired result.

Otto accepted the ride and slid easily into the woman's midnight blue BMW sedan. They pulled away from the curb, leaving Lucas behind on foot.

He memorized the BMW's license plate number. He'd check ownership later, should it become necessary.

Lucas stood for a moment on the sidewalk. He was in good physical condition. He could hurry along to Otto's apartment and arrive in less than twenty minutes, but rushing would draw attention he wanted to avoid.

Oh, well. It was a lovely night for a walk, after all.

He slid his hands into his front pockets and sauntered along the sidewalk as the BMW increased the distance between them.

The cell phone in his right front pocket bounced against his leg. He carried only one other item.

Lucas hit the redial button on the phone.

He answered right away, slightly breathless, as if he were hustling somewhere. "I've got a lead. It's not solid. But promising."

"Okay. What is it?" Lucas asked.

"Let me check it out first. If it pans out, you can join and maybe even bring Otto with you," he said.

Lucas heard an announcement in the background. "Are you at a train station?"

"Airport. And they're calling my flight. I'll call you as soon as I know something."

"Okay, but—" Lucas stopped speaking when he realized he was talking to dead air.

He disconnected and returned the phone to his pocket, picking up his pace. He wanted to believe he was closer to locating his brother. Which wasn't likely.

His brother was a genius. But he could also be incredibly stupid about normal risks of daily living. Such as protecting his personal safety from those who would harm him.

Lucas had been defending his brother against physical attacks since they were boys. Some things never changed.

As he approached the entrance to Otto's building, Lucas considered hiding the burner phone behind a bush in one of the oversized flowerpots near the front door. He could pick it up again on his way out.

But after he told Otto everything, she'd want to talk privately to his contact. Reacher had spoken directly to him, not to Lucas.

Thus, the phone's sophisticated encryption and the extreme care with which Lucas handled the burner. This one couldn't be lost or stolen or damaged before Otto had a chance to use it. His brother's life depended on Lucas's particular skill set, and it was ever thus.

Lucas stood across the street from Otto's building, watching those who entered and departed. He noted nothing of concern.

He crossed the street in the crosswalk at the traffic light on the corner along with half a dozen pedestrians. He followed along behind them past the front entry door.

He looked through the glass.

A long reception desk was opposite the door. A doorman was normally posted there, but right now, the desk was unmanned. The doorman wouldn't be away very long.

Lucas seized his chance.

He turned his back to the security cameras, neutralized the locking mechanism using the cloned key card in his pocket, and ducked through.

Inside, CCTV cameras were strategically placed and continuously recording. Lucas turned up his collar and dipped his chin, avoiding the cameras as much as possible to conceal his identity.

He hurried toward the elevators.

He'd studied the building's blueprints and property records. Otto's apartment was on one of the higher floors, with a north-facing panoramic view of the city.

The elevator would be easier than the stairs, but more dangerous, too. The doorman was more likely to notice the elevator's movements on one of the screens at his desk. And Lucas could be trapped inside an elevator with no easy escape routes.

He'd lived a good long time in this business precisely because he didn't take unnecessary risks.

Lucas slipped into the stairwell and skipped up the stairs two at a time.

When he reached Otto's floor, his heartbeat was barely elevated, breathing easily.

Lucas adjusted his clothing, patted the burner and the counterfeit key card still resting in his front pocket, opened the heavy fire door, and exited from the stairwell into the hallway.

Otto's apartment was four doors down on his right.

He moved purposefully. As if the doorman had called the resident for permission and he'd stepped out of the elevator on the correct floor. Should nosy neighbors be watching through their peepholes.

Lucas approached Otto's door. It was recessed slightly. There was a doorbell on the right and a wide-angle peephole in the center of the door, fifty-six inches from the floor. Which meant at or near Otto's eye level. She could easily see him by looking through it.

Of course, she'd check first since the doorman hadn't buzzed him up.

Seeing Lucas there, she might not open the door at all. Perhaps she'd call the police or her friends at the FBI allowing him no chance to explain.

Lucas had considered all of the ways this could go wrong. But he'd missed her at her club, and she was in for the night now. Nothing else he could do at this point. Only one choice. Plan B it was.

He stood in the center of the doorway, facing forward, allowing Otto to see him clearly. He wanted her to believe he was no threat to her.

He raised his hand and pressed the doorbell and dropped both hands to his sides.

Lucas heard the bell ringing inside her apartment.

Then he heard a squeaky hinge somewhere behind him on the opposite side of the hallway. Probably a nosy nelly checking on Otto's late-night visitor. An older woman with nothing better to do than watch out for her neighbors, perhaps.

Lucas turned to his left, facing the doorway behind him, intending to reassure the old woman.

He never made it.

The first bullet hit him above his left cheekbone.

His body slumped against Otto's door with a solid thump before he slid down to the carpet, landing on his right side.

The second bullet entered his left temple and exited onto the thick carpet.

Lucas never felt anything again.

CHAPTER 2

Thursday, June 2
Detroit, MI

FBI SPECIAL AGENT KIM Otto had finished her shower and flipped on the television in her bedroom to catch the news, increasing the volume while she dried her hair.

The story was mostly a rehash of what they'd been reporting for days. Deputy Secretary of State Derrick Braxton's controversial trip abroad to the island country of Quan.

North Korea considered Quan a rogue nation belonging rightfully to The Democratic People's Republic of Korea. The United States and the rest of the western world disagreed.

When they first reported Braxton's trip, reporters were mistakenly focusing on Quan Lan, a vacation island paradise owned by Vietnam located in the South China Sea. Fairly quickly, they corrected the error.

Quan, the country, was located in the Sea of Japan. Which made more geographic sense, at least. North Korea had claimed ownership of Quan more than seven decades ago.

But Quan wanted nothing to do with the North Korean regime and steadfastly maintained its independence.

Tensions between Quan and North Korea were high and always had been.

Braxton's current trip to Quan seemed to be pouring fuel on the fire, drawing sharp criticism as well as shining a dangerous spotlight on the tiny country.

Like everyone else, Kim had wondered why Braxton made the trip and what he hoped to accomplish because the cover story simply made zero sense. Kim had operated in Washington, DC long enough to know that there was more going on here than the world was being told.

Not that she'd figure it out tonight.

Kim pressed the off button on the remote and dressed for bed. At home, she wore the same brand of red silk pajamas as when she was on the road. She belted the matching red silk robe and slid her feet into flat red silk mules.

She glanced in the mirror as she passed. "Sometimes you do look like Suzy Wong," she murmured, amused.

After dinner at the club and socializing all evening, she was too wired to sleep.

Kim padded into the kitchen to pour a glass of wine, planning to read for a while before sleep. As she recorked the bottle of Brunello, she heard a solid thump against her front door.

"What the hell?" she murmured, cocking her head to listen for any further disturbance.

Her apartment building was quiet as a tomb. She'd been living here for years and had never met a single one of her neighbors.

Exactly the way she liked it.

No questions asked, no lies told.

Which also meant the noise was definitely not a neighbor looking to borrow a cup of something. Unless the woman liked coffee or wine or microwave popcorn, Kim had nothing to offer anyway.

Kim wasn't expecting a visitor. And if an unexpected one had arrived, the temporary doorman installed downstairs at the front desk would have called up to warn her. That was his job, after all. He was well qualified to perform it expertly.

The regular night guy's replacement might have called while she was in the shower or when she had the television too loud, though. Possibly.

She set the wine glass on the counter and walked to the door. She peered through the peephole into the dimly lit corridor.

Empty. Same as always.

Still, she'd heard the noise. No doubt in her mind.

A dull thud, like a suitcase or a heavy parcel making solid contact with the lower third of the solid steel.

Kim moved toward the small table near the entry and retrieved her off-duty pistol. She lived in this building because security was the tightest she could buy close to the FBI's Field Office.

But she had no illusions about personal safety anywhere in her city.

She lived in Detroit, where the weak were killed and eaten.

Any woman who didn't carry a gun and know how to use it here was a fool with a death wish. Just ask the mayor and the chief of police.

Kim returned to the front door with her weapon and leaned against the door while she used her palm print on the biometric panel to release the door lock.

The mechanism clicked into the open position and the door was immediately shoved inward. Kim braced her feet to use all of her weight against the force of the heavy door, but it pushed her backward relentlessly.

She was losing the battle.

She couldn't shove the door closed again. All she could do was slow its momentum while using it for cover.

When the door opened wide enough, Kim leaned around and looked down.

She blinked to clear her vision. She looked again.

Yes.

A dead man's heavy body and bloody head.

On the floor.

Pushing against her front door.

He was too heavy for her to successfully resist his weight and pressure on the door.

This guy was coming inside.

One way or another.

Kim stepped aside and allowed the body to push the door all the way open.

As the door moved, so did the body.

When the steel hit the doorstop, the man's upper body flopped across her threshold, leaving his lower torso in the hallway.

Kim knelt and checked his carotid pulse. Nothing.

His skin was still warm. He hadn't been dead long.

Kim whipped her head back and forth, peering into the darkened hallway, checking for the shooter.

No one there.

Which didn't mean he wouldn't come back.

She couldn't close the door with the body blocking the threshold. For a moment she considered leveraging his upper torso back into the hallway somehow.

No. A dead man leaning against her door would prompt actions and reactions she wanted to avoid.

Too risky.

Or she could call her boss. Request an extraction.

Cooper would send a small army of agents and technicians to swarm the place like flies on a dead fish.

The briefest of thoughts flashed into her head. Once she'd absorbed it, she couldn't shake the idea.

Cooper watched Kim like a hawk watches a mouse. Since she'd been assigned to find Reacher with that first four o'clock phone call seven months ago, she'd barely had a minute free from Cooper's prying eyes.

Which meant Cooper probably knew about this dead guy already. He'd probably known before she did.

What if he was one of Cooper's guys?

Or what if one of Cooper's guys had killed him?

The shooter was probably long gone. But what if he wasn't?

She couldn't leave her door open indefinitely.

Questions continued to flood her thoughts until she shook her head violently to clear them

"Cooper can wait," she murmured and made a different choice.

She found a pair of surgical gloves in the same drawer where she kept her handgun and pulled them on before she stepped into the hallway.

Blood and brain matter had splattered against her door and onto the carpet, but there was nothing she could do about that now. As the human tissue dried, the mess would be slightly less visible to casual glances in the dim lighting. If she could get the body out of the hallway, the murder might remain undiscovered for a few hours. She hoped.

First things first.

After what seemed an eternity of backbreaking work of shoving and maneuvering the dead weight, panting with the effort, she was able to get him inside and secure the door again.

Kim enabled and reset all of her alarms.

Then she plopped down onto a chair, placed the gun on the table beside her, and stared at the corpse of a man she'd never seen before.

"Who are you? Where did you come from? What did you want? What am I going to do with you?" She asked the first set of a thousand questions as if he might actually answer.

He said nothing.

"Okay. Let's figure this out." Kim found her phone and snapped several photos of the body. The side of his face would be unrecognizable to his own mother, but maybe the tech wizards could reconstruct it well enough to identify the man.

She opened the app on her phone and used it to record his fingerprints and ear prints. She pulled DNA swabs from the drawer, swabbed his blood and the inside of his mouth.

After that, she paused for a couple of sips of the wine. She'd be lucky if she could get him out of her apartment before he started to stink up the place. She really didn't want to move.

Fortified with liquid courage, Kim took a deep breath and bent over the corpse again. She patted him down.

Nothing in any of the jacket pockets. No wallet. No keys.

Nothing in the two back pockets of his trousers.

In his left front pocket she found a flimsy generic key card with no identifying marks on it. The kind hotels issued to unlock electronic door locks. Which was probably how he'd gained entry to the building.

When she had the chance to examine the CCTV footage, she'd confirm. But how could he have come inside?

And where was the damn doorman, anyway? They paid him a small fortune to be sure intruders *never* came inside. When she found the doorman, he'd better have a damn good explanation.

In the man's right front pocket, she found a high-end encrypted burner cell phone. Nothing else.

The phone had been used several times. Kim thumbed through three pages of call logs, beginning six days ago. Friday, May 27.

Every call, coming and going, connected to a single phone number, as if the burner was nothing more than a long-distance walkie-talkie.

The calls were short. None lasted more than ten minutes.

There were no voicemail messages, although the phone seemed to have that capacity. No text messages, either.

The obvious thing to do was to call the number on the call log. But not yet.

She needed to be better informed when she made the call. She might need backup, too, depending on who answered and where he was at the moment.

Hell, the guy at the other end of the phone could be the one who shot the dead man.

She was tired and sleepy, and she needed caffeine. No reason not to knock it back. She wasn't likely to get any sleep for a while anyway.

Kim went into the kitchen and set her phone, her gun, the DNA kits, and the contents of the dead man's pockets onto the table while she made coffee.

When the coffee began to brew, sending the delicious nutty aroma throughout her apartment, she returned her backup pistol to the table near the door.

After that, she took another quick shower to wash off the imagined stench of the dead man.

By that time the coffee was ready and she had developed her preliminary plan.

She poured a cup of hot black java. While it cooled, she collected a special encrypted cell phone from her bag and then returned to her seat.

First things first.

Get the dead body out of her apartment with as little fanfare as possible.

What was the best way to make that happen?

CHAPTER 3

Friday, June 3
Detroit, MI

KIM'S NEIGHBORS WOULD BE sleeping by now. People had to go to work tomorrow.

If the body was extracted in the next couple of hours, she might avoid witnesses posing too many questions.

It might help to know who the man was, but learning his name was her second priority. She already knew the most important essentials.

Mr. X was smart enough to breach her security and make sure he couldn't be easily identified if something went wrong.

He was an operative. No doubt in her mind. But an operative for whom? Government or private citizen? Foreign or domestic?

More importantly, what was his mission? And why did his mission get him killed?

Lastly, for now, what did any of this have to do with Kim?

She tapped her front teeth with her knuckle as she thought about these questions and a slew of others. She sipped her coffee, which had gone cold, making her notice the time.

Her window of opportunity was closing. This guy, whoever he was, had to go.

She flipped on the sophisticated anti-surveillance devices she'd installed to block surveillance inside her home, drew a deep breath for courage, and made the call.

Kim dialed a number she rarely called to reach the second most powerful man she knew.

Special Assistant to the President, Lamont Finlay, PhD, answered Kim's call on the second ring.

"It's very early in the morning, Agent Otto," he said in his deep, rich baritone, over the background noises she couldn't immediately identify.

The kind of voice that belonged on late night radio, she had often mused.

He didn't sound like a man who had been jolted by the phone's ring.

"Did I wake you?" she asked, assuming she had not, even as she was fully aware of the hour.

"We're just landing in Detroit," he replied. "I have a few minutes while we taxi to the gate. What do you need?"

Cell phone calls were electronically jammed while commercial planes were in the air. So he wasn't arriving on a commercial flight.

Which meant he'd be landing at one of the private executive airports nearby.

She'd met with Finlay in a northern suburb of Detroit a few weeks ago, but normally he worked out of DC or New York.

So why was he here in her city this time? And did his visit have anything to do with the dead Mr. X?

Kim ignored the questions her nerves kept piling on. Plenty of time for all of that later. For now, she said directly, "I need an extraction."

"For yourself?" Finlay asked without hesitation.

Which she took to mean he'd forego the embarrassing matters for now. Including the one likely to be top of mind for Finlay. Why didn't she call Cooper?

"No. Mr. X.," she said.

"Does he need medical attention?"

"No," she replied.

Finlay paused slightly. "Where is he now?"

He didn't ask for the man's name or any identifying characteristics.

"Inside my apartment."

She'd hoped to startle him. He gave no indication that she'd succeeded.

But the pause before his response was half a beat longer this time. She imagined he was thinking about logistics.

Finlay was familiar with the city and her building's layout. Removing Mr. X without drawing unwanted attention would be a challenge.

Her building opened onto a busy pedestrian sidewalk, even at this late hour. Traffic along the boulevard out front would be reduced, but still significant enough to pose risks. More risks than any of them wanted to take.

Which meant that Mr. X couldn't be carried or rolled out on a gurney.

There was a back exit leading directly to the parking garage. But that also meant taking Mr. X downstairs in the elevator and through the back lobby on the first floor.

The best option was to lift the body onto the roof and put him in a helo. Which was why Kim had called for the extraction. She could have organized a paramedic team with a gurney and an ambulance easily enough. Acquiring a late-night helo off the books was a bigger problem.

Of course, the next question was where to take the body and what to do with him once he was delivered.

Finlay would be thinking all of this through, just as Kim had already done.

"Okay," Finlay finally said. "Anything else?"

"Yeah," Kim nodded. "We'll need cleanup."

"Okay."

Finlay took everything in and asked no unnecessary questions, as expected. He had proven himself reliable several times before. And he kept secrets for a living.

Kim nodded. She'd made the right choice to call Finlay. Cooper would still be chewing her out at this point.

"I'll meet you at the helipad. What's your ETA?" Kim asked.

She heard him talking to someone else, but the conversation was muffled, and she couldn't make out the words over the background noises the private jet generated as it taxied.

A couple of seconds later, Finlay replied, "Thirty minutes. Max."

"Copy that." Kim checked her watch after he disconnected the call.

She hustled into her bedroom to pack her bag. She pulled her hair back into a ponytail and then twisted it into a low chignon at the base of her neck.

She dressed in jeans, boots, and a leather blazer. She settled her duty weapon into its holster and slid three cell phones into her pockets.

Finlay would be arriving soon.

She sat on the bed, pulled out her laptop, and clicked a few keys to bypass security to get into the CCTV system on the encrypted server.

Kim located the files containing video surveillance for the entire building. She began with the past forty-eight hours. She needed a place to start that made sense.

Mr. X or his killer could have entered the building earlier. But the system was set up to hold forty-eight hours of video in memory and then archive at hour forty-nine.

After she'd located and downloaded the current video, she searched the archives. She accessed and downloaded files for the past thirty days.

She saved the files to her laptop and uploaded them to her secure server. She'd always been a belt-and-suspenders agent. Redundancies had become a staple of her life. They had saved her bacon many times.

After she'd uploaded the video, she sent the fingerprints and the photos she'd captured on her phone to the same place.

She stuffed the DNA tubes with their samples into her breast pocket. She wasn't worried about degradation from her body heat. Samples had lasted more than six million years, even under adverse conditions.

Kim checked her watch.

Finlay would be here soon.

But she had time for a quick look.

She rewound the current video stored on her laptop. She stopped at a point four hours ago, which was an hour before her friend had dropped her off out front.

She remembered the time because she'd glanced at the clock in the BMW just as she left the car.

Kim gulped the last of her cold coffee as she used the fast forward to skim through the footage, looking for three men.

Mr. X.

The man who killed him.

And the lax security guard who was to blame for conditions on the ground.

CHAPTER 4

Friday, June 3
New York, NY

NIGEL MORIN WAS SEATED alone at the bar in the back of his favorite restaurant in New York City when the text came through from Detroit. He'd placed the phone on the bar near his drink when he arrived, where he could easily see the screen.

He looked rumpled and unshaven and tired. Which he was.

It had been a long week. With Braxton's trip to Quan, the media spotlight was shining its blinding glare on everyone at the State Department. The plan was for Brax to use his considerable charm, along with the full power of the US Government, to calm those fears.

For now.

Morin resented the unwanted attention from all sides, and it fell to him to deflect the attacks. Brax didn't give a crap what Morin had to deal with to do his job.

Brax never had cared and never would.

Morin shrugged. Brax was a jerk. Always had been, even back in college. No chance he would change after all these years.

Came with the package. Simple as that.

The bartender set the Perfect Manhattans he'd served while Morin waited to the left of the phone, keeping Morin's line of sight clear.

Eventually, the phone's screen had lit up with the message: *Done.*

A photo was attached. A big chunk of the man's head was blown away. Morin could easily confirm the kill with a single glance.

He sipped the cocktail and held the slight bitterness on his tongue for a few seconds, savoring the result as much as the booze.

Fox was good at his job. The outcome had been assured. Morin had found Fox at the end of a long, tedious, thorough search of the dark web a few years back.

Fox deserved his reputation. He had never failed. Not even remotely.

So Morin hadn't been worried about the elimination of Lucas Stuart.

But Fox's text had come later than expected. Briefly, Morin had wondered about the delay in the way a man wonders why the sun shines or the wind blows. Purely rhetorical.

The job was finished. Nothing else mattered.

Morin pushed the button on the phone to deliver the contract payment to Fox's offshore account. He sipped the Manhattan, waiting.

Twenty minutes later, Fox replied with a thumbs-up.

Payment had been completed, received, and acknowledged. The Lucas Stuart transaction was completed.

Morin nodded and drained his glass.

He wondered vaguely where Fox was now and when he planned to finish the next phase. Fox said the less Morin knew about his means and methods, the better for everyone.

Morin had always accepted the wisdom of those words and Fox had never let him down.

Not once.

Morin pulled two unmarked one-hundred-dollar bills from his pocket and tossed them onto the bar. He gathered the phone and slipped off the stool. The bartender was busy at the other end of the bar, but he acknowledged Morin's cash. Morin waved over his shoulder on his way to the exit.

He stepped outside where the spring evening weather was pleasant but not warm enough. Another month and the concrete jungle would be hotter than Hades.

Morin turned his collar against the cool wind and walked the few blocks toward his favorite riverside park.

A few lovers walked arm in arm along the riverfront. Otherwise, the place was deserted.

Morin stood watching the stars for a few minutes, as if the tranquility was why he'd come here. From his position in the shadows, he took another look around. Then he raised his arm and tossed the phone as far out into the river as he could throw it.

The lightweight plastic arched and fell a satisfying fifty feet or so, plopping down into the deep water. He imagined it floating slowly to the bottom where the river would destroy the electronics and bury the cheap plastic in the muddy garbage already piled there.

Morin shoved his hands into his pockets and set off to walk the last few blocks to his apartment. He pressed the buzzer and waited for the midnight shift doorman to release the door. When the lock clicked open, Morin went inside and trudged to the elevator.

He wouldn't get much sleep tonight and he'd be hung over in the morning. Which would be okay.

He was scheduled to attend another mind-numbing committee meeting at the UN early tomorrow. Keep up appearances, Brax had ordered. Morin had no choice. His was not to reason why and all that claptrap.

Still, committee meetings were nothing but a waste of time. Political theater. Designed to show that the US State Department was willing to play the game.

Nothing of consequence ever happened in those meetings or anywhere else at the UN for that matter. Morin planned to sleep through it.

Unless Fox needed assistance.

Morin didn't expect that to happen. Not for a while, at least. Had the search for Liam Stuart been simple, Morin would have done it already.

Instead, he'd brought Fox into the situation, for good reason.

First things first.

Fox had to find the journalist, on the other side of the country. Which would lead Fox to the foolish scientist.

He had some breathing room before Brax returned. But not much.

CHAPTER 5

Friday, June 3
Near Cleveland, OH

FINLAY HADN'T TURNED UP at Kim's apartment after all.
He'd sent Travis Russell, his Secret Service agent, instead. Which
was much better. Russell didn't make her nervous.

Russell was a member of Finlay's protective detail. Kim had
met him several times before and he was aware of her black ops
Reacher assignment.

All of which made dealing with Russell easier. He asked
few questions and offered little extraneous conversation. Kim
appreciated the focus.

"Where are we taking him?" Kim asked when Russell entered
the security of her apartment.

"Finlay suggested a private mortuary in Cleveland to preserve
secrecy until we identify the body," Russell replied, scanning the
doorway and the body. "Unless you have another preference?"

"No. I'm good with that," she said.

"Cleaners will be along shortly," Russell said. "They'll find
their own way in and out. No evidence will survive. Don't worry."

Kim nodded. "Weekly maintenance service comes on Friday. Your team needs to be done before the regular crew arrives."

"Roger that," Russell replied. He pulled a phone from his pocket and sent a couple of texts. "Looks like he took two gunshots to the head. No exit wound for the forehead shot. Big exit wound for the temple shot. Did you find the bullet?"

"The weapon must have been fitted with a silencer of some sort because I didn't hear the gunshots," Kim said, shaking her head. "Ask your cleaners to look for the bullet in case there's something special about it. Which isn't likely."

"Not likely, I agree. And the pathologist can remove the other one. But sure." Russell sent a third text and then dropped the phone into his pocket.

Russell was younger, bigger, and stronger than Finlay. Which meant Russell had simply brought along a body bag, placed the dead man inside, zipped the bag and lifted the body.

Kim opened the door and followed him down the hallway to the elevator that would take them straight to the helipad on the roof.

Russell had spent not more than five minutes inside Kim's apartment. Another few minutes to load the waiting helicopter with the body bag and Kim's travel and laptop bags.

Russell took the co-pilot seat. Kim was seated behind the pilot. They donned headsets and kept chatter to a bare minimum.

The pilot lifted off and they were in the air while Kim's neighbors should have been sleeping.

She watched as the city of Detroit faded into the distance.

Flight time across Lake Erie from Detroit to Cleveland in the helo would be slightly more than an hour, wheels up to wheels down. A commercial jet would have been faster. But speed wasn't the most important consideration.

The helo landed atop a low-rise concrete building on the eastern outskirts of Cleveland. An orderly hustled out to the helo pushing a gurney, bending low under the rotor wash, and using hand gestures to convey his words, which were blown away in the noise of the big bird.

Russell stepped to the cargo door, opened it, and pulled the body bag toward him. He and the orderly lifted the body bag on each end and placed it solidly on the gurney.

Kim patted her pockets to confirm she'd lost nothing and then pulled her travel bags from the helo. When she was solidly on the ground, Russell flagged the pilot the all-clear-to-depart.

The orderly pulled the gurney toward the entrance door. He swiped the key card hanging around his neck to open the door.

He pushed the gurney inside and held the door open until Russell and Kim followed, unable to talk loud enough to be heard over the roar of the helo lifting into the night sky.

The heavy door closed behind Kim with a solid clang as the locking mechanism clicked into place. She stood still for a few moments in the surreal silence like a deep-sea diver slowly decompressing before reentry.

"The morgue is this way," the orderly said, leading the way through a maze of hallways, pushing the gurney forward.

Russell and Kim walked side-by-side behind the orderly until they came to another locked door. This one had a small sign posted on the wall near the door handle: Authorized Personnel Only.

The orderly swiped his key card again to unlock the room. "Can you hold the door open?" he asked Russell.

"Sure," Russell replied, grabbing the door at a spot several inches above Kim's head.

The orderly wheeled the gurney inside.

Kim followed into a modern morgue decked out with gleaming stainless steel everywhere. If there was a spec of dirt in the room, she didn't see it.

Russell had closed the door behind them and caught up just as the orderly parked the gurney beside one of the exam tables.

"I will leave you here. The pathologist is on his way. You won't need to wait long," he said, nodding on his way out.

"What is this place? Secret lab or something?" Kim asked, not kidding.

"We'll find a spot for talking shortly," Russell said before Kim could ask any more questions. "No ID on this guy. Did you check his pockets and come up empty?"

She nodded. Not quite a lie. Not quite the truth, either.

Russell frowned. "You collected his biometrics back in your apartment, I assume. Have you run everything through the databases?"

Kim shook her head. "Not yet. Haven't had the chance. I thought you could help with that."

Russell gave her a knowing look and a firm nod in response. "Let's see what the doc can tell us. Then we'll get him identified and go from there."

"Sounds like a plan," she replied, just as the mortuary door opened and a man dressed in a white lab coat walked in.

He looked mid-forties. Short blond hair, brown eyes, clean shaven. If he was wearing his own lab coat, the embroidered text over his left breast pocket declared he was Dr. Ryan Samuel.

"Sorry to call on you so late, Dr. Samuel," Kim said when he joined them.

"Let's get this guy on the table and see what we can see," Samuel replied, unzipping the body bag as he talked and pointed with his chin. "Gloves on the cart behind you."

They gloved up and Russell helped Samuel with the heavy lifting. They moved the body from the gurney to the table, leaving the bag behind.

Samuel viewed the man's body carefully from crown to soles without touching him. "Cause of death seems obvious. We don't need a postmortem to know what happened here. Unless you have reason to be skeptical, I'd call it homicide rather than suicide."

"It's rare to see a suicide with two gunshot wounds to the head, but I have seen it happen," Russell said.

"We found no weapon anywhere near the body," Kim replied.

"We're all in agreement, then," Samuel said, standing back from the exam table. "Tell me why you're here."

"The first thing is to identify him," Kim said. "We found no identification in his pockets. We've never seen him before."

"Okay. We can run fingerprints and DNA against the databases quickly. Fingerprints can be done now. DNA will take a bit longer. We can't check dental records unless we have something to compare them to," Samuel replied. "We'll check for birthmarks, tattoos, healed injuries, implants, anything that might give us a positive ID."

"I'm sure it goes without saying that we appreciate your discretion here," Russell said.

"Of course." Samuel nodded. "When do you need the results of the autopsy?"

"What we really need is the ID," Kim exchanged glances with Russell. "After that, we'd like to run ballistics on the bullet when we find a weapon to compare it to. And if there's anything special about the bullet or anything else you find. Otherwise, the full autopsy can wait a bit longer."

Samuel looked at the body again. "I'll let you know when I have something to report."

CHAPTER 6

Friday, June 3
Near Cleveland, OH

KIM FOLLOWED RUSSELL OUT of the mortuary. They walked silently through the building, down the elevator, and into the night.

A slight breeze had picked up while they were inside, moving cold air across Lake Erie and reminding Kim that she should have brought a coat.

"How about coffee?" Russell asked, tilting his head toward a sign down the street advertising an all-night diner.

She nodded and fell into step beside him. What she'd have preferred was a few hours' sleep while Samuel did his work. But she owed Russell now, so if he wanted to talk, she could sleep afterward.

"You've worked with Samuel before?" She asked as they walked west along the sidewalk.

She was pulling her travel bag with her laptop case secured and resting against the long handle. The bag was heavier than it looked, and the sidewalk was cracked, and the wheels caught in the uneven surfaces, jerking her to a halt now and then.

"Yeah, we've used him a couple of times on classified matters. He's reliable enough. We can trust him." He reached the glass door first and pulled it open, allowing Kim to walk through ahead of him. "He might have some answers in a few hours."

The diner was unoccupied, which wasn't surprising given the hour. Too late for dinner. Too early for breakfast.

The cook was in the kitchen behind the counter. His booming voice suggested they take a seat anywhere.

"Coffee?" the cook bellowed over the big griddle's exhaust fans, as if there was no other reason to be in the place at this hour. He was probably right.

"Great," Russell replied with a wave, following Kim to a table in the corner where she could sit with her back to the wall.

They got settled and the cook brought a plastic carafe in one big paw and two thick porcelain mugs in the other. "Cream and sugar?" he asked.

"No thanks," they replied.

"No servers on duty. Just yell if you want anything else," he said on his way back to the kitchen.

Russell sipped his coffee and said nothing as if to convey this was her show and he was playing a supporting role only.

"You're wondering why I didn't call Cooper instead of Finlay," Kim said. "You're also wondering who the dead guy is and why he was shot in my doorway."

Russell nodded. "For starters."

"Right. Well, me, too," Kim said before laying out the facts as she knew them. "I've never seen that guy before. He had no identification on him of any kind. And I didn't know he'd been shot until the shooter was already gone."

"Easy things first. I heard what you told Samuel. You really didn't run his prints or facial recognition? Didn't get the DNA working either?" Russell asked, as if she might have held something back. He saw the answers on her face and shook his head. "You did none of that. Because running things through the FBI could have alerted Cooper."

"Exactly," she replied.

Russell was a federal agent and he worked for Finlay. He was well aware of the capabilities and limitations she operated under.

"You're worried that the guy was either sent by Cooper or killed on Cooper's orders," Russell said as he worked his way through the list of reasonable inferences. "Why do you think Cooper is involved here?"

"My building has tight security. Nobody can walk in off the street unless they have help," Kim replied with a shrug. "Cooper knows where I live, and he knows how to get inside. He watches me every minute of every day. Sometimes I'm gone for weeks at a time, but Cooper would have known I was home. Occam's razor. The simplest answer is probably true."

Russell nodded. "I could play devil's advocate here and argue with you. But let's say you're right. You think this situation has something to do with Reacher?"

Kim lifted her coffee for a sip to cover her surprise.

She hadn't for a moment considered that Reacher might be involved here. She'd had a career, a whole life, before Cooper forced Reacher to become her constant focus.

Did everything in her world need to be about Reacher now?

Kim swallowed and cleared her throat. "Hard to say. Possibly."

"If Cooper's involved, he'll have a flag on the biometrics. I could run them through our systems, but we're all employed by Uncle Sam. Cooper has access to everything I've got, one way or another," Russell said, talking it through. "Want me to try?"

"I have other options. I'll try them first." She shook her head. "But I need to get some sleep. Is there a hotel around here?"

"Yeah. But it's not the Four Seasons, I'll warn you."

"I don't need a full spa experience tonight," she grinned.

"Let's go." Russell pulled a bill from his pocket and tossed it on the table.

He waved to the cook as they left the diner. Russell strode purposefully westward for another block and then turned north. Kim struggled to yank her bag along behind.

They stopped in front of a brick building housing the historic Harrison Hotel, complete with dormers and a turret. They climbed the stairs to the front porch. He opened the door and Kim walked back in time about a hundred years.

The lobby might have been redecorated about 1975. The carpet looked that old and the avocado and gold color scheme confirmed her guess.

"Wait here. And don't worry," Russell teased. "They have indoor plumbing."

He approached the antique reception desk manned by a costumed clerk dressed appropriately for the era. He booked two rooms, collected the room keys, and led the way toward the elevator. He punched the button for the second floor.

"There's no restaurant or room service. But we can go back to the diner in the morning," Russell said when he escorted her to her room, unlocked the door, and handed her the key. "I'm across the hall. You have my number if you need anything."

He turned to go.

"Russell," Kim said. "Thanks for your help tonight. If you talk to Finlay, thank him for me, too."

"Will do," he replied as he unlocked his room and stepped inside.

Kim moved her bags inside and closed and locked the door behind her.

The clock on the bedside table said it was now after five o'clock in the morning. Her former partner, Carlos Gaspar, would be awake and at his desk.

Gaspar rarely slept well. Pain in his right side kept him alert and exhausted most of the time. Which meant he'd probably been available last night, but she'd had no opportunity to contact him before now.

Even if she'd tried.

Which she hadn't.

Because the possibility that Reacher was involved with the dead Mr. X had not occurred to her until Russell mentioned it. Now that the question had been posed, Kim couldn't shake the feeling that Russell was probably right.

She opened her travel bag and found the fresh burner phone she'd stashed there before she left her apartment. She fired it up and dialed one of the encrypted burners she'd sent Gaspar a few weeks ago.

Neither burner phone had been turned on before. Which should mean that Cooper wasn't tracing calls. Not yet anyway.

The phone rang three times before Gaspar picked up, slightly breathless. "Sorry, Sunshine. I had to dig you out of the bottom drawer. Took me a minute."

"No worries, Chico." Kim's tired smile stole onto her face and made her feel a bit better. She pulled her laptop out and fired up her encryption equipment. "I've got a situation. I'm sending you fingerprints, ear prints, and photos of a guy. I need to know who he is."

"Hang on a sec."

She heard a few clacking keystrokes as he prepared to receive her intel. Steady, reliable Gaspar. He'd proven himself more times than she could count. Once again, he didn't disappoint.

"Ready when you are."

"Coming now." Kim connected to her secure server, pulled the data she'd stored there, and transferred it to Gaspar. He'd been her first partner on the Reacher assignment. For medical reasons, he'd retired a few weeks back and taken a job with a high-end private outfit called Scarlett Investigations in Houston.

Kim was devastated when Gaspar left the FBI. But she soon realized that he was a much more valuable asset to her on the outside of the FBI than he'd been on the inside.

Scarlett Investigations was well funded with a client roster of heavy hitters and the means to handle everything Kim could do inside the FBI and a lot more.

Gaspar was no longer handcuffed by the rules and constraints a working FBI Special Agent was subjected to. Which meant he was about a thousand times more valuable than before.

"Got it," he said, clacking the keys on his keyboard. He mumbled the steps as he received the files, opened them, stored the data, and began the real work. "Uploading the fingerprints first. Searching now. Ear prints, more reliable than fingerprints, as you know, going next. Photos last, and going now."

"Anything else?" Gaspar asked. "How about the CCTV in your building. See anything helpful there?"

"No chance to check it yet. But affirmative on physical evidence," she said slowly, looking at the only items she'd pulled off the body. "I've got a key card and no idea what it opens. A couple of DNA swabs. And a burner phone with only one number in the call log. Anything you can do with those?"

"You know I can. But I need physical possession of the DNA and the key card to run them." Gaspar slurped loudly over the phone, which made Kim smile.

He was drinking the sweet Cuban coffee he loved like a kid would drink it. He'd made the noise to lift her spirits and she appreciated it.

She gave him the phone number.

"I'll figure out how to get you the DNA and the key card," Kim yawned. "Can we talk after I get a few hours of shuteye?"

"You bet. I'll be here," he said as he rang off.

Kim glanced longingly at the bed, knowing she was too wired to sleep. She opened her laptop and pulled up her building's CCTV footage. She ran the recordings at triple speed, scanning for the dead man and the shooter.

CHAPTER 7

Friday, June 3
New York, NY

MORIN FIRST AWAKENED WITH the alarm clock blaring in his face half an hour ago. Sunlight entered the room from large windows without blinds. He tried, but he couldn't get back to sleep.

He dragged himself into the shower and downed a couple of cups of coffee while he ignored his wife's droning report of her latest family drama.

There was always something going on with her big extended family and most of it was neither positive nor interesting. Today's babbling report was no exception.

He tuned her out and focused on his own issues.

Morin had heard nothing from Fox since the completion of the first transaction. Flight time from Detroit to Los Angeles on a non-stop Delta jet was less than five hours. He must have reached Los Angeles.

Fox had booked the red eye, departing after midnight. Even with the usual air travel snafus, he'd be on the ground by now. He'd have connected with his ground support and acquired the weapons and equipment he needed to complete the job.

But it was three hours earlier in California where the world was just waking up. Which probably meant Fox hadn't approached the target yet.

The target should be easy to locate and even easier to eliminate.

Ashley Westwood was a journalist. Worked for the *LA Times*. Once upon a time, maybe five years ago, he'd been the science editor.

Until he was demoted for "failures in journalistic integrity." Whatever that meant.

Curiously, the *Times* had kept him employed while shuffling him off the front pages and out of supervisory roles.

Now he called himself a science reporter, a description that seemed to cover a variety of frivolous in-depth reporting slated for the lifestyle and classified sections of the paper.

Three weeks ago, Morin had pulled up the journalist's last dozen articles online.

Most were what Morin would call junk science. Health reports based on fraudulent weight loss supplements and baldness cures and the like.

Westwood's other recent articles were so called "whistleblower accounts," claiming corporations were polluting the drinking water or poisoning employees or pushing bad nutrition for dogs and babies. Things like that.

Click bait. Alarmist and inflammatory and poorly researched and designed to generate the ever elusive buzz that kept the national conversation lively and vacuous.

Nothing new or particularly threatening in most of Westwood's whistleblower pieces.

But Morin *had* found two articles that concerned Brax.

One was published five years ago. It purported to be an exposé of the Dark Web, which the journalist had seemed to confuse with the Deep Web. That alone made Morin wonder how thorough and knowledgeable the guy really was.

But Westwood's shortcomings didn't stop there. His alleged exposé had failed to explain how the Dark Web was a depraved and scary sub-set of the Deep Web.

Five years ago, the Dark Web was a known haven for the kind of illegal activities the *Times* editorial board probably didn't deem suitable for exposure in a family newspaper.

Hell, the Dark Web wasn't a family-friendly place. If anything, the cesspool had grown exponentially more depraved over time.

Because the journalist's Dark Web article was old, Morin might have ignored it. But the internet's search engines made finding old reports like that one a simple matter of a few keystrokes these days.

Which meant Morin simply couldn't afford to let the old one go.

Any barely computer literate intern could find the journalist's poorly drafted article and twist it to suit and destroy. Worse, the journalist might take it into his head to update the prior article. He could write a much better one this time.

No, the stakes were too high to take that risk, on the first Dark Web article alone. Even if that had been the only problem. Which it wasn't.

The bigger problem was presented by the second piece.

The journalist's second article was more recent and based on facts allegedly gleaned from another whistleblower.

This one was an exposé about secret weapons in development by private contractors inside the US.

The gist of it was that government funding was illegally funneled to private firms for the purpose of avoiding oversight and building what the press liked to call the war machine.

Not that this was new information or startling in any way to the well informed.

Most of the world, friends and foes alike, believed secret weapons development was ongoing among warmongers and the scientists who supported them.

Which was actually true.

Governments barely bothered to refute the crazy conspiracy theories. Mostly because those theories were useful.

As long as tinfoil hat types were jousting at fictitious ideas, they were not focused on finding the real threats.

But the real development programs were much more deadly than the fictitious ones. The journalist had come too close to several ongoing projects with the help of his unnamed sources.

There were substantive mistakes in both the older Dark Web and the newer Secret Weapon articles. Which made the whole pieces somewhat less threatening.

Counterintelligence operatives could point out provable errors and cast doubt on the remaining facts.

The mistakes were there. They couldn't be denied. The *Times* did have defenses. Could have been related to bad intel from the whistleblowers. Or maybe the journalist was just plain sloppy.

None of the excuses mattered. The articles were out there for anyone to find. And they did, one way or another, contain top secret intel that simply must not be exploited.

Morin extracted and eliminated both articles from the world wide web, the deep web, and the dark web as well.

Which wasn't like the old days when papers could be burned out of existence.

Digital pieces couldn't be totally removed. People who had already discovered them still existed. The articles had been downloaded and stored in places Morin couldn't even hope to find.

Morin was tracing them as best he could, but the process was difficult. As a practical matter, it would take too long to eliminate all traces of the two articles.

But he could close the loop at the open end and ensure that the journalist didn't write more drivel on the sensitive projects.

Morin knew precisely how to make that happen.

He had hired Fox. Who targeted the journalist, along with his sources, for removal.

The first phase was done. The first target had been eliminated last night in Detroit. Lucas Stuart.

Phase two was well under way. Fox would find the journalist and eliminate both the man and his work soon enough.

Morin eventually noticed the silence in his kitchen. His wife had finally wound down and headed toward the shower.

He flipped on the TV and ran through the various news reports, looking for last night's story.

Several murder reports led the broadcasts in various places around the country.

Not surprising.

Crime rates had been rising for a while almost everywhere.

None of the reported murders Morin found during his quick channel surf were committed in Detroit.

Which could mean that the body hadn't been discovered.

Or the report could have been suppressed.

Or maybe there were too many murders in Detroit last night to report them all.

Could Morin possibly be that lucky?

He grinned briefly.

No chance of Lady Luck striking Morin anytime soon.

He found the new burner phone and checked it for a text from Fox.

Nothing.

Lack of fresh contact from Fox made Morin nervous. He tapped his finger rapidly on the table as he considered what to do next.

Which was when he noticed the time.

Morin dropped the phone into his pocket and refilled his coffee. He put the lid on the cup and took it with him when he left his apartment.

He couldn't be late for his committee meeting at the UN. People would notice. Brax would find out.

There were bean counters and attendance takers everywhere.

And a CCTV camera to record every waking moment around New York City, it seemed.

Morin's alibi would only be established if he showed up and people present at the meeting remembered seeing him there.

He'd need to talk to some of them. Make sure they remembered the conversations.

The best way to make his entrance memorable was to show up after they'd already started. But he couldn't be any later than that.

Morin had hustled halfway to his destination when Fox's phone rang.

Even amid the morning cacophony of traffic and bells and horns and voices along the sidewalks, the sound of the phone's ring tone was jarring.

Fox never called.

Never.

Until this moment, all communication had been disappearing texts only.

Morin fished the phone from his pocket and picked up the call. "Yeah."

"He's headed to Niagara Falls. He's in the air. I'm several hours behind him," Fox said without preamble. "You'll need to set things up."

"Understood." Morin nodded, already worried. This development presented several serious problems.

Fox couldn't fly commercial while carrying weapons and other necessary equipment. He'd need supplies in Ontario.

Which would be challenging.

Guns and ammo and suppressors and all manner of explosives were strictly controlled in Canada.

Morin's thoughts were already tumultuous.

He could arrange things.

But he'd need solitude to do so.

Privacy he wouldn't have for most of the day.

"You've got nine hours to get what we need. I'll send you a list," Fox said, interrupting Morin's chaotic worries. "Leave everything in the back of the SUV parked at the Niagara airport. Text me the exact location. I'll take it from there."

Before Morin could respond, Fox disconnected.

The words and the assumptions were beyond arrogant.

Fox was well aware that even Morin's invisible fingerprints couldn't be found on the methods, means, or results. The job was strictly hands off as far as the State Department or Brax were concerned.

That's why Morin had hired Fox and agreed to his outrageous demands.

Niagara Falls was way too close to New York City for comfort, geographically, diplomatically, and several other ways, too.

Yet, Morin had no choice.

Fox needed support in Niagara.

Without it, the operation would fail.

Failure, Brax had made crystal clear before he left for Quan, was absolutely, positively not an option.

CHAPTER 8

Friday, June 3
Cleveland, OH

AFTER STARING AT THE video footage for a while, Kim had nodded off. When she awakened, the laptop had slid off her lap and onto the bed. She closed the lid and stretched her aching muscles.

She'd left the drapes open, and the morning sun filtered weakly through the dirty windows. Diffused lighting didn't make the decrepit space appear better or cleaner. There was no room service, but a one-cup coffee maker rested on the dresser.

She set the coffee to brew and headed to the shower, wishing she'd brought shower shoes and hoping she wouldn't catch a fungus.

When she emerged from the shower, drying off with the threadbare towel, the weak and tasteless coffee was ready. One sip was all she could stand. She poured the rest down the bathroom sink.

Kim dressed, packed up, and was ready to head out when hard knuckles rapped twice on her door.

"Room service," Russell said.

"You're a lifesaver." She opened the door and offered a grin, accepting the paper cup of hot coffee he offered with an appreciative whiff of its heavenly aroma.

Russell entered her single room and immediately it became too crowded. He left the door open and retreated to the threshold. "Samuel called. He's finished the autopsy. Wants to brief us now because he's headed out of town. Won't be back for a few days, he said."

"I can drink coffee and walk at the same time." Kim nodded as she tossed her hotel room key card onto the dresser. Housekeeping would pick it up later.

He stepped aside as she pulled her travel bag through the door and into the hallway to prove the point.

"You're grumpy when you don't get your coffee," Russell teased as he followed, closing the door behind them.

They walked to the end of the hallway in silence, took the elevator to the first floor.

"I paid the bill already," Russell said, and they walked outside, retracing the route they'd walked last night.

This area of Cleveland seemed mostly abandoned. The sidewalks were not busy. Nor were the streets. Which was okay because it meant she could easily pull the travel bag along without dodging pedestrians, even in the crosswalks.

As they approached the diner, Russell kept walking. "No time for breakfast, I'm afraid."

"I'm not much of a breakfast person," she replied, anxious to reach the private mortuary. "Samuel give you any preview of his findings when he called?"

"He said he'd rather report only once. I didn't get the feeling that he had a lot to say." Russell paused briefly at the corner and then crossed the street.

"I reviewed the CCTV videos from my building yesterday."

"Find anything?"

"Possibly. The victim entered the building about thirty minutes before I found him."

"How'd he get inside? Don't you have a doorman? Was he sleeping or something?"

"All good questions," she grimaced, swigged the last of the coffee, and tossed the empty cup into a trash barrel on the way past. "Wish I could offer equally good answers."

Russell led the way up the stairs to the front door and pressed the call button for Dr. Samuel's suite of rooms. A video cam, correctly positioned, offered someone inside a clear view of the entrance. The door lock was released with a buzz.

Russell opened the door and Kim walked through, pulling her bags across the threshold.

"The doorman was away from the desk. He's a temp. Our regular guy has been out sick for a couple of weeks. I don't know the temporary guy," Kim said, answering Russell's questions while waiting for another elevator.

"Maybe he needed a bathroom break or something," Russell replied.

The elevator arrived. He stepped inside and held the door with his arm while she pulled her bags into the car.

"Possibly." Kim lifted her gaze to the elevator buttons. Samuel's offices were on the fourth floor.

"You think there's a nefarious explanation?"

The elevator door closed slowly, and the old elevator began its creaky ascent.

Kim shrugged. "Mr. X entered using a key card. He kept his face hidden. The cameras didn't get a single clear view of him. Not even after he fell against my front door."

She waited for Russell's analysis, which she expected would confirm hers.

"So not a hapless visitor wandering the hallways looking for the home of a friend or colleague," Russell said slowly. "Not a crime of opportunity, either. He was prepared. He had advance recon on your building and where you lived, how to gain access, and how to avoid discovery once he was inside."

"That's how it looks," she said as the elevator bounced to a stop at the fourth floor and the doors opened wide.

She pulled her bags toward the entrance to Samuel's office.

"What about the shooter? Did you locate him on the video footage?" Russell asked.

Kim stopped at Samuel's door and turned to face him. "I went back two weeks. Couldn't find where the shooter entered my building. He was able to avoid the cameras in my hallway last night, too. Not even a partial view of him before, during, or after the shooting."

Russell cocked his head, pressed the bell, and waited. "So you're thinking the shooter and the victim are both pros. They know what they're doing. They both successfully, but separately, breached your state-of-the-art security, for reasons unknown. One died. The killer escaped."

"Seems like the only reasonable explanation at the moment," Kim replied just before Dr. Samuel opened his office door wearing a clean lab coat and paper booties over his shoes.

"Good morning. Follow me, please," he said, leading the way to the morgue.

Samuel pressed a pass card hanging from a lanyard around his neck, followed by his left palm, to a biometric reader. The frosted glass door lock released with a loud click.

"You can leave your bags there," he said, pointing to a nearby corner where spare personal protective equipment hung on hooks. "You'll want to slip those lab coats and booties on, to save your clothes and reduce trace in the mortuary. Grab gloves as well."

They did as he suggested. The lab coat supplied to Kim was way too big. It covered her from shoulder to ankle. The one Russell donned barely closed in front and hung just above his knees.

"This way," Samuel said, pushing through another set of double frosted glass doors using the same security measures.

They approached a man's body covered to his shoulders by a green paper drape lying prone on a stainless steel table. Dr. Samuel had cleaned the blood from his head, which made him look slightly better than when Kim had found him dead in her doorway.

Seeing him with his head wounds again was startling. She'd almost expected to see the altered images she'd created on her laptop last night.

Human faces are fairly symmetrical. Specialized software could copy the intact side of the face and duplicate it to match on the injured side. Then the software automatically manipulated the images to create a full-face image of her would-be visitor.

The software Kim used wasn't as sophisticated as forensic facial reconstruction systems used by pathology labs. But it served her quick needs well enough.

The computer-generated image could then be run through specialized facial recognition software. The database would rapidly shoot through driver's licenses, passports, mug shots, social media sites, and more to find a match that would identify the corpse.

Gaspar was running the software now, but he had not called with positive results thus far.

Once they got a list of possible victims, they'd seek confirmation using DNA, fingerprint, ear print, or dental records. And anything else they might have access to.

With luck, Kim could know this man's identity in the next few hours.

Or she might never know.

But there was no reason to be fatalistic about this.

At least, not yet.

CHAPTER 9

Friday, June 3
Cleveland, OH

DR. SAMUEL STOOD IN the cold room with both hands stuffed into his pockets, looking at the body on the stainless steel table as if he might simply by force of will cause the dead man to release his secrets.

"So far, he's still a John Doe. We ran his prints and DNA through the various databases we have access to and got no hits," Samuel said. "We have requested dental records from the usual sources, but again, no hits yet."

"Which means he wasn't in the US military, prison system, or the other criminal or civil databases?" Russell asked to clarify.

"Correct. We also checked the INTERPOL AFIS systems," Samuel nodded. "So he's never been arrested or had a job that required fingerprinting, inside the US or in any of the INTERPOL member countries."

"Or if he was, his identity has been removed from the system," Kim said.

Russell nodded. "But he could be a regular Joe who has never had a reason to get his prints on file. There are millions of those people, males and females, walking around the US, not to mention dozens of other countries in the world."

"In which case we may never know who he was," Dr. Samuel said flatly. "Obvious cause of death was two gunshot wounds to the head. The first shot was fatal. There was no need for the second."

"What else can you tell us about him?" Russell asked.

"Nothing to tell. There's nothing unusual about him, medically speaking. He's well nourished, well developed. Mid-forties," Dr. Samuel recited as if he were dictating the autopsy. "Reasonably good muscle fitness. Not a bodybuilder or a runner, but he was in good shape. Nothing remarkable in his tox screen. Nothing in his pockets."

"What about the labels in his clothes?" Kim asked.

"Just your basic global brands made in the far east and worn by everyone everywhere." Dr. Samuel shook his head. "If you'd gone searching for an average white male, this guy would fit the profile in every respect."

Kim looked at Russell, arching her eyebrows in question. He nodded in return.

Bottom line was that they didn't know who this guy was or why he'd been killed after sneaking into Kim's apartment building.

Presumably he'd made the effort to connect with her. Whether he had sinister or benign motives remained unknown.

But Mr. X definitely was not an Average Joe.

He was much too clever in a way that came from expertise and experience with current surveillance equipment and techniques.

He'd known he'd need a key card to enter her building, and he'd figured out how to clone one that worked.

He knew how to hide himself from visible and invisible cameras installed throughout her building. He knew not to take the elevator and how to enter and exit the stairwells without being seen or caught.

All of which proved he had well beyond average skills.

"What about the bullet and bullet wounds, Dr. Samuel?" Kim asked. "Any luck with those?"

"Nothing yet. Both bullets came from the same gun. But we'll need a weapon to compare them to. Find me one to test and I'll put a rush on it," Samuel shook his head, glancing at the clock. "I have a plane to catch. I'll call you as soon as we know anything more."

They followed him out of the mortuary, slid the PPE into a hamper near the exit door, and left Dr. Samuels alone in his office.

"How about I eat some eggs and you tell me what you know so far. Maybe I can help with whatever this is," Russell said after he'd pushed the button to call the elevator car. "If you're worried about Cooper, and you feel he's tracking Finlay, we can avoid both of them for a couple of days. Although it's easier to do this sort of thing when we have some resources."

Kim hesitated. She liked Russell. He'd already proven he was capable and could be trusted.

But he was Finlay's right-hand man. For now, her instincts were to keep both Finlay and Cooper out of the loop. Could she trust Russell to do that?

They walked out into the sunlight again. Russell stopped at the bottom of the stairs, hands at his side, waiting for her decision. "Eggs? Or not?"

"I hate eggs. But the coffee was damned good at that place last night." Kim grinned and headed toward the diner. Russell fell into step beside her.

"Two things I haven't told you," Kim said as they walked.

He smiled. "Only two?"

Kim shrugged. "I found the key card that he used to enter my building in Mr. X's pocket. It's a generic gray plastic electronic card about the size of a credit card. It has no markings on it of any kind. I didn't have a chance to test my theory, but the video surveillance suggests he used that card to bypass the exterior door locks."

"Finlay could probably find out where it came from and who cloned it," Russell said as he held open the door to the diner.

Kim flashed him a warning look on her way to the table they'd occupied a few hours ago. They were the only two customers in the diner, which suited her just fine.

The same cook who had served them before brought coffee and quizzed them for their orders. Russell asked for eggs, bacon, and pancakes. Kim ordered wheat toast and more coffee.

When the cook went back to the griddle, Russell said, "What was the second thing you haven't told me?"

"I found this in his pocket, too." Kim pulled out the special encrypted burner phone that had only been used to communicate with one number. She placed it on the table between them.

Russell did the same quick checks Kim had completed last night. He picked up the phone and ran through the call log. He checked the voicemail and the texts screen, which were both empty. Then he handed the phone back to her and she returned it to her pocket.

"You know Carlos Gaspar, right?" Kim asked.

"Your former partner. Now working with Michael Flint and Scarlett Investigations out of Houston. Solid team. Well trained. Reliable. Committed," Russell replied, sipping the coffee.

Kim nodded, draining her coffee and refilling the plastic mug from the plastic thermal carafe. "I asked Gaspar to run down the guy's phone and the number he's been communicating with."

"What did he find out?"

Just as Russell asked the question, the cook brought the food. After the usual plate shuffling and refill questions, he retreated to the griddle again where the loud exhaust fans would make it impossible for him to hear their conversation.

"Gaspar's only been working on it for a few hours. No results yet," Kim replied, munching her toast. "I wanted to know more about whoever Mr. X was calling before I went any further. But now that we are where we are with the card and the phone and the body…"

She allowed her voice to trail off and waited to see whether Russell might have a better idea.

He shoveled the eggs and bacon into his mouth like a stevedore. The pancakes disappeared with the flourish of a magic act.

Kim smiled. Gaspar ate like that. As if he were starving and every meal would be his last and he only had thirty seconds to finish it.

Russell swallowed hard and gulped coffee. "So why don't we just call the number and see what we get?"

"That's what I thought, too. Gaspar can trace my call. See where it goes, possibly," she said. "So even if the guy doesn't pick up, we might be able to locate him."

"And go from there," Russell nodded. "Okay. Let's do it."

"Okay. But not here," Kim said. "The Harrison Hotel is a safe zone, isn't it? Operatives can use it securely, without the usual concerns."

"Can't get anything past you." Russell smirked.

CHAPTER 10

Friday, June 3
New York City, New York

MORIN HAD SUFFERED THROUGH two dull, lengthy meetings before he'd been able to sneak out the back of the UN building and find a suitable location. He contacted his counterpart in Canada for help with fulfilling Fox's wish list.

The SUV was relatively easy. Morin rented the vehicle over the internet, using secure channels, fake names, and cloned credit cards.

His Canadian operative moved the vehicle from the rental lot to one of the long-term passenger parking garages nearby. He left the keys under the mat and sent a confirming photo.

Two pistols, suppressors, and two boxes of bullets were procured and hidden in the back of the vehicle. Rope, plastic sheets, protective gear, surgical gloves, and so on were also stashed in the SUV.

The last items on Fox's list would have been easy enough to supply from New York City. Morin guessed they'd be simple to get in Niagara Falls as well if he had a reliable operative on the ground there.

Which he did not. His Canadian counterpart had denied the wherewithal to provide them. Turned Morin down flatly. No wiggle room at all.

Which meant Morin had exhausted his covert connections. Inside every country in the world, fentanyl was simple to find, easy to use, and a perfect legal weapon. Fox wouldn't like it, but he'd need to acquire the drugs himself.

He sent a confirming text to Fox and returned to the last UN sub-committee meeting of the day. Morin trudged to his seat and plopped down hard.

He swigged bitter, cold coffee because he needed the caffeine. The day's activities had been exhausting. And they weren't done yet.

A message pinged his personal cell phone. Morin swiped to open and watch the attached video. It was a quick recap of Deputy Secretary of State Derrick Braxton's controversial remarks on the island country of Quan a few hours ago.

The speech as well as the commentary that followed was translated and printed on the screen.

Morin shook his head, restarted the video, and watched it again. The recording was no less alarming the second time through.

War was coming to the small country. Bigger, bolder, more ruthless fighters would stop at nothing to wipe Quan off the map.

Brax wasn't helping to avoid the inevitable.

Indeed, his remarks seemed calculated to encourage the United States Armed Forces to counterattack.

The translator's droning voice continued to babble the sub-committee's speeches into Morin's headphones. He'd stopped listening long before. He cared nothing about water rights in Africa. He had more pressing problems closer to home.

The world was on the brink of yet another forever war, destined to drain American blood and treasure. Brax seemed to be doing everything he could to make that happen.

His speech was designed to make the dictator show his hand in response. Even as the dictator denied his own war mongering and renounced the west for interference, the dictator was preparing to invade Quan.

There was only one way to thwart the little man's ambitions. For the first step, Brax made sure the world saw the dictator for what he was.

When the dictator was killed before he could invade, no one in the western world would object or care.

The plan was illegal and brilliant and likely to succeed. Which was why Brax was the boss, frankly. Morin wouldn't have the balls to put cold blooded murder of a world leader in place.

Moments after the video ended, the phone pinged with a text.

He was on the ground in Niagara Falls.

Morin responded with a smile and a thumbs-up emoji. He dropped the phone into his pocket, pretending to listen to the droning testimony before the UN subcommittee for another hour.

Then he left the building and made his way back to the same bar as last night to wait.

CHAPTER 11

Friday, June 3
Cleveland, OH

KIM WAS ALREADY ON her way to the door when Russell stood and tossed a few bills onto the table to pay the cook both for the food and the discretion. He followed her out into the crisply cool afternoon.

The Harrison Hotel was a few short blocks away.

Russell checked in while Kim waited. The hotel required proper authorization, and she had no way to acquire it. But Russell did. She tried not to focus on the reasons.

He waved her toward the elevators and they rode up to the sixth floor this time.

"I got a suite. We need more space," Russell said, opening the door. "Wait here."

Kim waited in the hallway.

"All clear," he said, holding the door for her to pull her bags inside. He made a sweeping gesture with his arm. "Two bedrooms if we decide to stay."

"Who knows we're here?" Kim asked, chewing her lower lip as she glanced around the space.

"Not as many people as if we checked into any hotel using our personal credit cards. That said, Finlay could find out if he wanted to. So could Cooper, with a bit more digging," Russell said. "But I doubt either of them have this place on their regularly watched radar. No reason to worry about it at the moment."

"Okay. But as soon as we figure out where to go, we're leaving."

Kim unpacked her laptop and secure hotspot and connected to her server. She sent a secure text message to Gaspar asking for the results on Mr. X's phone.

"Nothing yet," was the instant reply. "Can you talk?"

Kim located the special encrypted burner phone she was currently using to connect directly to Gaspar and placed the call. He picked up.

"Are you alone?" he asked.

"Russell's here," she replied.

Silence. Gaspar didn't trust Finlay and he wasn't all that thrilled with Russell, either. Mainly because Russell was Finlay's closest personal detail.

To Gaspar, talking to Russell was an open pipeline to Finlay.

Kim couldn't argue with the logic, but she couldn't wait forever, either. She put the call on speaker. "Russell knows about the dead man's phone. Tell us what you have discovered so far."

After a bit more silence, Gaspar stated his terms of engagement. "No questions about means and methods."

Kim glanced at Russell for agreement. He nodded, and she said, "Understood."

After another few moments of silence, Gaspar said, "It took a while, but we eventually isolated general locations for both numbers."

"That's more than we had before," she said.

"Yes, but it's not much. Both phones are encrypted burners. End-to-end encryption. Disappearing text technology."

Kim frowned. "So our Mr. X was a lot more sophisticated than we'd hoped."

"It gets worse," Gaspar said. "The two phones, let's call them Alpha and Bravo, are using commercial cell towers in busy areas, which makes them kind of like finding two needles in an arena-sized hay barn. Isolating dates and times for individual calls will be tedious work."

Kim cocked her head. "You mean both phones were *only* used in specific locations?"

"Not totally stationary, but they didn't move around much. Which could be the good news," Gaspar confirmed. "Bravo phone, the one you took off your dead Mr. X, was purchased in New York City only six days ago."

"And the other one, Alpha phone?"

"Los Angeles, originally. Also first used six days ago."

Russell said, "What happened six days ago to set this thing in motion?"

"Good question. I've got no idea." Kim shrugged and shook her head. "Where is the Los Angeles phone now? Still in L.A.?"

"Alpha phone has been quiet," Gaspar replied. "Nothing incoming or outgoing in the last twenty-four hours that we've been able to find."

Kim kneaded the creases in her forehead with her fingers. "Do we think the L.A. guy ditched his phone?"

"Only one way to find out at this point," Gaspar replied.

"We'll have to check the numbers," Russell said.

Gaspar agreed. "I'll give you a specific number and you make a call from Bravo phone. If Alpha phone is still in L.A. I can quickly determine whether your call pings the same cell tower as the other calls."

"Okay," Kim nodded, understanding the plan. "What if Alpha phone has left the area?"

Gaspar said nothing. The answer was obvious.

No way to trace the location of Alpha phone immediately if it wasn't being used in the same general area.

"What if, instead of a call, I send a text to Alpha phone's number? Can you locate the tower closest to where the text is eventually picked up?"

"Maybe," Gaspar said. "But since we can't interrogate your dead spook, calling the L.A. number is probably a faster way to find the handler."

"Probably a more dangerous way to do it, too," Russell said.

"Copy that," Gaspar acknowledged. "Let's do this one step at a time. Get past the first step. Then we'll decide. Ready to try my test number for the first call?"

Kim memorized the digits, picked up Mr. X's phone and dialed as Gaspar directed.

"Okay. Your call is hitting the correct tower. Try the real number for Alpha phone next," Gaspar instructed.

Kim dialed the number she'd pulled from Mr. X's call log and waited while the call connected to the cell tower. The electronic noise coming through the earpiece from the other end simulated a ringing phone.

The ringing noise continued ten times, but the call never clicked over to voicemail. Which could explain why there were no voicemail messages on Bravo phone.

"Go ahead and hang up. He would have answered by now," Russell said.

"Let's try a text message. Even with disappearing text software, the message should hang around at least a few hours. That would give us a longer opportunity to catch the fish," Russell suggested.

Gaspar's exasperated sigh traveled through the speaker as if he were sitting across the room. "Let me get set up."

"I didn't know you could actually trace disappearing texts like that," Kim said, eyes wide. "Some sort of new tech?"

"No questions about means and methods, remember?" Gaspar replied, clicking his keys for a few seconds. Then he said, "Wait for my signal. Then send a text with three words. *Where are you?* Nothing else."

Kim punched the words into the text box and paused with her thumb above the send button. When Gaspar gave the signal, she sent the text.

No immediate response.

"Now I guess we wait," she said aloud. "Unless one of you has a better idea."

CHAPTER 12

Friday, June 3
Cleveland, OH

AN HOUR AFTER SHE sent the text, the dead man's phone rang. The ringtone was a loud buzzing sound which she heard across the room.

She sent Gaspar a quick text to be sure his trace was active on the call. He sent an immediate thumbs-up.

Kim pushed the speaker button, started the recording, and then picked up the call. She said nothing while waiting for his opening gambit.

The man's voice traveled rapidly across the miles.

"Sorry I didn't answer before, Lucas. I was in the shower." The voice was mid-range and sounded middle-aged. He was somewhat breathless, as if he might have rushed through that shower. "How did it go with Agent Otto?"

Gaspar had asked her to keep the line active as long as possible, giving him time to work his magic and locate the other phone.

Kim paused a long moment before she spoke.

"Thank you for calling me back. This is Kim Otto," she said. "We've been trying to get in touch with you."

Her response seemed to startle him. Not surprisingly. He'd been expecting the dead man to answer, not an FBI Agent.

Kim waited for his reply.

After a few moments, he cleared his throat. "Agent Otto. Sorry. I was expecting Lucas. I've been traveling. Which is why I didn't get your call earlier."

"I have a lot of questions, as you can imagine," she said, rapidly processing the facts he already confirmed.

He'd named the dead man.

He knew Kim was an FBI agent.

What else did he know?

"Reacher said you were thorough," he replied. "Are you on your way?"

Reacher? How did this guy know Reacher? Why and how had Reacher been discussing her with him?

Kim glanced across the room toward Russell, raising her eyebrows. He shrugged and shook his head.

She took a deep breath. First things first. Find the man on the other end of the line. Go from there.

Gaspar hadn't located the caller. He needed more time.

"Not on my way yet. Working on it," she replied, stringing him along. "Is Reacher with you?"

"Lucas knows where to find me. You're in Detroit. Not that far away. The witness is here. You can see what we have and talk to the witness yourself," he said, ignoring her question about Reacher. "How soon can you get here?"

"I need to get paperwork and authorization," she stalled, giving Gaspar as much time as possible to complete the trace.

"I can set up the interview for later tonight," he said, dangling the bait.

"I'll need to reserve a hotel room," she said. "What's the address there?"

"Lucas can give it to you," he replied. "I've already got a suite we can work from."

"Okay. I can probably convince my boss to let me do that, under the circumstances." She took a pause and pushed the envelope just a bit. "What name did you use to register?"

"My real name. It's not like the front desk subscribes to the *LA Times*, you know? No reason to make something up. Plus, I had to show them my passport. I don't have a fake one to splash around," he replied easily, as if he were not nervous at all. "Just ask reception to call up when you get here."

Passport. Which meant he'd left the country.

He'd said he wasn't far from Detroit. Which had to mean Canada. Perhaps Montreal. Or Toronto.

Why had he mentioned the *LA Times*? Was this man recently featured in the media?

"Okay. I'll let you know as soon as I make arrangements," she replied.

"That'll give me time to finish up," he said. "Let me talk to Lucas."

Kim's breath caught. Now was not the time to tell him Lucas was dead. If he knew, he might disappear again. She might never find him a second time.

She said the first thing that popped into her head. "He's in the shower."

"Ask Lucas to call me when he's done. See you soon," he said and disconnected.

Kim punched the disconnect button and glanced at Russell. Half a moment later, a text message from Gaspar pinged.

"We've located the guy." She read the text aloud. "Niagara Falls, Ontario, Canada. Confirmed."

"Sounds like Reacher's involved now, too," Russell replied. "Good to know."

"Yeah," Kim said.

Reacher said you were thorough. Lucas knows where to find me. The witness is here. Have Lucas call me. See you soon.

So many unknowns in those short sentences. Lucas, whoever he was, had been sent to talk to her last night, not kill her.

Sent by Reacher. Why?

The attempt to find her had caused someone to kill Lucas. Had he known he was putting his life on the line?

What was going on here?

"Reacher's involved. Now we know. You need to get Cooper on the line?" Russell asked.

She shook her head slowly. "Not yet."

"Okay, but we have to get there somehow." Russell nodded. "I can call Finlay for a jet. It'll take a while to organize. And I'll have to explain some things. That okay with you?"

"Not yet." Keeping Finlay in the loop wasn't necessary now. If she accepted help like that from him, she'd be obligated to explain things she didn't want to share. Another text pinged from Gaspar.

She read the text aloud for Russell's benefit. "The caller's name is Ashley Westwood. Senior technology reporter. *LA Times.* Checked into the Clark Hotel in Niagara Falls last night."

"Still no clue who Lucas is, though?" Russell asked.

"I thought it might spook him if I started asking him questions Lucas could easily answer if he weren't dead." Kim shrugged. "We'll break the news once we find Westwood. Then he can tell us more about Lucas. And whatever the hell is going on here."

"What's the connection to Reacher?" Russell asked.

Kim considered a few possible angles before she shrugged again. "I don't know. But I'd like to find out before Cooper does."

She called Gaspar.

When he picked up, he said, "Way ahead of you, Suzie Wong. Nothing in Reacher's army records ties him to Westwood. Westwood never served in any branch of the military."

"So whatever the connection between them, it's more recent and probably not related to Reacher's military service," Kim said slowly.

"Fastest thing to do is to ask Westwood. Get a few more details. Maybe I can find a link to Reacher along with a way to locate him now," Gaspar replied. "But I need a place to start unraveling the bird's nest."

"Yeah. Which means I have to get on the road. It's a three-hour drive and I need to rent a car first." Kim turned her head toward Russell. "Bring your passport?"

"Always," Russell nodded. "You never know when you might have to take a quick flight to Paris."

"Or a quick drive to Canada," she replied. "I haven't been concerned with paperwork and travel permissions for a while. Cooper usually handles my details."

"What about Cooper?" Gaspar asked. "He'll be pissed when he finds out about this. Now that you know Reacher's involved, might be better to get him on the inside, don't you think? You might need help down the road. Help I can't get fast enough or maybe not at all. I don't have much support in Canada."

Kim knew what he meant. *Support* was a euphemism for easy access to weapons and equipment and personnel to use it expertly when the situation went south.

Which it would.

With Reacher in the mix, things always went south.

Gaspar operated outside the confines of the FBI, but he avoided breaking the law. He had a job and a license to protect. And a family, too.

He was telling her she'd be operating without much of a safety net.

She couldn't rely on Gaspar in the same way that she relied on Cooper. Cooper had the full force of the U.S. Government at his beck and call, one way or another.

Gaspar couldn't possibly compete with that, even if he wanted to.

Cooper's strength would be seriously diminished outside the U.S., but he'd have more resources than Gaspar.

Still, Kim hesitated.

Instincts had saved her far too many times.

She'd learned to trust her gut. At the moment, it was flashing a big red neon "NO."

No Cooper.

She had Russell and Gaspar.

They would have to be enough.

At least for now.

If the authorities found her weapons at the border crossing point, she'd have no choice. Bringing unauthorized weapons into Canada would probably land her in prison for a long, long time.

At that point, Cooper, or maybe Finlay, would have to be her first call. Until then, she'd stay under the radar. She was used to operating down there.

Gaspar's phone pinged with another text. She read it quickly.

"Come on. Our ride is downstairs," she said, pulling her bags toward the door with Russell following close behind.

CHAPTER 13

Friday, June 3
Niagara Falls, Ontario, CA

GASPAR HAD ARRANGED AND delivered an SUV to the hotel. Kim and Russell had hit the road to Canada shortly afterward. The two-hundred-mile drive along Interstate 90 through Erie and Buffalo was uneventful.

The first time Westwood called, Kim ignored the ringing phone.

Russell said, "He might have something helpful to say."

"He's probably looking for Lucas."

"No way to head off Westwood's questions indefinitely. He's gonna notice Lucas is missing and there's only two of us when we get there."

"Yeah, and not answering will raise his internal radar and make him suspicious," Kim shrugged. "But that can't be helped. We'll deal with it when it happens."

At the border checkpoint, a single agent sat alone in a booth vetting would-be visitors before he allowed them through.

"Looks like things are moving along well enough," Russell said, glancing at the clock on the dashboard. "We're right on time."

Vehicles were stopped behind a swing arm gate until the agent pressed a button to lift the arm. The single line of vehicles waited quietly, approaching the gate one at a time.

When it was their turn, Kim held her breath as she passed through the gate.

"Passports, please," the agent said, looking into the SUV.

Kim handed the blue US passports into the booth.

"What's your reason for entering Canada today?" the agent asked pleasantly as he swiped both passports through the electronic reader.

"We're visiting Niagara Falls," Kim replied.

"How long do you plan to stay in Canada?" he asked while briefly checking the results of the passport scan on his screen.

"Couple of days," Kim said.

"Have a great visit," he replied with a welcoming smile as he returned the passports and waved permission to pass through.

Kim cleared the checkpoint and followed the nav system guidance across the Peace Bridge into Canada. After that, she followed the signs toward Niagara Falls.

Russell had punched the Clark Hotel address into the navigation system. Estimated travel time from Cleveland was three hours and thirty-two minutes.

Kim's lead foot had shaved twenty minutes off the estimate while they'd traveled on the interstate, but now traffic in the town was moving at a crawl.

It was exactly eight thirty-two, just as the nav guidance had predicted.

"Machines will be the death of us all," she said with a grin.

"I'm surprised there's still so much traffic," Russell replied, as they advanced toward the majestic Horseshoe Falls.

Kim had been to Niagara Falls before. With her parents on a family vacation when she was a teen. And a couple of times since then for conferences and business trips. The Canadian side boasted much for tourists to love. Stellar views, a zip line, boat tours, good restaurants, a couple of casinos, and more.

"You shouldn't be surprised about the traffic. The views of the falls and outdoor activities are popular with international travelers and locals alike. It's another hour before sunset, and it won't be dark for almost an hour after that," Kim replied. "No way to avoid the crowds for a few hours yet."

"Then we'll need to contend with tourists enjoying the nightlife," Russell said. "There's fireworks scheduled and who knows what else going on out there."

"More than ten million people visit here every year from all over the world, according to the PR department," Kim replied with a grin. "Let's just hope they're not all here tonight."

There were two tall buildings ahead with red Clark Hotel signs lighting the tops. One hotel was obviously taller and newer than the other. The older one was positioned for stunning views of the Niagara Falls area, including both Horseshoe Falls and the US Falls, as well as the Niagara River.

The SUV's navigation system routed them toward the older hotel where they expected to meet Westwood.

Kim turned into a one-way street. Two blocks down, the Clark Hotel entrance was on the left. A knot of tourists stood near the valet stand waiting as runners delivered and removed their vehicles.

"This place is busy, too," Russell said, craning his neck to observe all sides of the street. "We can use that to our advantage."

"We can try to melt into the crowd. But surveillance cameras are everywhere around here," Kim replied. "The Niagara Falls area is always a potential terrorist target. Power stations, bridges, and drinking water plants are vulnerable, among other things."

"With any luck, these tourists are all self-involved and no one will focus on us."

"We're meeting Westwood in his suite on the twenty-second floor. It's not likely the elevators will be full all the way to the top," Kim replied. "Someone will notice us, either now or later when they review the CCTV. Count on it."

There was no street parking, and she didn't want to use the valet, so Kim drove around to the attached parking garage on the northeast side of the building.

She embassy parked the SUV on the first floor near the elevator and emergency stairs.

Kim slipped cell phones into her pockets and checked her weapon. Russell did the same.

They climbed out of the SUV and Kim pushed the alarm button on the key fob to set the anti-theft device. She glanced around the immediate area to embed the location into her memory.

"Take the elevator to the lobby?" Russell asked, jerking his thumb in that direction.

"Let's walk. Check out the area from the front entrance. See what we're dealing with," Kim said, already moving toward the street.

"Westwood is likely to be nervous. He's got to have figured out that you lied to him by now since Lucas never called him back after that shower," Russell said as they walked.

She shrugged. "Not much I can do about it. Lucas was dead before I knew either he or Westwood existed."

Outside the front entrance, Kim overheard conversations in four different languages that she could identify and at least two more that she couldn't immediately place.

English and French, since Canadians used both languages. Spanish. Italian.

The unfamiliar words might have been Farsi and Hebrew, but she wasn't certain.

They bobbed between groups of guests talking together while waiting for the valet. On the other side of the crowd, the front doors slid open automatically, allowing Kim and Russell to enter the busy lobby.

One glance straight ahead was enough to explain the popularity of the hotel.

The entire south side of the building was a wall of glass overlooking an astonishingly mesmerizing view of The Great Niagara Falls.

Hotel guests stared in awe as more than 680,000 gallons of water tumbled over Horseshoe Falls every second. The US Falls and Bridal Veil Falls added another 75,000 gallons. The roar was nothing short of exhilarating.

Water cascading over the falls provided the deafening background soundtrack inside the hotel which raised the volume of conversation to annoying levels.

Kim made no effort to talk over the noise. Scanning the crowd for threats, she tapped Russell's arm and moved toward the registration desk.

Guests were lined up to reach the harried personnel at the front desk.

Subtle differences in haircuts, clothing, posture, and language suggested an international mix of tourists and employees. Checking in, checking out, making hotel reservations, setting touring schedules for tomorrow, and on and on.

She didn't see anyone she recognized, but she hadn't expected to.

To the right of the desk was the elevator alcove housing. People were waiting to enter one of the six cars as they landed and ferried passengers both up and down.

Kim headed in that direction and Russell followed.

The first two elevator cars emptied and then refilled with people and luggage. Kim and Russell were able to squeeze onto the third car.

As the elevator stopped at each floor, guests filed out, until only one family of four was left facing the front of the car.

CHAPTER 14

Friday, June 3
New York City, New York

THE MIDTOWN RESTAURANT BUZZED with activity. All tables were full and a line of patrons waited to be seated. The usual upscale banter and laughter accompanied the live musicians playing softly in the corner. The air conditioning struggled to cool too many warm bodies crammed into too small a space.

Friday night in Morin's favorite New York City restaurant was as predictable as sunrise. Which was exactly the way he liked it.

From his usual perch at the bar, Morin had placed the four cherry stems parallel on the cocktail napkin beside the cell phone. He'd tied knots in the stems with his tongue after he chewed the boozy fruit floating in his drink.

He preferred a Rye Manhattan, but tonight, he'd specifically requested Canadian whisky in tribute to the task at hand.

The bartender had offered food several times, but Morin declined. His head was too clear already because he'd received three brief texts.

The first when Fox arrived in Canada. Another when Fox had collected the necessary supplies.

The third had said simply, *target acquired*. Which meant Fox had located Westwood.

Nothing since. Which was not what Morin had expected. If Fox had located Westwood, why was the man still alive?

The delay was nerve-racking.

Which was why Morin had consumed the four Perfect Manhattans. So far.

The bartender offered food again and this time Morin ordered steak and fries with his fifth drink, simply to avoid the disapproving stares from hungry patrons expecting him to vacate his seat.

Before the bartender had a chance to deliver the cocktail, the guy occupying the stool next to Morin left.

A tall, exceptionally attractive woman slid gracefully onto the warm black leather. The sort of woman every man sees the moment she enters the room.

Morin noticed everything about her, all at once.

Her little black cocktail dress, standard New York evening attire for a certain set. Red pumps with four-inch heels. Sleek dark hair styled by the most expensive cutter in Manhattan.

Morin's judgment snapped her into the proper box. Sophisticated, educated. Wealthy, of course.

And pure poison.

She was the kind of woman who, in another time, would have smoked her cigarette from an opera length slender silver holder resting between pouty red lips.

In short, she was exactly Morin's type. An old-fashioned femme fatale. A seductive woman certain to cause disaster for any man involved with her.

Morin knew for sure.

Because they'd been lovers once, a long time ago.

When they were young and foolish and unattached.

She'd attached herself to a series of more successful men since then, while Morin had married a woman more suited to be a diplomat's wife.

She had become Audrey Ruston, Special Assistant to Assistant Secretary of State Derrick Braxton.

After half a moment too long, Morin felt like slapping himself on the forehead. Maybe he'd had one too many cocktails. Of course, he should have anticipated the play.

Brax was a belt and suspenders guy.

Naturally, Fox wouldn't be the only assassin deployed on this assignment. Maybe Morin had had too many Manhattans after all. Not that he'd admit it.

"Audrey," Morin said while signaling the bartender on her behalf. "Aren't you supposed to be globe-trotting with Brax at taxpayer expense, saving the world and all that?"

The bartender arrived. Audrey ordered a dirty gin martini.

"I *was* with Brax in Quan. Horrid place, by the way. Can't figure out why anyone would go to war over it," she said, wrinkling her nose as she turned to face him. "He sent me back to check on you. You're making him nervous."

"Why?" Morin asked, as if her words hadn't sent a painful chill straight through him like an icy spike to the groin.

"He's heard disturbing rumors," Audrey said quietly, offering an appropriate smile of gratitude to the bartender as he placed the martini on a cocktail napkin near her elbow. "Too disturbing to trust to electronic communication."

But not too disturbing for pillow talk, her body language practically screamed. At least, any man who knew her as well as he did could read her like a children's book.

Audrey raised the martini toward Morin in a quiet toast before she sipped. She closed her eyes and nodded. "Best martini in the world right there. Can't get one even remotely close to it in Quan."

"Best bartender on the planet. I agree," Morin said shortly, annoyed with her affectations. "You've come all this way to tell me something. So let's have it."

"Actually, I came to ask you something. Specifically, where's Stuart?"

"Which one?"

"What do you think?" Audrey snapped. "Both of them."

Morin had been in the game a long, long time. The small hairs raised on the back of his neck sending a sharp electrical frisson of disquiet down his spine.

The feeling was familiar.

Comforting in its own way.

He'd learned to heed the warning. He cocked his head and narrowed his gaze to sharpen his thinking, which had been fuzzed by alcohol.

Jousting with Audrey Ruston hadn't been on his agenda tonight. Not even remotely. He was unprepared. Which gave her another advantage.

Audrey had always been a spectacular liar.

She wouldn't exclaim the truth even if it bit her on that very nice ass.

She was lying now. Morin had reported mission status appropriately through channels. Brax already knew the full situation.

They were running a little behind schedule, but the project was on track. Nothing to worry about here.

The test would take place as planned.

Krause. Ottawa. Two days hence.

The unimportant, meddling Stuart brother, Lucas, was dead.

The essential Stuart brother, Liam, was missing. Temporarily.

The journalist had interfered in Morin's plans to find Liam Stuart, but Fox would eliminate that problem shortly.

Fox would find the missing brother and Morin would get him back on track. Liam Stuart would produce and test the prototype as planned.

Brax knew all of this. He'd approved the plan. Just this morning.

So why was Audrey Ruston really sitting here grilling him about it?

She must have intel that Morin didn't.

Which was unacceptable.

And worrisome.

Give Audrey a nibble of anything and she gobbled everything in the whole kitchen, tossing carcasses aside as she went. He'd seen her do it too many times before.

"Fox has served us well. He's half-finished already," Morin told her through clenched teeth.

"Fox is out of his depth here. There are things about the situation that you don't know."

"Such as?"

She shook her head. "Sorry. Above your clearance level."

Which was bullshit. His clearance was higher than hers. She was bluffing. Flouting her relationship with Brax. Testing Morin.

But to what end?

"The *situation* is *totally* under control," he said, mocking her with cold certainty.

"Seems like the opposite of *under control* to me," Audrey replied with a saucy, flirty grin. "Where's the scientist? Where's the prototype? You've had plenty of time to find them. Do we need to assign the job to someone else? Do we need a plan B here? Things are worse than we thought in Quan. Brax wants to go immediately after the test. No wiggle room. Tick tock. Time is running very, very short, Nigel."

Morin burned with cold anger. He gave her a hard stare. "You think you can do better? Is that it?"

"Better than eliminating the only person who might have lured Liam Stuart from hiding? Better than traveling six thousand miles in the wrong direction chasing a journalist who knows nothing?" Audrey shot back hotly. "Bet your ass I can do better, Nigel. Just stay out of the way and watch me."

Morin's anger flared. She had always been ambitious. And capable. And ruthless. She had something to prove.

Brax didn't send her to check up on him. That was a flat-out lie.

Audrey intended to succeed where he'd failed. She'd been after Morin's job for a while, and she must have figured now was her chance to move in. Simple as that.

"You're wasting your time, Audrey," Morin said calmly, jaw clenched. "Fox is already in place. The journalist will spill what he knows and then be eliminated within the hour. We'll have the scientist and the project back on track before you can change out of those ridiculous shoes. Better luck next time."

Audrey smiled like a pinup girl, as if she knew worlds more than he did.

She lifted her martini and drained the glass. Then she slid off the stool and stood three inches from his face.

"It's cute that you think so, Nigel. You know I like you. Always have. But fifty bucks says I'll have the scientist and the prototype before morning." She nodded and leaned forward to whisper in his ear. "Get out of the way. Save yourself. Don't screw this up if you want to stay on the bottom of the team."

Morin frowned but said nothing.

Audrey turned to deliver her parting shot. "My helo's waiting. Wait here. I'll call you when I'm done."

She moved like a slender reed in the breeze, blending with the glittering patrons crowding the bar.

Morin watched her slide effortlessly amid the throng on her way to the door. He texted the operative he'd placed at the exit, just in case, to keep track of her. He sent another operative to connect with the first. Two men on Audrey was probably not enough. But it was all he could call out with zero notice.

When Morin could no longer see her retreating form, he turned to glance again at the black cell phone screen on the phone assigned to Fox.

Still no word. The silence made Morin antsy. And nervous.

Audrey had a point.

Maybe Fox was losing his edge.

The scientist went missing five days ago. Which was way too long. He should have been apprehended already.

The journalist and the brother should have been minor complications, easily dealt with. Another failure.

Brax probably *was* worried. The stakes couldn't get any higher. On top of everything, the situation in Quan had deteriorated more rapidly than expected. Leaving zero wiggle room in the schedule.

Brax must feel like the tail was wagging the dog. Not good.

Morin might have been too forgiving because Fox had done good work before. Maybe Audrey was right. Maybe he'd made a mistake with Fox.

He'd give Fox another couple of hours. That's all Morin could afford to wait. He could repurpose the two operatives again, take them off Audrey. He could also get personally involved. If he had to.

Audrey would move in quickly, like she'd promised. She'd be in Niagara and on Fox's tail before Morin finished his dinner.

If Audrey found Liam Stuart and the drone before Fox did, Morin was done. Brax would shut him down like a bad date.

Audrey was determined to end Morin's career. Terminal right now. That's what she wanted.

Unless he could end Audrey's career first.

The thought curled the corner of his lip into a snide smile. Nothing would make him happier.

"Steak and fries. Man, that smells great," the bartender said as he delivered Morin's food. "Where'd that woman go? She owes me for the martini."

Morin shrugged as if he had no idea who she was or where she went. Audrey could pay her own damned bar bills.

He picked up the steak knife and glared at the empty black screen on Fox's silent phone.

CHAPTER 15

Friday, June 3
Niagara Falls, Ontario, CA

AT THE TWENTY-SECOND FLOOR, the family left the elevator and turned in the same direction Kim and Russell were planning to walk.

Kim hung back until the family reached their room and went inside, leaving Kim alone with Russell in the hallway.

Gaspar had said Westwood's suite number was 2226, which was almost at the end of the corridor. As they walked, Kim reached into her pocket, retrieved a pair of surgical gloves, and pulled them on. Russell did the same.

When they reached the suite, Kim rapped on the door, facing the peephole so Westwood could see her.

No answer. The door stayed closed.

Kim knocked again.

Same result.

She murmured, "What's he doing in there?"

A key card reader was embedded into a sensor above the lever in the door handle mechanism. She pushed down on the lever. A red light flashed on the sensor to confirm the lock was engaged.

Kim glanced at Russell. He pulled a cell phone-sized black device from his pocket and pressed a few buttons.

A flat circular image appeared on the screen.

He held the screen close to the sensor in the door's locking mechanism.

A moment later, a green light flashed on the sensor. Russell lowered the lever handle and the lock clicked open.

He pushed the door inward and Kim went inside.

Russell followed Kim, closing the door behind them. He returned the black box to his pocket.

Kim drew her weapon. Russell did the same.

They quickly swept through to clear the three-room suite.

A common room with a small kitchen. Two bedrooms. Two and a half baths. The suite had a spectacular view of the Niagara River, Horseshoe Falls, the US Falls, and Bridal Veil Falls.

When they were sure the suite was unoccupied, they holstered weapons and returned to the common room.

"That's a handy lock picking device you've got there," Kim teased, scanning for evidence that Westwood expected to return soon. "Is it official issue? I'll ask Cooper to get me one."

Russell shrugged. "Modern spy gadgets are not quite as good as James Bond movies, but we do okay."

She nodded, as a random thought passed through. "Does that one do anything else?"

"Like what?"

"Can it read a key card, for example?" She showed him the key card she'd taken from Lucas's pocket. "I think Lucas used that to get into my building. But maybe it's something else."

Russell took the gray plastic card and examined it. "I might be able to read this. Want me to try?"

"Later. Right now, we need to locate Westwood," Kim nodded. "He was expecting us, yet he's not here. Why would he leave? Where did he go?"

"I didn't see him in the crowds downstairs and I looked," Russell said.

"He wasn't there. He'd have stuck out, even in that group," Kim replied.

Gaspar had sent four official headshots for Ashley Westwood posted by the *LA Times* in the paper and on its website. He'd also included some candid photos Westwood posted on social media.

Westwood was an outdoorsy type. He looked and dressed like a naturalist or an explorer.

Short unruly hair. Blond once but going gray. A beard of the same length. Squint lines around his eyes. Maybe fifty-five or so. No younger.

Exactly the kind of guy that would choose Niagara Falls as a meeting spot. Contrary to Lucas, who had the appearance of a man used to less rugged activities. Kim figured Westwood was the man in charge of their little team.

"What makes you think he left voluntarily?" Russell asked, still checking the place out. Opening drawers and doors. Riffling through clothes.

"No reason to think otherwise, is there? I don't see any evidence of a struggle. Nothing obviously missing," Kim replied as she examined the suite herself.

She glanced outside the large windows. Darkness was gathering over Horseshoe Falls outside. Spotlights were already trained on the spectacle to please the tourists.

Westwood was a journalist. He was likely to have brought a laptop as well as his cell phone. Maybe more equipment, too.

Would he have taken the laptop with him?

Kim went to check the closets again. Each of the two bedrooms were equipped with a closet. Inside each was an ironing board, iron, extra pillows, and a blanket.

She stood looking from the common room toward the two doorways.

One of the bedrooms had not been used. Perhaps it was meant for Lucas.

Westwood had occupied the other room. His bathroom towels were damp on the floor. The small bars of soap had been unwrapped and used.

His travel bags were stashed in one corner. There was a rolling carry-on and an empty canvas laptop case.

Westwood's clothes were hanging in the closet. More outdoor wear. High-tech fabrics with many zippers. Old and creased, as if he lived a lot of his life in them.

No shoes. He was probably wearing his travel footwear. Hiking boots, most likely.

Kim swept the clothes aside on the closet pole.

She found what she'd been looking for.

A wall safe. Set into the back wall. The safe was closed and locked.

"Russell?" she called out.

He came into the room. "Yeah?"

"Does your gadget open this digital lock on the safe?" Kim asked.

"Maybe." Russell approached the closet.

He punched a few buttons on the screen and then studied the safe.

It was the standard type often found in hotel rooms. Large enough to hold a laptop and a few other items along with it. Jewelry. Other electronics.

The safe's door had a punch button keypad similar to a push button desk phone. Above the keypad was an LED screen to display.

At the moment, the display said, "locked" in red LED letters.

"I'll give it a try. But this safe is old and pretty low tech. Probably installed at least twenty years ago. See if you can find the master code to unlock it online," Russell said, kneeling near the keypad to get a better view. "Hell, we might get further just busting it open."

He pulled the black device from his pocket and put the flat screen close to the keypad. He held it there as he'd done with the electronic door lock earlier. Nothing happened. The safe did not unlock.

He punched a few buttons on his device screen and tried again. The door remained locked.

Kim used her phone to search the internet. She found a video hack for opening the old safe on the first try. "Try this. Press and hold the lock button until the battery indicator comes on."

"Okay. Got it. Now what?"

"Press zero until the word 'Super' appears," Kim said, still reading the listed steps. "When it disappears, press in all nines."

"Done," Russell said. "Didn't work."

"Okay, try the sequence again. But this time, press all twos."

Russell did as she'd asked. This time, the safe flashed the word *open* and the door unlocked. "That was easy."

"Sometimes low-tech is the answer, I guess." Kim grinned. "For these old systems, it's better to find a hiding place in the room and rely on stealth."

"Yeah, well you should have told Westwood that. His laptop is in here. A couple of zip drives. An unopened burner phone still in the plastic," Russell said, pulling the laptop and the zip drives from the safe and handing everything to Kim.

"Guess he wasn't in a huge hurry when he left, if he had time to stash stuff in the safe," she said. "Probably also rules out someone forcing him to leave."

Kim slipped the two zip drives into her pocket, carried the laptop into the common area and placed it on the table.

When she lifted the lid, the screen came to life. The display opened a web page Westwood must have been using when he closed the laptop. A page on the dark web.

Before she had a chance to examine anything else, Lucas's cell phone rang.

Kim pulled it from her pocket.

She recognized Westwood's number.

This time, she answered his call.

CHAPTER 16

Friday, June 3
Niagara Falls, Ontario, CA

WESTWOOD'S FIRST WORDS WERE, "Where is Lucas? Why hasn't he called me?"

"We're at your hotel, as promised. Lucas is not something to discuss now. Phone conversations can be overheard," Kim replied reasonably. "Where are you?"

She heard the roar of the falls and scratchy interference through the handset as he considered what to do next. His silence lasted too long.

"Look, Mr. Westwood, I don't understand your lack of cooperation here," Kim said irritably. "I'm an FBI agent. You sent Lucas to contact *me*. At Reacher's suggestion. I came here to meet with *you*, at your request. What was the point of all that if you won't talk to me now?"

Westwood cleared his throat. "Are you alone?"

He sounded unsure about what to do next, as if he might bolt. Which meant she had a chance to tip the balance.

104 | DIANE CAPRI

"Of course I'm not alone. FBI agents travel in pairs. My partner is with me. Agent Russell." She paused to let the information soak in and then asked, "Where are you?"

"I'll meet you in a public place. You'll tell me about Lucas. Then I'll decide," Westwood said, as if he was controlling the situation. Which, for the moment, he was.

"That's fine. Make it somewhere within walking distance." He probably hadn't gone far from the possessions he'd left in his suite or the witness he'd claimed was close by.

He paused a long agonizing time before he said, "It's a holiday here. The Journey Behind the Falls tour is running late tonight for a special event."

"How far away is it?"

"Ten minutes. Maybe less," he said. "Get directions at the information desk in the lobby. Table Rock Centre. I'll be waiting at the first observation deck below ground level. Near the retaining wall opposite the tunnel."

"Sounds like it'll be busy. Lots of people around," Kim said, "Can we talk privately there?"

"The fireworks will be starting soon. Visitors will be focused on that," Westwood replied.

"How will I find you?"

"I'll find you," he replied before he hung up.

Russell had completed his cursory search of the suite while she was on the phone. He walked into the room just as Westwood disconnected. "Where is he?"

"He wants to meet us outside, at the falls." Kim dropped the phone into her pocket and retrieved Gaspar's phone. "Bring his laptop and the charger. We'll leave it in our SUV on the way out."

"Copy that," Russell said, closing the heavy draperies against long-distance surveillance. Just in case.

Kim headed toward the exit, calling Gaspar on the way.

When Gaspar picked up, Kim said, "Westwood just called me on Lucas's phone. Can you trace the call? He wants to meet at the falls level observation deck, Table Rock Centre. I think that's where he called from. I could hear the falls roaring in the background. He had to raise his voice, so he's close to them somewhere."

Gaspar clicked the keys on his keyboard.

After a couple of moments, he said, "Yeah. I've got him. He's standing on the lower deck. On the side closest to the city. Away from the falls cascade. I can't tell if he's alone."

"Can you get access to CCTV out there?" Kim asked, waving to Russell and heading toward the door.

"Possibly. How much time do we have?" Gaspar asked.

"Ten minutes. We're on our way now. Do what you can," Kim said as she hung up and followed Russell out the door and into the hallway.

"I've located Table Rock Centre," Russell said when she met up with him at the elevator.

He'd removed his gloves after he punched the call button. The elevator car was headed down instead of up, which meant a longer wait.

"The hotel sits on a bluff. Table Rock Centre is down the hill. There's a stairway from one to the other," Russell said. "After we stash the laptop in the SUV, we can walk through the hotel, down the stairs, and across the parking lot."

"Can we make it in ten minutes?" Kim asked, shucking her gloves before the car stopped to avoid curious glances.

The doors opened. Passengers stepped out. Kim moved inside. The elevator car descended.

"Did you get the vibe that he'd rabbit if we're late?" Russell asked under his breath.

"Hard to say." Kim shrugged.

The elevator stopped on the twentieth floor and another couple entered.

Kim tilted her head to acknowledge them and said nothing more.

The ride down was terminally slow. The elevator seemed to stop at every floor, admitting passengers each time.

When they finally reached the lobby, Kim and Russell were pressed against the back of the crowded car, facing forward.

People standing in front of Kim emptied the car as slowly as they'd entered, maneuvering luggage and strollers and wheelchairs until finally, the car was clear enough to exit.

"We're running later than planned. Westwood could bolt," Kim said as they hustled toward the front door. "We can make better time on our own. Easier to move through the crowds. I'll go on ahead. You run the laptop out to the SUV. Meet me at the observation deck."

"Sounds like a plan," Russell nodded. "See you in ten. Fifteen at the latest."

"Copy that," Kim said with a grin.

Russell peeled off left at the front door. Kim picked up her pace to move around the knot of giggling girls in front of her on the right.

The corridor to the Falls Incline Railway was clearly marked. Kim headed through the doors and out onto the walkway bridge. At the end, instead of turning toward the jam-packed incline railway car, she took the stairs down, two at a time.

The roar of the water tumbling over Horseshoe Falls at those seven-hundred-gallons-per-second was deafening. Heavy mist soaked the air. The added humidity enhanced the early spring cold and sliced her skin even through her clothes.

Kim clamped her teeth together and shoved her hands into her pockets. Without a hood for warmth, she tilted her head down and kept going.

The wind picked up closer to the river, whipping spray from the falls like pellets. Water stung her eyes as she struggled to remain fully engaged with her surroundings, scanning for Westwood.

And whoever might be hunting him.

Crowds of tourists moved like a herd of bison ever closer to the river, lining the retaining fences, seeking good vantage points to view the special fireworks. Laughing, chatting, enjoying the adventure.

Several people behaved foolishly, but none seemed overtly suspicious.

Construction work had closed two of the walkways, one on each side of Table Rock Centre. The retaining fences had been removed and flimsy temporary barriers erected.

An ever-growing mob moved around the orange cones and barriers and continued toward the Rainbow Bridge connecting the US to Canada.

The lower observation deck where Westwood waited would probably be one of the busiest fireworks viewing locations. With luck, perhaps the proximity to the cold, wet spray would persuade some to watch the show from a more distant location.

Kim entered the warmth of Table Rock Centre and pushed through the crowd to the ticket counter. A twisty queue of pleasant tourists waited, credit cards in hand. Kim slid along the ropes behind their backs and made it to the cashier. The jovial group didn't seem to mind.

At the checkout, she bought two tickets. One for her and one for Russell. She hurried along to the line waiting for the elevator to the lower level.

She pulled her phone from her pocket and sent a quick text to Russell, telling him to skip the ticket line and where to find her.

The queue moved with glacial speed. Only one elevator car. Ten tourists packed in each time. The rate of descent painfully slow.

The system was designed to regulate and limit the number of people occupying the lower observation deck. But for special events like tonight, it seemed the numbers had been adjusted to allow the space to fill beyond normal capacity.

When Kim was close enough to spy an emergency stairway, she slid along the back wall to the exit door and stole inside. She stashed Russell's ticket behind a trash barrel and sent a quick text to update him. Then she took the damp, slippery stairs down to the tunnels below.

CHAPTER 17

Friday, June 3
Niagara Falls, Ontario, CA

KIM LEFT THE STAIRWELL and merged into the group of tourists sporting cheap yellow rain ponchos milling about like twinkie snack cakes or minions in a kid's movie.

The oversized hooded ponchos protected wearers from the breath-stealing, relentless cold shower thrown from the waterfalls, which was okay.

They also effectively disguised and concealed sex, size, and shape, which wasn't okay. Not even remotely.

The oversized yellow ponchos concealed too well.

Any one of the yellow-clad could be Westwood.

Any of the others might be armed and dangerous.

Kim considered waiting for Russell. In situations like this, two agents were better than one.

Her natural instincts leaned toward self-preservation. When she had the option. Which she didn't have here.

People poured into the tunnel at the speed of racing turtles. Soon, the already congested observation deck would be at full capacity.

Propelled by urgency, Kim snagged a yellow poncho and slipped it over her head. As she walked, she slid her arms through the plastic sleeves and raised the rain hood.

The poncho concealed her appearance as effectively as the others. Westwood wouldn't see her coming. Which could be helpful.

As she crossed the tunnel rock, Kim slid along the edges of the crowd. She walked through deep cold puddles that soaked her shoes and sent shivers through her body. She clenched her teeth to stop the chattering.

Weaving carefully along the wet stone floor toward the open observation deck at the end of the tunnel, she continually scanned for Westwood's sturdy shape and curly beard beneath the yellow plastic hoods.

She slipped twice. Only the tightly packed bodies swarming through the tunnel kept her upright.

She finally broke through the tunnel's exit and emerged onto the frigid, wet air of the observation deck.

Along the outside edges, the deck was surrounded by a decorative safety barrier. A short concrete wall ran along the edge. Decorative stone pillars were placed at regular intervals. Vertical wrought iron fencing was placed between the pillars.

On the other side of the barrier was a sloped apron of green space and sporadic rocky outcroppings leading straight down to the rough shoreline of the Niagara River beyond Horseshoe Falls.

Younger kids climbed on the iron railings slicked by the relentless spray while their parents chatted among themselves, ignoring the obvious danger.

Nearby, exuberant teens engaged in good-natured horseplay sat astride the rails and pillars, daring each other to jump.

A determined suicide could easily climb over and plunge down into the Great Niagara Falls before anyone could stop him. There was no official count of suicides from this point, Kim guessed. The Chamber of Commerce didn't like to publicize such things.

Out of sight, out of mind, perhaps. Even so, suicides were not rare.

Was Westwood planning to jump? Why would he do that? He'd sounded okay on the phone. He was a journalist tracking a story. Nothing he'd learned so far should have made him suicidal. Surely.

Kim glanced back toward the tunnel. The horde of yellow ponchos bobbed and weaved and pushed toward the cascade of water falling close to the north side of the wrought iron barrier. Phones were poised for photos of soaked visitors.

The throng of plastic-clad spectators continued to funnel through the tunnel's opening from the elevators, increasing the growing mass packing the observation deck like canned meat.

The milling herd didn't feel threatening so far. They seemed to be content to socialize and wait for the show to begin.

But panic could lead to a deadly stampede through the tunnel elevators from which there was no exit. Or over the railings to the slippery, wet ground. Everywhere she looked, Kim saw disasters waiting to happen.

She shivered uncontrollably now, from the cold and wet as well as the imminently dangerous vibe she felt all the way down to her bones.

Kim needed to find Westwood and move to a safer location to interview him. Sooner was better.

She turned a slow three-hundred-sixty degrees, scanning the yellow-clad tourists, seeking a glimpse of the man she now imagined a harmless nebbish.

Her eye level settled about mid-chest for the men and somewhere around the yellow hoods on most women. Faces were mostly obscured by the brimming ponchos packed in on all sides.

She turned a second slow circle, this time scanning below the ponchos at legs and shoes. Most were wearing damp jeans and wet running shoes. A few hearty souls wore sandals and paid for it with wet blue feet.

Kim squinted skyward toward the outer edge of the observation deck, catching brief glimpses of the Rainbow Bridge where the fireworks would originate. She lowered her gaze, seeking Westwood again.

Which was when she saw a man wearing cargo shorts and hiking boots with speckled laces like miniature mountain climbing ropes among the crowd ahead.

She'd seen similar sturdy legs and boots before. One of Westwood's articles showed photos of him in the field wearing the same type of shorts and footwear. Could the sturdy legs belong to him?

Kim moved toward the boots. Before she reached them, she glanced back toward the tunnel's exit.

Russell had emerged, head and shoulders above the others in his cohort, clad in a massive yellow poncho, scanning the crowd just as she had done.

Reassured by his presence, she turned back and continued moving toward the hiking boots, threading slowly through the crowd, making slow progress. The man wearing the boots was now surrounded by gawkers, tightly packed together.

Conversation volume out here was raised several decibels to be heard above the roar of the falls.

The area's night lighting dimmed in preparation for the fireworks show. The observation deck and all surrounding areas, north and south, became darker, shadowed and foreboding.

Before Kim could reach Westwood, without warning, the first explosion filled the sky with an almost supersonic boom that shook her teeth. Followed by sparkling fireworks near the Rainbow Bridge.

The spectacle drew awed gasps from the crowd, along with pointing, shouting, applause, and laughter.

More explosions followed quickly after the first.

The chaos had raised Kim's internal threat meter into the red zone and held it there. Her heart pounded and her ears rang with the aftermath of each new explosion.

Rapidly, her mind ran a threat assessment.

Had she been lured here by false promises of vital information?

Did Westwood mean to harm her?

Possibly. What did she know about Westwood, after all?

He claimed Reacher had sent him.

Which was possible, but not likely. Why draw her to a place where no conversation could possibly happen if his intent was to discuss vital matters? The plan was preposterous on its face.

Still, perhaps Reacher did send him. Westwood's claim couldn't be confirmed or disproved because Reacher was, as always, unreachable.

Meaning Westwood's story could easily be a lie.

He might have discovered Lucas's death.

He might even be responsible for Lucas's murder.

Kim's natural skepticism and wariness increased as conditions on the ground became more threatening. Westwood seemed dangerously threatening to her now.

Why didn't he wait in his suite, as they'd planned?

If Westwood had lured her here to harm her, he could easily escape capture.

The observation deck tonight, with the crowds and the falls roaring and fireworks bursting in batches of gunpowder blasts overhead, was a perfect set up to cover an attack and get away.

Was Westwood that clever? That calculating?

Kim took a quick look over her shoulder seeking another glimpse of Russell. A solid batch of yellow ponchos filled the space between the tunnel's exit and where she stood.

She couldn't see Russell anywhere in the crowd. Mentally, she crossed her fingers, hoping he was there somewhere. Hoping she could rely on him if she needed to.

Kim reached inside her jacket and pulled her weapon from its holster.

She held it concealed by her side as she plowed through the spectators, headed toward Westwood, continuing her slow, relentless forward momentum.

Three batches of fireworks exploded, one immediately following the other, drawing Kim's attention to the sky. Boom! Boom! Boom!

The crowd whooped appreciation with loud applause and screaming high-fives for the spectacular color bursts, paced rapidly, growing more intense with each volley.

Westwood's boots with the speckled laces were only a few feet away from her now. She was almost there.

One of the tourists shoved toward an opening in the yellow ponchos for a better view of the show. A momentary gap opened in the crowd just as he slipped on the wet pavement and caromed into Kim, knocking her to the ground.

She landed hard on her left side, holding her weapon off the wet pavers. The man who knocked her over didn't seem to realize what he'd done. He kept going without a backward glance.

From her position on the ground, Kim's focus returned to the boots. Craning her neck for a clearer view of Westwood from a new vantage point, seeking a chance to confirm his identity.

This time, her effort was successful. Definitely the same man whose photos she'd found online. The *LA Times* science reporter. Ashley Westwood, PhD.

She saw him clearly through the gaps between legs and boots beneath yellow plastic ponchos.

Westwood's body rested on the ground against the wrought iron fencing on the edge of the rowdy horde.

Eyes open. Lips slack.

Rivulets of water ran down his lifeless face from the falls' unrelenting mist.

The yellow plastic hood was bunched around his neck.

Curly gray hair was plastered to his scalp.

His wiry beard resembled wet steel wool.

The bullet had come from a distance, entering through his back. Blood soaked his clothes inside the opaque poncho and ran beneath the clinging plastic onto wet concrete.

A pink-tinged pool of watery blood widened beneath the body.

People had shifted aside providing him space to crumple.

No screaming. No panic. Nothing.

No indication that nearby revelers had noticed the man die.

Before she could rise from the cold, wet pavement, another round of fireworks exploded overhead, sending showers of red, white, and blue sparklers raining across the night sky.

CHAPTER 18

Friday, June 3
Niagara Falls, Ontario, CA

KIM PUSHED HERSELF OFF the wet pavement. She whipped her head around to look for Russell. No luck. She couldn't wait.

"Move!" she ordered as she shoved and elbowed her way through the crowd toward Westwood's body. "Coming through! Out of the way!"

Spectators, eyes toward the sky, engrossed in the show, moved aside with annoyed glances.

One guy shoved back, declaring, "I was here first."

Kim left him blocking her path when a gap opened briefly to one side. She slipped through. The gap closed rapidly behind her as she thrust forward, making slow progress.

Finally, she reached Westwood's cold, wet body. She knelt to check for a carotid pulse to confirm.

He was dead.

He'd been dead when he dropped to the pavement. By this time, he'd been lying there long enough to get cold as stone.

A flash of movement caught her periphery. One of the yellow ponchos. Awkwardly out of place.

She glanced toward the yellow flicker just in time. A tall, thin man placed his foot on the short retaining wall, gripped the wrought iron railing with one hand and vaulted over the top.

In a quick moment, he landed solidly on the greenspace outside the fence, prepared to run. When he hit the wet ground on the other side, he slipped and lost his balance.

He slid along the hill toward the river, flailing his arms to stay upright. The yellow plastic hood held snug by the falls' constant shower.

Using both long arms and legs, he managed to stop his descent and scrambled up to a level spot on the wet earth. From her vantage point, she couldn't see his weapon.

He paused for breath before he began to run southward, outside the safety barrier, along the rough natural edge of the pedestrian walkway.

His feet slipped every time he hit a muddy patch of ground, but he stayed upright and kept going.

Kim scanned the area ahead, beside, and behind him. His options were limited. The crowds and the terrain operated as a barrier to escape.

He was headed toward the Rainbow Bridge. There was an open walkway up from the river to the street at that point.

If he reached the exit before Kim could stop him, he'd be gone.

Was he Westwood's killer? Maybe not. But he was the only man risking life and limb to run away from the murder scene.

Flight was an indicator of guilt, in Kim's experience.

If he had another excuse, he could tell her when she caught him.

Quickly, Kim patted Westwood down and grabbed his wallet and two phones before she stood up. She grabbed an arm nearby and shook the spectator to attention. He frowned and glared at her.

"What?" he demanded in a short, sharp snap of impatience. "Find another place to watch the show, lady."

Kim pointed to Westwood's body. "He's been shot. Call the police."

"Call them yourself," he replied without looking, still annoyed.

What a jerk. Kim had no time to argue. She gave him a sharp elbow jab to the bicep, hard enough to hurt.

Which pissed him off.

He drew back to return the punch, but she moved out of reach before he could lay her out cold.

"Call the police! Just do it!" she yelled to be heard over the cacophony as she shoved her way to the railing.

She didn't bother to yell at the fleeing man on the other side of the retaining wall. Waste of breath. He wouldn't have stopped running even if he could hear her yelling over the deafening noise.

Kim grabbed the cold, wet, slippery railing with her free hand. The barrier was almost as tall as she was.

She stepped up onto the retaining wall, threw her right leg over the wrought iron railing, and stepped onto the retaining wall on the other side. Still holding the railing, she lowered her feet to the muddy earth.

When she felt steady enough, she released the railing and headed across the rocky outcropping as rapidly as she could move.

She kept one eye on the running man and the other seeking secure footing. The rain-slicked and uneven surface made speed impossible in the darkness.

Sporadic fireworks illuminated the sky and revealed the ground ahead.

Her quarry landed in mud and slipped on the grass. More than once, he went down on one knee and struggled to stand again.

Relentlessly, steadily, slowly, she closed the gap.

The crowds at the observation deck behind her and along the pedestrian walkway to her left, still watching the fireworks at the Rainbow Bridge, seemed oblivious to the desperately slow chase.

Kim was barely winded by the exercise. She was a runner. She lived in Detroit. Where she trained in inclement weather most of the year. Snow, wind, rain, bone-chilling cold. She was used to it.

She could beat this guy.

She knew it as well as she knew anything.

All she had to do was outlast him. She wasn't even breathing heavily.

Kim shoved her awareness of the roaring falls, exploding fireworks, and cheering crowds out of mind.

She focused solely on two things.

The runner.

The precarious terrain.

Nothing else entered her consciousness as she reduced the distance between them.

Near the middle of the long distance, the running man slipped again and went down. This time he landed on both hands and knees.

He stayed down for a couple of seconds. Kim was gaining on him.

Her focus was disturbed by Russell's voice calling behind her. She kept running carefully over the rocky ground, not even casting a quick look over her shoulder. Russell could see her. There was no reason to look toward him.

Russell's longer legs and heavier bulk carried him faster and more securely forward. "I've got this," he said as he sailed past her.

Kim kept her steady pace.

Russell was half a block ahead.

The shooter must have heard Russell calling out. He jumped up from the darkness and sprinted forward. He turned when he landed on a patch of flat grassy earth, holding a handgun.

As the fireworks shot up from the stand, he set his stance and waited for the flash to perfect his aim.

"Russell! He's got a gun!" Kim shouted a moment later, looking for cover.

Russell saw the shooter's intention a split second later. He stopped and dropped to the ground, rolling down the hill toward the frigid Niagara River below.

Russell scrambled behind a boulder outcropping for cover.

When the burst of bright fireworks lit the sky and the ground below, the shooter aimed toward Russell and released two quick rounds under cover of the explosions.

The blinding flash of the fireworks imprinted on Kim's retinas. She squeezed her eyes closed and opened them again. Nothing helped.

She returned fire, trusting her memory to pinpoint the shooter's location.

Unnatural quiet between the fiery bursts settled over the scene.

When the next rounds whistled upward and exploded the night, Kim's vision had cleared enough to see that the runner had made good use of his time. Somehow, he had disappeared. Where had he gone?

She whipped around in all directions, peering into the crowd above and the river below. Another break in the fireworks display had plunged the hillside into darkness again.

The shooter could be hiding anywhere in the shadows. Kim kept her pistol at the ready, searching while she waited for her partner.

Russell climbed up from the boulders below, sliding along the muddy incline, adjusting his feet for purchase on the muddy embankment. Twice, he slipped down a few feet and struggled to retake the same ground.

When he reached Kim, muddy and shivering, Russell asked, "Where is he?"

"Dunno," she replied quietly, watching for unnatural movement.

"Did you get a good look at him? A photo, maybe?"

She shrugged. "No such luck."

The grand finale fireworks shot up from the launch pad. A group of a dozen rockets whistled high into the sky and burst apart in rapid succession. Bright, colored light flooded the hillside as well as the areas above and below it like floodlights.

Kim looked frantically while she could.

When the last of the fireworks had sputtered into darkness and the applause died down, the nighttime lights illuminated again, casting contrasting shadows across the hillside.

She scoured the area again.

The shooter was nowhere. He had simply vanished.

"Let's go get cleaned up. Catch some sleep." Russell gestured toward the Rainbow Bridge, the only viable exit point. "There's CCTV cameras everywhere around here. One of them could have caught a good image of his face. I'll make some calls. Maybe we'll get lucky."

Kim had already asked Gaspar to search the CCTV. He might have spied something useful, too. But she found no fault with the plan and fell into step with Russell. She continued her vigilant scanning for the tall, thin man.

No luck.

CHAPTER 19

Saturday, June 4
New York City, New York

WHEN THE TEXT FROM Fox finally came, Morin was seriously worried. He'd long ago finished his steak, downed another cocktail, and placed five knotted cherry stems on the small square napkin.

A notification finally slid across the dark screen. Morin punched it with his index finger. The message opened instantly.

Only one word: *Done.*

No photo attached. Meaning no proof of death. Which was absolutely necessary.

Audrey Ruston had wiggled her gorgeous ass right into his head. She was right, dammit. Proof of death was required. Before he reported success to Brax, Morin had to confirm.

He replied: *Terminated?*

Several long seconds later, Fox sent a thumbs-up emoji.

Still not satisfied, mostly because he knew Brax would demand absolute certainty, Morin replied: *Photo?*

He waited an interminable number of seconds this time before a photo from Fox finally appeared on the screen.

A photo of what, exactly? Poor quality. Bad lighting. Resolution too low for clarity when he tried to enlarge the image.

Morin could make out only a dark background image, a few darker vertical lines in the foreground, and a barely visible man-sized lump on the ground among them.

The vertical lines could have been legs.

A crowd, maybe, standing outside at night.

Perhaps near Niagara Falls, since Fox had said Westwood was there.

Why did Fox choose such an exposed location? A kill in a place like that wouldn't go unnoticed. Fox had taken a hell of a risk.

The man-sized lump could have been Westwood's body lifeless on the wet pavement. Or it could have been a bulging black trash bag. Or a tired kid taking a nap.

The shot was snapped quickly and without Fox's usual level of care. Even after several attempts to manipulate the image, Morin couldn't definitively see that the lump was Westwood, dead or alive.

Morin shook his head. The cocktails had infiltrated his brain, making his thinking too fuzzy.

He could not confirm that Fox had killed the right man from this bad photo.

Which meant he couldn't authorize payment. Brax would have his head.

The downward spiral of his thoughts gained speed as he reached the inevitable conclusions at the bottom.

Morin couldn't pay Fox for unconfirmed services rendered.

His failure to pay meant Fox would discontinue the hunt for the scientist and the prototype.

Not good.

Brax would be pissed.

Which would give Audrey Ruston the advantage.

Also not good.

On the other hand, if Morin did pay for the kill and Fox had failed to eliminate Westwood, Brax would be livid.

Morin wouldn't stay on the team for sure. Brax couldn't and shouldn't allow such incompetence to stand.

Audrey Ruston was one ruthless bitch. Always had been. She lacked whatever gene that gave most humans the capacity for forgiveness and remorse.

Which was the main reason he'd ended his relationship with her years ago. She was, simply put, too cold. No man had ever left Audrey before. She wouldn't stand for it. She had vowed to make him pay.

Audrey's quest to replace Morin had become a matter of personal pride for her. She would have Morin's job. For sure. No matter how long it took or what was required to accomplish the feat.

If Morin managed to thwart her this time, her thirst for vengeance could become even worse.

He shuddered.

Without asking, the bartender brought another Manhattan. Morin should have sent it back. He didn't.

He sipped slowly, crunching his gray cells to concentrate and think things through, discarding every option that popped into his head.

He could imagine no viable alternatives.

He needed proof of Westwood's death. Nothing less would suffice. He couldn't move forward without confirmation.

How could he get it?

A notification flashed across the phone's screen. Another terse message from Fox, demanding payment. Morin heard the icy cold tone in his head.

Well?

Morin swigged the last of his cocktail, tied the sixth and final cherry stem, and tried to find a better answer. No luck.

He sent his response text to Fox, brooking no argument.

Need proof.

Morin waited a few seconds while the bartender processed his credit card for the night's tab. Evidence that he'd been here the whole night. Should he need to prove it.

After he signed for the charges and slid off the bar stool, one last text came through from Fox. A thumbs-down emoji this time.

The phone rang.

Morin picked up. "Yeah."

Fox was slightly breathless, as if he were moving fast. He demanded, "Payment in full. Now. You know the rules."

"So do you," Morin replied, struggling to keep the panic from his reply.

"Send full payment or suffer the consequences."

Morin said nothing.

Fox exhaled heavily, his voice jerky, as if he might be running up a steep incline. "You have a wife, Morin. Kids."

The threat to his family was unmistakable.

Morin's breath stopped, depriving him of oxygen. His heart rate tripled.

Trembling made conversation impossible. He became lightheaded, dizzy. Pulsing pain pounded his chest hard like a dozen cannon balls shot from close range.

On the line, he heard a heavy door close, and Fox's conversation became terse and less cryptic.

"You have access to CCTV. You can find a better image of the journalist if you need it," Fox said. "His face will be all over the local news soon enough. Use your resources. Get the proof you need. But send my money now. When I have it, I'll find the scientist and the drone. As we agreed."

Stalemate. No proof, no money. No money, Fox quits. Right here. Right now.

Westwood was probably dead. Morin had seen the lump.

He had no reason to believe Fox had lied about the identity of the body.

Killing Westwood was Fox's job. A skill Fox had mastered long ago. He'd never failed before.

Beyond that, Fox was at least as ruthless as Audrey. Maybe more.

Fox would kill Morin's family if he didn't pay. Morin was certain of that.

But Fox couldn't survive without protection from Brax. The assassin business often led to vengeance and Fox had made too many enemies over the years. Morin was certain of that, too.

Indecision was killing time and leading them no closer to resolution.

Morin took a deep breath to steady his nerves. "The journalist is done?"

Fox swore under his breath. He seemed preoccupied again. "Of course he's done. I promise you that."

Morin climbed onto his seat at the bar and signaled the bartender for another drink with a shaky hand.

He was more afraid of Fox's threats to his family than Audrey's vengeance. His first attempt to respond was little more than a croak.

Morin cleared his throat and tried again. "I'll send payment now."

"See that you do," Fox said. "I'll be in touch after I've found the scientist."

"You know where he is?" Morin asked, realizing he sounded pathetically hopeful.

"I know where he's going. I'll wait," Fox said.

"When will that happen?" Morin asked but Fox had already disconnected.

He pushed a few buttons on the phone to pay the kill fee.

He waited for Fox to confirm receipt.

The bartender brought another Perfect Manhattan and placed it on the bar.

While Morin waited for payment confirmation, he gulped half of the numbing sweetness from the glass as he watched the big clock mounted over the back of the bar.

Too many minutes passed.

Still no word from Fox. Did he get the money or not?

After another five minutes, Morin knew something was horribly, terribly wrong. He felt the disaster in his bones.

He slid off the bar stool and landed squarely on his feet. The pleasant alcohol buzz he'd been building was replaced by crystal clarity.

Brax didn't know anything yet. No reason to report failure. That sort of news travels fast enough on its own.

Morin realized now that he should never have sent Fox to do the job. He should have done it himself.

Maybe it wasn't too late to fix this.

Morin left the restaurant and headed toward the garage where he parked his Range Rover.

Morin knew where Fox had planned to go next. He could handle this personally. Brax would like that.

CHAPTER 20

Saturday, June 4
Niagara Falls, Ontario, CA

"THIS PLACE IS CRAWLING with people tonight because of the holiday, whatever it is," Russell said quietly.

Kim trudged behind the throng along the pedestrian walkway adjacent to the Niagara River.

From this vantage point tourists must have been distracted by the fireworks. They probably didn't witness her frantic pursuit of Westwood's killer.

Nor did they seem particularly aware of her muddy, disheveled appearance now.

Russell, being bigger and broader, attracted a few curious glances, but nothing alarming. No shrieks or frantic calls for police.

These people were the complete opposite of nosy.

Kim appreciated the lack of interest. The less explaining required, the better.

They walked past the entrance to Table Rock Centre, toward the stairs leading up to the hotel. There were no ambulance or police vehicles out front, which was odd.

Westwood's body might have already been recovered. Surely he wasn't still lying there on the cold pavement.

The stairway entrance and the Incline Railway were overwhelmed by the mob of people waiting to use them. Russell led the way around through the alley to the front of the building.

When they finally reached their vehicle parked in the garage where they'd left it, Russell grinned. "Are you feeling lucky?"

"Not especially," she replied with a long exhale. "Why?"

"We could go up to Westwood's suite. Take a look at his laptop. See if we can figure out what the hell is going on here. Decide what to do next. It's not like he's going to need the room," Russell said. "Or we can try to find another hotel now, get cleaned up, come back later when we're looking presentable and less likely to draw stares. Your choice."

The idea was beyond tempting. She was wet and cold and muddy. A hot shower and fresh clothes would be more than welcome. But even a quick wash would help.

Connecting with Gaspar now instead of later might solve a few other problems.

The laptop and the zip drives had become urgent. But the data Westwood had stored was likely to be encrypted. She'd need special expertise to access it.

Leaving the laptop a bit longer seemed like the better answer.

A closer search of Westwood's suite was a good plan, though. They might turn up intel they hadn't found before.

The only real risk she could think of at the moment was that local authorities might identify Westwood's body, run his passport, and show up at his suite before she had a chance to search.

But that probably wouldn't happen until later. She and Russell would be long gone by then.

"Okay," Kim said. "We'll do the search now and leave Westwood's electronics for later. We'll stay twenty minutes, max. If we don't find anything by then, we leave empty-handed."

"Worried that Westwood's shooter might show up?" Russell asked, cocking his head.

"Nothing would make me happier," Kim replied dryly. "But no. The Falls area is a top terrorist target. Every inch is crawling with security. You can't sneeze without hitting one of them."

Russell nodded. "The longer we stay, the more likely we are to attract the wrong kind of attention."

"If they found us, we'd be okay, eventually. Cooper and Finlay would intervene. But all of that would slow us down," Kim said. "Let's just get in and get out. We see anybody watching us, we split up and meet back at the SUV."

"Roger that," Russell said with a grin.

She pulled a baseball cap from her travel bag and snugged it onto her head, tugging the bill low. She was still wearing the yellow poncho, which was still good camo. She pulled the plastic hood over the ball cap.

"How do I look?"

"Like all the other tourists." Russell didn't have a baseball cap, but he arranged his poncho as artfully as possible.

"That's as good as it's gonna get." he said, viewing his reflection in the SUV's tinted window. He turned to her for inspection. "How do we look?"

"Like a couple of wet, exhausted tourists," Kim replied.

"Perfect, you mean." Russell grinned.

Kim shrugged and headed toward the busy front entrance of the Clark Hotel. The valet line was longer now that the fireworks had ended. Runners were bringing vehicles up four at a time.

The queue of bedraggled tourists wearing yellow or red plastic ponchos stretched all the way back and into the main lobby.

Instead of drawing stares, Kim and Russell easily blended with the others. What made them a curiosity now was swimming upstream like salmon during mating season.

Which couldn't be helped.

Russell led the way through the throng, elbows and forearms widening a gap large enough to slip through before it closed again.

The lobby had been crowded before the fireworks show and now, a sea of soggy bodies logjammed the exits. Russell continued plowing forward, but progress was like moving Mt. Rushmore with a plush toy.

He swiveled his head, spied an opening, tilted his chin to the left. Kim followed closely lest she lose the chance.

Eventually, they reached the elevator lobby on the left of the reception desk. Russell pushed beyond the bulging pack of shivering patrons.

On the other side of the elevator Russell climbed the open stairs to the Mezzanine level. A marginally lighter horde gathered here waiting to enter the restaurant that overlooked the falls.

Russell muscled his way to the rear of the pack. Elevator doors opposite the hostess stand opened, disgorging another twenty people into the lobby. Russell slipped inside the elevator and pulled Kim in with him.

The doors closed and the elevator began the long climb up to Westwood's suite on the twenty-second floor. Passengers disgorged on every floor until only six were left to exit at the top.

Russell and Kim were the last to leave the elevator car. They lingered a few moments to give the others lead time.

Kim led the way to room 2226.

She stood aside as Russell used his device to unlock the door while she gloved up. He pressed the levered handle with his sleeve and gave the door a shove.

Kim slipped inside first. Russell followed and closed the door.

The intruder had not opened the drapes, but he'd left all the lights on.

Inside the door, she stopped and stared.

The interior of the suite looked like it had been blown apart.

Russell halted immediately behind her. From his vantage point over her head, he scanned the damage as he gloved up.

Silently, Kim drew her weapon and stepped carefully into the common room. One quick glance around was enough to confirm that the intruder was done in this area.

He'd swept the entire room and tossed everything he touched onto the floor. The cushions were slashed and torn apart. Dishes lay in broken shards on the tile. Flatware was strewn in all directions.

Given the level of destruction, he'd probably been searching for more than a standard-sized laptop. He might have wanted the thumb drives Kim had already taken. Maybe he was looking for other things, too.

Russell drew his weapon and fanned out to Kim's left. Muffled curses interspersed with the sounds of breaking objects came from deeper into the suite.

They approached the short corridor leading to both bedrooms.

Simultaneously, Kim heard the intruder thumping around, throwing objects to the ground, and cursing inside the bedroom closest to her.

Russell's voice was louder and more bombastic than hers. Also more likely to make an immediate impact.

She gestured to convey the message. Russell nodded.

Kim assumed a shooter's stance while Russell took two steps toward the door.

All at once, he reached out, slammed the door open, and yelled, "Police! Drop your weapon! Hands up!"

CHAPTER 21

Saturday, June 4
Niagara Falls, Ontario, CA

THE MAN WHIPPED AROUND to face them. His features were sharp beneath pale skin. He was exceptionally thin, as if a character artist had drawn his accentuated skinny physique.

Dressed in black, head to toe.

Black knit cap covered his dark hair. Black leather gloves snugged long, slender fingers.

He'd have been nearly invisible in the darkness.

His black boots were wet and muddy, as if he'd been running along the hillside while someone chased him, perhaps.

Was Skinny the man Kim had pursued on the hillside and lost? She'd never had a clear view of his face out there, but the strong churning in her gut said he was the one.

No doubt his gloved hands had been searching Westwood's suite before Kim arrived. And destroying evidence as he went.

Half a second after Russell's shout filled the room, the skinny man looked up, saw the threat, and reached for his gun with his right hand.

Russell shouted, "Hands up! Now!"

Skinny lifted his weapon to fire.

Kim ignored her training and aimed her Glock at his right shoulder. She didn't want to kill him before he had a chance to answer a thousand questions.

She squeezed off a quick round before Skinny had a chance to aim or fire.

Her bullet struck exactly where she'd placed it.

He screamed and slapped his left hand over the entry wound. His gun fell from his right hand and thumped to the floor. His right arm hung useless at his side dripping blood onto the carpet.

Good. He'd be in pain, but still able to answer questions. Such as who the hell he was and why had he killed two men who only wanted to talk to her?

Half a moment later, before Kim had a chance to move, Russell fired off two rounds. Both slammed into the intruder's torso, center mass.

The skinny man went down instantly, his blood pooling under him for the slice of a second that his heart continued to beat. Then the blood flow, like his heartbeat, stopped.

"Why'd you kill him?" Kim cast a glare toward Russell. "We need to know what he knows. Why he killed Westwood. And probably Lucas, too."

"Because he was about to add both of us to his kill list." Russell snapped. "Not how I wanted to spend the rest of my night. You?"

She didn't argue with him in the heat of the moment. Russell's view of the skinny man had been partially blocked. He couldn't see the extent of the man's shoulder injury. He didn't hear the shooter's gun drop to the floor. No doubt, Russell's actions were justified.

"Security will be here any minute. The fireworks outside have been over for a while now. No chance those three gunshots will go unnoticed." Kim jerked her head sideways toward the body. "I'll search him. Look around. See if you can find what he was looking for. Quickly."

Kim approached the skinny man, pulling out her phone. She snapped several photos, taking care with the head shots. She might get lucky with facial recognition software.

She pulled his gloves off carefully and then used the app on her phone to take a quick set of fingerprints and ear prints. She swabbed him for DNA.

Still wearing her gloves, she patted him down. His ID was in an RFID wallet in his front pocket. She snapped photos of everything and returned it.

In his other front pocket, he carried a hotel key card and US currency. About five hundred dollars in bills of various denominations.

A burner phone was stuffed into his back pocket. No time to check it thoroughly. She slid it into an evidence bag and then into her pocket.

She grabbed the plastic bag from the ice bucket and dropped his pistol into it.

Then she placed the gloves into the bag as well.

With luck, she'd get better fingerprints and DNA from the gloves from the lab.

His phone could provide faster data and leads, if she got lucky.

The gun might reveal solid ballistics on both the Westwood and Lucas murders.

While Russell searched the other bedroom and Kim was busy with the body, she heard the heavy entrance door slam closed in the front room. Her breath caught.

"Russell!" she shouted as she jammed everything into her pockets and hurried toward the bedroom door. "Let's go!"

When Russell reached her, she said. "Someone else was in here. Maybe an accomplice. I heard the exit door close. We can't hang around. Locals could already be on the way."

"There's nothing to find here anyway," Russell said, jerking a thumb over his shoulder toward the dead man. "That guy have anything useful on him?"

"Maybe. We'll see. But he also had a key card to another hotel room."

"So we're going to check out his room? And maybe use his shower?" Russell suggested. "I'd like to get cleaned up."

Kim opened the door and stepped into the empty hallway. She swiveled her head and looked in all directions but saw no one hanging around making a hasty exit after slamming the exit door to Westwood's suite.

Russell followed, holding the door until it snugged quietly shut behind him.

They made tracks to the elevator lobby and ignored the elevator cars. Kim slipped into the stairwell and Russell followed close after.

Kim rested most of her body weight on her hands and slid down the rails, one flight after another, her feet barely touching the stair treads. Russell hustled along behind her.

When she'd descended ten flights, Kim paused to wait for Russell at the landing. He wasn't winded, but he seemed to appreciate the short break.

"Could have been someone from housekeeping. Maybe she opened the door, saw the mess, and hurried out again," Kim said. "She might not have heard the gunshots at all."

"Possibly," Russell replied, doubtful. "Or, your first thought, the skinny guy could have had an accomplice."

She nodded. "Also possible."

"We won't find whoever it was based on what we know now. Better to let them come to us, don't you think?" Russell asked.

"Agreed. Twelve flights to go and we'll be at the lobby level. Another one down to the parking garage." Kim said as she moved to the next flight of stairs and headed down.

"So we go to the skinny guy's hotel?" Russell asked on the way down.

"Could be it's not his hotel," Kim reminded him. "But yeah. The key card is our best lead right now. The key card has the hotel name but no room number on it. You game to keep going on this?"

"I'd really like to know what the hell is going on here."

"We can figure that out when we get there, possibly."

"Get where?" Russell said behind her, taking the steps two at a time.

On the fifth floor, a guest opened the door to the stairwell and started down. Kim was below him. Russell above.

He didn't make eye contact with either of them. Nor did he speak.

They descended three flights at a normal pace and in total silence.

At the mezzanine floor, the man opened the door and headed toward the restaurant. They were alone in the stairwell again.

Kim picked up her speed and the conversation where they'd left off.

"The key card is for the Father Louis Hennepin Hotel. The address is a small town called Niagara-on-the-Lake." She'd hit the landing and moved toward the next flight down. "I've been there before. It's about thirty minutes north of here. On Lake Ontario."

"And what, the door slammer actually was the cleaning lady?" Russell asked, slightly breathless after rapidly descending twenty-one flights.

"Then we'd better get the hell out of here before the local constabulary shows up." Kim slid down the last set of handrails, landed firmly on the pavement, and walked through the door to the parking garage.

Russell overtook her. He approached the SUV, used the key fob to unlock both doors and climbed into the driver's seat and started the engine.

Kim took the passenger seat quickly. Russell pulled out of the garage before she'd had a chance to put her seat belt on.

She punched the hotel address into the navigation system and hit the green button. The mechanical voice advised the drive was twenty-one kilometers and would be accomplished in twenty-eight minutes, door-to-door.

As Russell drove following the directions, Kim picked up the alligator clamp she'd left on the console earlier and attached it to her seatbelt near the retractor.

Russell seemed to breathe a bit easier once they were clear of the garage. "Any chance we can find a bite to eat at this hour?"

"Along country roads through farmland and wineries?" Kim grinned. "Not likely."

"Maybe skinny guy's room has a minibar," he grumbled.

CHAPTER 22

Saturday, June 4
Niagara Falls, Ontario, CA

AUDREY RUSTON HAD PUSHED the heavy door of Westwood's suite inward just in time to hear the unmistakable sound of gunshots in one of the bedrooms. Two guns fired.

One shot from the first, followed by two shots from the second weapon.

After the second shots, she'd heard a heavy thump, like a man falling to the floor.

Audrey crept closer to the bedroom and stood with her back to the wall. She turtled her head through the open doorway for a quick scan.

Three people across the room. Two were still vertical. One on the floor, obviously dead.

Audrey had never seen the big man and the Asian woman before.

Operatives of some sort, judging from their demeanor and the easy way they handled both the weapons and the situation.

Probably not private security.

More likely a couple of well trained members of Uncle Sam's team, one way or another.

For a split second, Audrey worried that Brax had sent backup to replace her. But that made zero sense.

Brax was a slimy bastard, but also a man of his word. He'd give her the twenty-four hours he'd promised to find Liam Stuart and the prototype before he sent someone else.

Audrey cocked her head. Two professionals standing over a man down.

All three looked like they'd been rolling in the mud. Faces and clothes were crusted with dried earth.

Even from this distance, Audrey easily pegged the unlucky recipient of the bullets. No challenge at all since she knew the guy.

If names were destiny, Ace Fox was fated to become a cunning killer the moment he drew his first breath.

His tall, skinny frame and pointed face conveyed his sly, feral, nocturnal habits.

Fox had perfected the art of murder for hire after a decade of successful contract hits, paid for by men who operated on the fringes of Uncle Sam's payroll. He was a very wealthy man. Which didn't make him any more likable.

Audrey had wondered why Fox stayed in the game. She shrugged. Now, she'd never know. She'd lost her chance to get any intel at all from his thin and narrow lips.

The two operatives were preoccupied with Fox and his activities. After a moment's quick scan of the situation, Audrey turned and crept silently away.

She made it all the way out of the suite.

But she'd misjudged her exit.

The heavy door slammed closed behind her, faster than she'd expected and loudly enough to raise the dead.

She'd had to move fast.

Instead of heading downstairs, Audrey scurried back to the observation post she'd commandeered across the hallway. She slipped inside the room and put her eye to the peephole.

She didn't wait long.

The big man and the Asian woman soon exited the suite, weapons still in hand. They'd heard the slamming door when Audrey had ducked out. Which meant they'd be looking for her.

She watched as they hurried along the hallway toward the elevator lobby, holding their weapons down at their sides. Their movements reflected Uncle Sam's textbook training.

The two were operatives. No doubt about it.

When they turned the corner, Audrey slipped into the corridor and followed a discreet distance behind them.

She arrived just in time to see the stairwell fire door close behind the big man. Half a moment later, one of the elevator cars dinged loudly before it stopped on the twenty-second floor.

Two couples got out.

Talking among themselves, they didn't seem to notice Audrey as they moved down the corridor in the opposite direction from Westwood's suite.

Audrey smiled. She'd always been lucky.

She slipped into the empty elevator car and pushed the button for the garage lobby. The big man and the Asian woman were likely to try to escape from there.

Predicting behavior was a necessary skill in this job. A skill Audrey had honed to perfection through countless hours of practice.

Audrey reached the garage before the operatives did. She scanned the license plates on vehicles parked within easy exit range.

She spied an SUV with an Ohio rental plate.

Vehicles parked nearby sported mostly Canadian license plates. Here and there, a few New York plates. Only one Ohio plate embassy parked near the exit.

She took the chance and put a tracker under the wheel well. She snapped a photo of the Ohio plate and the SUV, just in case.

Then she sauntered to the hotel's valet entrance and leaned casually against a pillar, phone held down by her side. A good photo of the two would help.

She wanted to know who they were and why they had been dogging Fox.

Because soon, they'd be dogging her.

Audrey liked to know exactly what she was dealing with.

She didn't wait long before the Ohio SUV pulled out of the garage. The big man was driving and the Asian woman rode shotgun.

Which meant the woman was number one on the team. Proper procedure again. Number two was always the driver. Simple as that.

As the SUV approached the valet stand, Audrey mingled with a group of tourists and shot a burst of photos toward the windshield. Shots good enough to identify the driver and the passenger.

The big man turned left at the street and merged into traffic. Audrey waited until they'd turned the first corner, blocking her view and also blocking the SUV's rear view.

She wasn't concerned about losing the SUV. Her tracker had good range. No need to rush.

When she was certain she was well beyond the driver's line of sight, Audrey sauntered to her rental and slipped behind the steering wheel.

She started the sedan's engine and activated the tracking software on her phone.

The pulsing blue dot on her screen showed the Ohio SUV heading north.

Nothing much up that way except the picturesque old town of Niagara-on-the-Lake. The tracker showed the town resting on the south shore of Lake Ontario at the mouth of the Niagara River.

Audrey remembered it as a small and sleepy place. The shops and restaurants would have closed hours ago. The only businesses that could be accessed at this hour were hotels.

Maybe these two needed a nap.

The operatives had to be at least a little annoyed at this point.

As far as Audrey could tell, they had made no progress of any kind. Which was good.

Even better, it was safe to guess that they'd been thwarted at least three times now. First, with Lucas Stuart. Then, Ashley Westwood. And now Ace Fox.

Three chances to find Liam. Three strikes. If this were a baseball game and there were two outs, their side would be retired.

Team Brax had acted promptly enough after Liam Stuart disappeared to deflect certain failure. So far, so good.

The opposition, whoever they were, had yet to give up, though.

Why would two of Uncle Sam's operatives be going to Niagara-on-the-Lake? Looking for further intel on Fox and his mission, probably.

Which meant the big man and the Asian woman, and maybe whoever they reported to, didn't know Fox or what his mission was. The drone project could still be saved.

Which would please Brax no end.

Were they headed to Fox's hotel? As far as she knew, Fox wasn't likely to have booked a hotel room anywhere. He liked to slip into places without notice. He used false names and counterfeit identification.

All of which meant these two operatives weren't likely to discover Fox's hotel room, even if he'd had one. Which Audrey continued to doubt.

Beyond that, Fox was a pro. He'd never have left anything remotely incriminating anywhere and certainly not where a hotel maid could steal it.

Audrey felt confident that whatever Fox had learned about Liam Stuart and the prototype had died with him.

She'd bet her heirloom diamonds on it.

And never worry for a moment about losing that bet.

Which meant Fox didn't know where the scientist was or where the prototype was hidden.

If he'd known, he wouldn't have been searching Westwood's room, probably.

And Fox would still be alive.

Which he definitely wasn't.

The only reasonable conclusion Audrey could reach was that nothing about Brax's project had been compromised. As a bonus, Fox was out of the picture, maybe without collecting payment.

Audrey smiled. Perhaps she could claim his fee. She didn't need the money, but she wanted it. Money was how these guys kept score. And she intended to win.

There were rules to the game and Audrey deserved no credit for removing Fox from the playing board. Unfortunately. His scalp was one she had no right to claim.

Collecting the fee Fox was owed would be a way to twist the knife of Morin's failure into his belly, though. Which was great. Morin had crushed her once upon a time. She wanted payback, and she'd get it. One way or another.

Nigel Morin was on his way out. Audrey meant to make that happen. Stealing Fox's fee from under Morin's nose would show Brax, once again, how incompetent Morin was.

All she had to do was finish Fox's job. Find Liam Stuart and the drone. Bring the drone back in time to complete the test. Have the project ready to be deployed.

When Audrey accomplished all of that, Morin would be done.

Brax had promised. And Brax was a man of his word.

His very life often depended on it.

Audrey smiled, quite pleased with the situation. No sweat. She'd completed tougher jobs many times.

She glanced at the screen on her phone again. The pulsing blue dot led her along behind the Ohio SUV. They drove through miles of grape vineyards. Wineries had popped up everywhere, one after another.

Audrey wondered how grapevines, or anything else for that matter, thrived in the frigid snow blanketing this area for months at a time. But she'd been served wines from the region and found them some of the best cool climate varieties around.

She shook her head. Krause had to be freezing his ass off up here. He'd had a solid and easy job down in New York. Why the hell did he leave it for this place? Ego? Pride?

"What a fool. Men can be so utterly and completely stupid," she said aloud, driving a safe distance behind.

Audrey followed the tracker's blue dot into town and along Main Street.

She spied the Ohio SUV parked across the street from the entrance to the Father Louis Hennepin Hotel.

The big man was sitting behind the steering wheel.

The Asian woman must have gone inside.

As if her thoughts had conjured Krause, his name flashed on the screen of her phone, casting an eerie blue light into the dark cabin.

Half a moment later, the special ring tone she'd assigned to Ira Krause sounded.

An involuntary shudder went through her.

As if *he'd* walked on *her* grave. Instead of *her* walking on *his*.

CHAPTER 23

Saturday, June 4
Niagara-on-the-Lake, Ontario, CA

THE FATHER LOUIS HENNEPIN Hotel sounded impressive, and it was. The plaque out front proclaimed the whitewashed Georgian structure was established in 1832. Kim imagined gracious hospitality, architectural excellence, and probably a great restaurant.

Her stomach growled at the mere thought of room service. Food that wasn't delivered in a paper bag through a drive-up window. Which she wasn't likely to get at this time of night. The hotel looked closed for the evening.

Russell pulled into a no parking zone across from the entrance on Queen Street.

"We're not sure about this key card," he warned. "The dead guy had possession of it, but that doesn't mean the room will be empty."

"Copy that. Find a legal place to park. I'll persuade the desk clerk to give me a room number. I'll text you when I have it," Kim said as she opened the door and stepped out onto the sidewalk.

"Wait for me. Don't go in without backup," Russell called out before she closed the door.

Kim scowled and said nothing.

"Seriously, Otto. We know nothing about that guy. He could have a date stashed in there. Or a partner. Or a zillion other things. You never know," Russell replied.

"Right." Kim closed the door to the SUV.

Russell couldn't help himself. He was a trained agent. He knew the book inside and out. So did Kim. But she'd also learned that not everything unfolded according to the book. Especially in the hunt for Reacher.

The temperature had dropped at least ten degrees and a stiff breeze blew off the lake with the kind of clean smell she'd only experienced from the Great Lakes.

The cold sky was clear and the full moon added brilliant light as well as ambiance.

The place reminded her of home. Not surprising, perhaps. Niagara wasn't that far from Michigan.

Kim looked both ways, saw no one loitering nearby, and hoofed across the street. Trotted up the steps to the front door.

She grabbed the heavy brass handle and yanked hard. She rushed across the threshold, chilled to the bone.

The hotel lobby was as charming as the exterior. A cozy fire in the big fireplace might have warmed the room earlier in the evening, Kim imagined. Subdued lighting, comfortable furnishings, and deep pile carpets under, she loved the hotel already.

At the same time, the cozy ambience nagged her. Intuition. The skinny man would have been grossly out of place here, even before he'd spend the night rolling in the mud.

Perhaps he'd stolen the key card. Russell's warning repeated in her head. Maybe another guest occupied the room.

Only one way to find out.

The desk clerk wasn't sitting behind the big desk out front. She didn't see him anywhere. But it was very late. Maybe he was napping on a cot in the back.

Kim took advantage of his absence to duck into the restroom off the right side of the lobby.

When she pushed the door open, bizarrely blinding ceiling lights bounced off the white marble tile and white fixtures as if she'd stepped from the 1832 lobby directly into a sterile space station five hundred years later.

She closed her eyes against the piercing glare.

After a moment, she opened her eyelids again, slowly allowing her pupils to adjust to the unforgiving blaze. Why the hell did the decorator make the lights so bright and unforgiving in here?

She glanced at her reflection and grimaced. She'd tidied her face in the SUV's small lighted mirror on the way here. This glaring light ravaged all illusions. No question. She looked worse than a vagrant.

If the desk clerk had been manning his station when she'd entered the hotel, he'd have been smart to summon the police.

Kim ran water from the faucet until the stream warmed. She splashed her face and neck, sluicing the last of the dirt down the drain.

She used a damp paper towel to remove the worst of the dried mud on her clothes and shoes. Then she unwound her long hair from its knot at the back of her neck, smoothed the straggling strands into a ponytail, and twisted the thick, black rope into place again.

When she'd finished, Kim gave herself a critical inspection in the big mirror and frowned.

She looked like she'd wrestled with an alligator in a mud pit. Probably smelled like it, too.

She shrugged. Nothing more she could do here. Maybe Russell would bring the travel bags with him and she could do a proper job.

Kim returned to the lobby. The desk clerk was back at his post. She stood away from the desk, hoping the clerk couldn't see her very well and wasn't squeamish about the stench.

Truth was, he didn't look a lot better than she did. Messy brown hair and rumpled clothes made it look like he'd been sleeping. Perhaps a doorbell of some sort had sounded in the back to wake him when she'd first entered.

The tag fastened to his green shirt said *Todd*.

Kim sidled up to the desk and displayed all the pathetic charm she could muster. "Todd, I'm so sorry to wake you."

Which was true enough. She'd have preferred to let Todd sleep at least another couple of days while she approached the dead man's room undetected.

"No problem," he said, rubbing his eyes with his knuckles the way a six-year-old might. "How can I help?"

"I can't remember which room is mine." She smiled as she pulled the key card out of her pocket.

She displayed the card with what she hoped was charming chagrin and forgivable incompetence. "The number isn't written on here anywhere."

"Yeah. We do that for security. We write the number on the little paper sleeve we gave you for the card at check in," he said, palm out to receive the card. "Don't worry. Nobody ever remembers the numbers. I'll look it up for you."

He swiped the plastic through a reader of some sort attached to the screen of his computer system. As the data came up on the screen in front of him, he frowned.

"What's wrong, Todd? Can't you figure out the room number, either?" Kim said, half flirting with him as if she were clueless. Which, in this instance, she certainly was.

"It's not that." He cleared his throat and peered at the screen as if the print were very tiny and his vision simply wasn't up to the task. "Your visitor profile hasn't been filled out here. Like, how many people are in your party. You've got a two-room suite, but we didn't swipe your passports and—"

"I'm sorry." Kim used her hand to cover a big fake yawn. "It's late. Can we do the rest tomorrow? I'd really like to get to bed."

"Okay, well, yeah, we can deal with this stuff in the morning, I guess." Took him a minute to locate a pen to write the room number on a sticky note and hand both the note and the card back to her.

"Thanks, Todd. I'll come down tomorrow with everything else, I promise." She glanced at the room number. Two twelve. "Oh, and my friend is parking the car. I'll just text him our room number so he doesn't have to bother you again. You can ignore the bell when he comes in. Get some sleep."

"Okay. That'd be great," Todd replied.

"Again, I'm really sorry to bother you. I can't believe how scattered I am sometimes."

He yawned. "No problem."

Kim waved with the back of her hand and felt his sleepy-eyed gaze following her, but she didn't turn around. When she reached the elevator, she looked again to confirm that Todd had left his post. With luck, he was already snoring on his cot.

She envied him. She'd like to be sleeping right now, too.

Kim pressed the elevator button for the second floor. There was a third floor, but a special card was required to access that one.

She texted the room number to Russell. He sent her a thumbs-up emoji in response. She frowned. He should be here by now. How far did he have to go to park, anyway?

At the second floor, Kim left the elevator and waited until it began the return trip to the lobby.

As she expected, no one else was walking around the halls at this time of night. Aside from the creaks and groans of historic buildings everywhere, the place was quiet.

Room 212 was on the right, near the end of the corridor.

Kim crept forward and stood to one side of the doorway. She gloved up and then held the key card firmly in her left hand.

Mindful of Russell's warning, she readied her weapon. He wasn't wrong. Better to be paranoid than dead.

Searching a dark room when an armed person could be inside was a dangerous task. Entry doorways were choke points and they weren't called fatal funnels for nothing.

In this case, the fatal funnel was on either side of the doorway, as deep as the door was wide and just as high.

The bottom of the fire door snugged tightly to the carpet beneath it. So tight that interior light, should there be any, couldn't possibly escape.

Which was a good design for fire protection and control, but not great for Kim's purposes. No way to know whether the room was completely dark or brightly lit. Either way, she'd be vulnerable as soon as she opened the door.

Kim listened for noises inside. She heard nothing, but not everyone snored as loud as her father. The occupants might be light sleepers. They could wake up at the slightest noise.

According to the desk clerk, this was a two-bedroom suite. Both bedrooms could be unoccupied. Which was okay. Or either room could be occupied, which was definitely not okay.

What did Westwood's killer need with two bedrooms? Accomplices. Simple as that.

It made sense that the skinny man's posse might be waiting here for his return.

Or maybe he'd planned to bring Westwood back with him and now that they were both dead, both bedrooms of the suite were vacant. Which also made sense.

She glanced at her watch.

Russell should be here by now. Where was he?

Another five minutes passed.

Kim was antsy now. Her gut said she'd been standing there too long. Another guest or the hotel's CCTV could find her actions odd enough to call the police. Which was, right at the moment, the last thing she wanted.

She needed to move. But where?

Russell knew where she was. Something must have delayed him. He'd be there as soon as he could.

Odds were the room was empty. And if it wasn't, she'd deal with the situation as it happened.

Kim took a deep breath and swiped the key card. The lock clicked open. She breathed a bit easier.

Todd had been right. This was the correct room. So far, so good.

She took a second deep breath and prepared to clear the interior of the suite. She patted her pocket to confirm the flashlight.

Kim waited another minute.

When she opened the entry door, she'd be backlit by the lights from the hallway. Which would give occupants of the room a chance to see her. She'd be an easy target.

Still no Russell. He must have run into a problem.

She heard the elevator bell ding, announcing the car had arrived.

Maybe Russell.

Maybe someone else.

Like hotel security.

Kim swiveled her head for a quick look around.

Nowhere to hide while she waited. She stood fully exposed. At this point, she had only one real choice.

Time to go.

She pushed the levered handle down to unlatch the door.

Then she gripped her weapon with both hands and used her foot to shove the door all the way open. Fast.

She flattened her back to the exterior wall next to the doorjamb and waited outside the room another moment.

Nothing rushed toward her.

She heard no noises inside.

Kim moved quickly into the dark.

She flattened her back against the interior wall and scanned the entrance using the brief light from the corridor while the door slowly closed behind her.

CHAPTER 24

Saturday, June 4
Niagara-on-the-Lake, Ontario, CA

WHEN THE DOOR CLOSED, the room was darker than a grave. No ambient light at all. Instant blindness.

Kim stood still, barely breathing, willing her eyes to adjust enough to reveal the shapes and shadows she'd glimpsed only briefly.

Darkness was both an offensive and defensive weapon. She could neither see nor be seen. Like all weapons, the tactical question was when and how to use it.

A flick of the light switch on the wall where she stood would brighten the room. And also make her an easy target.

She had a flashlight in her pocket and if she turned it on, she'd have control over the beam. But the beam would draw attention directly to her.

The night vision app on her phone was a better option than the flashlight, but if she lifted the phone from her pocket, the screen would illuminate automatically. Same problem as the flashlight.

Kim stood motionless. Waiting. Listening. All senses dialed up to red alert. Never relaxing her two-handed grip on her gun.

Another full minute of hyper-awareness for movement or breathing or scents or anything to indicate she was not alone.

She sensed nothing.

Kim took a deep breath and raised her elbow to flip on the lights. Before she reached the switch, a woman's calm, husky voice emerged from deep into the dark room.

"We've got a few options," the woman said, with a hint of amusement. "We could stay as we are indefinitely. We could just shoot each other now and be done with it."

She paused as if she expected Kim to respond. She said nothing.

After a few moments, the woman continued. "Or we can flip the lights on and have a civilized conversation."

She waited again. Same non-response. "Before you decide, you should know that I have several advantages."

"Such as?" Kim replied evenly.

"I could have killed you already, if I'd wanted to."

"You think so?"

"You're literally in the dark. I'm not. I can see you."

"That so?"

"You're standing against the wall just inside the door. You have a pistol gripped in your right hand. A Glock. Same as the one I have pointed toward you." She laid things out plainly, as if to show Kim she was truthful and perhaps even trustworthy. "You're alone. You're wearing dark clothing but your pale skin is not covered."

Kim had collected enough data. She'd placed the voice slightly to her right. Maybe twenty feet away.

She could shoot toward the voice and hit her dead on before the woman had a chance to return fire.

Probably.

"Okay. You can see me. But I know where you are. And, as you point out, I'm armed."

"Me, too. That doesn't make us evenly matched, though, does it?" The woman laughed. A small, quiet chuckle.

"Why not?" If Kim kept her talking a bit longer, she could confirm the target's location with pinpoint accuracy. Even in the dark.

She'd trained for such situations. Her skills were excellent. She was also well aware of her limitations. Shooting into the dark without night vision was never anybody's first choice.

"You don't know me," the woman said. "But I've been expecting you."

The assertion jolted Kim, as it was no doubt meant to do. Her stomach was already churning. The woman's words made her belly hurt. Sharp pain right in the center of her torso. Which she ignored.

Who was this woman?

Even if she'd seen Kim's face as she entered the room, how could she know Kim's identity?

Her thoughts zipped through her mind faster than a Formula One racer.

Only one person knew she was anywhere near Niagara-on-the-Lake. Russell. And there's no way he'd have revealed anything to this woman.

But she quickly realized Russell wasn't the only one who knew Kim was in Canada.

There were others.

Ashley Westwood. He'd talked to Kim on the phone. Invited her to his suite. Arranged to meet her on the Falls Observation Deck.

Westwood could have called this woman and read her in. He'd had plenty of time. Or reported to her if she was already more knowledgeable than he.

In fact, Westwood had claimed to have a witness he wanted Kim to meet.

Was this woman that witness?

And witness to what, exactly?

And the skinny man lying dead in Westwood's suite back in Niagara Falls. He seemed to know more than he should have about Westwood. Maybe Westwood had told him about Kim, too.

The skinny dude knew Kim was in Niagara, since she'd chased him all over the hillside. He could have called a whole list of contacts between the time he lost her and the time she found him in Westwood's suite. He'd had plenty of time.

The list of those who knew Kim's general whereabouts was way too long.

Gaspar knew she was here. Cooper or Finlay might know by this time, too. They had made no attempt to contact her, but that meant nothing. They watched her constantly. Of course they could know.

And then there was Russell, of course. She hadn't been with him every minute. He also had a job. He could have been reporting to his bosses. Where was he, anyway?

The methodical process calmed her. Her breathing evened out. Her stomach calmed a little. The situation seemed slightly less threatening now that she'd thought things through.

She smiled. So many possible contacts in the loop. No way could this woman kill Kim and get away with it.

Small comfort. But better than she'd felt just minutes ago.

Kim didn't lower her weapon.

"Why were you expecting me?" Kim asked, to keep the conversation going. Give Russell a chance to get here.

Keep the woman talking and not reacting for a while longer, maybe.

"We could continue talking about this in the dark, Agent Otto. Or," she said, pausing to make sure Kim was paying attention, "We could turn on the lights. Have a civilized conversation."

"You already know I have a gun pointed directly at you," Kim warned.

"Right back atcha, girlfriend." The woman gave her dry chuckle again.

Which pissed Kim off. Nothing about the situation was the least bit amusing.

But this woman sounded sure of herself. As if she were prepared to do whatever was necessary. Which she probably was.

"Killing each other will solve nothing," Kim replied.

"Just the opposite, actually." The woman said and paused, waiting for Kim's consent or something.

Kim said nothing.

"Time is of the essence here, as you lawyers say. I know things that you want to know." Her patience seemed to be wearing thin. "If I were going to shoot you, don't you think I'd have done it already?"

Kim gave her more silence for a couple of seconds, but once again, there was really only one choice here.

"Okay. Turn the lights on. We'll see what you've got," Kim said, raising her left hand to deflect glare and thwart temporary light blindness.

"I've got a lamp over here. We'll try that first. Are you ready?" she asked, as if she cared. Maybe she did.

"Yeah," Kim replied, keeping the pistol pointed toward the voice. Just in case.

"Here it comes," she said.

Kim closed her eyes just before she heard the flip of the switch. A wide cone of dim yellow light cast out from the far corner.

Kim blinked once and lowered her hand from her eyes and returned to her two-handed grip. Her eyes hadn't fully adjusted. That would take about thirty minutes. But she could see well enough.

The woman was seated on the chair near the lamp. She was wearing dark glasses. She must have slipped them over her eyes just before she turned on the light. Before that, she'd probably worn night vision.

As promised, she was holding a Glock pointed at Kim. After a moment, she removed the sunglasses to reveal dark lively eyes. She waited to let Kim take a good look at her.

She was Asian, but not petite. Five-nine maybe or even five-ten. And built to match. Not a bone in sight. Not the least bit willowy. Maybe forty-five. Long, black hair hanging down her back. Jeans and a T-shirt and lace up shoes.

Kim said, "Let's level the playing field. Who are you?"

"My name is Michelle Chang. I'm a private detective based in Seattle. Previously, I was with the FBI. Just like you, Agent Otto." Her accent was regular American midwestern. The kind Kim heard everywhere. "I tell you this so you'll know I wasn't bluffing. I'm really good with the Glock. Even in the dark. You can check bureau records for my test scores if you like. I've checked yours."

Kim steadied her hands and willed her stomach to stop flipping over like a happy dolphin. "Anybody else here or expected to show up?"

"I'm assuming you're not alone since FBI agents travel in pairs," Chang said, lowering her weapon first as some sort of show of good faith or something.

She placed the Glock on the table next to her chair and moved her hand out of reaching distance.

"You're sure I won't shoot you, then," Kim's lip turned up in a slim smile.

"Absolutely positive. FBI agents don't shoot civilians in the absence of an imminent threat," Chang displayed her empty hands, palms out, and replied with the husky humor she'd displayed several times already. "I'm definitely a civilian. And I've been assured that you are a good agent. Is that true?"

Kim cocked her head. "Who told you that?"

Chang smiled. "He said you'd ask that question."

CHAPTER 25

Saturday, June 4
Hamilton, Ontario, CA

LIAM STUART LAY WIDE awake, hands behind his head, staring at the knotty pine ceiling in the dark. A strong breeze whistled across the roof and around the sharp corners of the old cabin.

He was tired and weary and desperately needed sleep. The last time he'd slept well enough was the night before he'd been told the target's name.

The same night he'd argued with Lucas because the target's identity had soured everything that came before and after.

The overwhelming euphoria he'd felt when he completed the most difficult project of his career had been dashed beyond resurrection. It would take his cold, shriveled heart years to move past this failure.

Liam could barely remember the uncontained joy he'd felt just a few weeks ago, when he'd felt he owned the world and every possible future was his for the taking.

The Stiletto 100 drone was a spectacular breakthrough. The only one of its kind.

Stiletto 100 would give those who possessed it unparalleled advantages on the ground. He'd already imagined a dozen uses for the new weapon.

But he was required to demonstrate Stiletto 100 under field conditions as the final test of its functionality.

The successful final qualifications test, or FQT, of the Stiletto might be the highlight of his entire career. He imagined the feeling would be like winning the World Cup or the first man to walk on Mars or circumnavigating the globe faster than anyone had ever done before.

The FQT was usually the most exciting part of bringing any new weapon to market for Liam. He'd worked toward FQT for several products over the years as a junior and then senior member of the development team.

But this was the first new design for which he had been totally responsible. The Stiletto 100 was his baby, from conception to completion. He was proud of the work he'd done and excited to move from testing into production. The FQT was the last hurdle.

The Stiletto 100 would bring millions of dollars from buyers around the world. Liam would become famous in certain circles, infamous in others. No other weapons engineer on the planet had achieved such success in Liam's lifetime.

He had been floating on pure joy whenever he imagined how the Stiletto 100 would change the world.

Liam couldn't have been happier.

Until the target for the FQT was selected.

"We can't do that," he'd said, slack jawed.

"We can and we will," Morin had replied coldly. "Either you can do it or someone else will."

"But surely we can choose another target?"

"There's no reason to do that. We've made the right decision," Morin repeated. "Are you on board or not?"

"And if I say no, what are you going to do?" Liam replied, jutting his chin forward in defiance. "It's not like you've got a backup plan, now is it?"

Morin frowned. "You're right. I was wrong. This is your job and you'll do it. Period."

Morin hung up and Liam had pitched the phone across the sidewalk. The hard plastic rectangle slammed against a brick wall and bounced onto the sidewalk. Liam didn't bother to retrieve it. The damned thing would never work again and that was just fine with him.

Liam had stuffed his hands into his pockets, head down, and walked toward his SUV. He wished Morin had never told him.

He felt as if he'd been asked to eat his own family.

He couldn't reconcile his euphoria with such despair.

Feelings were always a problem for him. Feelings caused chaos, anger, frustration. Sometimes, violence. He'd learned simply to ignore them.

But he couldn't compartmentalize his feelings this time either. Which was not normal. Not even close.

Despair was not an emotion he'd experienced before. He quite simply didn't know how to handle it.

He closed his eyes, breathing deeply, and allowed his mind to wander, taking a mental break. The technique worked better than anything else to help him relax.

To the extent he was capable of relaxation.

Lucas had been quite irritated with him. "Try meditation. If that doesn't work, try something else. Not sleeping is making you crazy. And it's not great for the rest of us who have to deal with you, either."

"Right," Liam replied, because he'd already tried, and the effort was useless. He had never been able to quiet his mind. Not since he was a child.

Stifling the constant churning of his thoughts was simply impossible.

Eventually, he'd developed a technique for watching his thoughts. He knew how to detach himself. He'd been doing it all his life. Detachment from all things was his usual default position.

The first face that crossed his mind tonight was Lucas, his kid brother. Lucas had always been the head of their little family of two.

Which made no logical sense, really. How could that be?

Liam was older, smarter, wealthier, and dammit, better looking. He grinned in the dark.

But the point was he should have been taking care of Lucas all these years. Instead, Lucas was the stable one. The caring one.

And yes, the reliable one.

"Where are you, Lucas?" he said aloud. The question nagged him.

Liam visualized his brother in the arms of a worthy woman who adored him and wanted to have his babies and live in familial bliss forever more.

Not that Lucas ever mentioned such a creature. But Liam hoped she existed. If anyone deserved happiness, it was Lucas.

Maybe there were better brothers in the world. Liam had no frame of reference for that. He had Lucas. No one else.

And Liam was quite sure that no other brother would have put up with him all these years the way Lucas had. For that alone, his brother deserved several medals.

Lucas was the normal one. The one most likely to make a good father to a passel of young Stuarts. It wasn't too late for Lucas.

Lucas was only thirty-eight. He had plenty of time.

Liam, on the other hand, was already forty-two. And after the final Stiletto 100 test, he'd be busier than ever. By the time he could think about settling down with a family, he'd be an old man. Which was just fine with him anyway.

Wives required care and handling. He rubbed his arms through his sleeves. Just thinking about kids made him itchy.

He had no desire for wives or kids. He rarely spent time with his own brother. Which was exactly the way he preferred things.

A booming clap of thunder directly overhead blasted Liam from semi-consciousness. He scowled.

Storms had been forecast. He hadn't expected any sort of follow through from Mother Nature. Millions were spent on state-of-the-art equipment. Sparkling television personalities were paid to deliver weather reports with bright smiles and certainty. Yet meteorology lacked the very accuracy and precision that any sort of science demanded.

Liam never trusted weather to perform as predicted.

A flash of too-close-for-comfort lightning briefly illuminated the cabin, followed by more way-too-close thunder.

A moment later, the rain started. Howling wind picked up speed. Within three minutes of the first thunderclap, his warren in the woods was engulfed in a full-on storm.

Which reflected his mood perfectly. As if a Greek chorus had been added to a movie to enhance his annoyance.

Liam had nowhere to go for a good long while. He closed his eyes again and listened to Mother Nature's outrage mirroring his own.

The force of the storm was comforting, somehow.

Maybe like trying to sleep in a foxhole, mortar shells landing close by, the screams of soldiers providing a soulless soundtrack.

The storm was also infuriating. Anger rose in his gut with every thunderclap, which made him want to lash out like an avenging god.

Because he'd been waiting for the right conditions to run two more field tests on the Stiletto 100 prototype before the FQT. Tests he definitely could not do in a raging storm.

The one image he'd tried to erase from his memory stormed his defenses like a band of invading marauders. Again.

Ira Krause, his mentor, colleague, and the only real friend he'd ever had, flashed into his mind. The specter of Krause simply would not leave Liam alone.

When the choice was initially announced, Liam had instantly made up his mind.

He could not betray Krause so viciously. He would not do it. Consequences be damned. Simple as that.

Which was when Liam took the Stiletto 100 and disappeared. He was sure Morin and the entire team were experiencing a full-on freak-out. Too bad.

They wanted the Stiletto 100 and they'd only get it on Liam's terms.

Liam had called Krause earlier. They'd planned to meet here, at the cabin. Liam promised to show Krause the Stiletto 100. Offered him a private demonstration.

Krause had been curious, despite their recent estrangement. Liam heard the excitement in his old friend's tone even as he'd tried to conceal it. Krause had agreed to come at first light.

Krause had no idea what Liam planned to do at the parade in Ottawa. Which was one condition of the FQT, of course. An obvious point. Conditions on the ground must reflect actual conditions of use.

If Krause had known what was coming, he'd have avoided the parade and the test would fail.

And too many had worked too hard for too long. The parade must happen as planned and the test must succeed. Failure was not an option.

Only the target would change. Whether Morin liked it or not.

CHAPTER 26

Saturday, June 4
Niagara-on-the-Lake, Ontario, CA

AUDREY WATCHED THE OHIO SUV a few moments longer. The big man idled the engine for about ten minutes before he rolled onto the street and drove away.

Briefly, she wondered where he was going and why the Asian woman didn't return to the vehicle first.

But Audrey was already late.

She could waste no more time on these two curious operatives. She'd taken clear headshots and sent them off to Brax.

Brax would figure out who they were and why they were hanging around Westwood and Fox. That was the best she could do right now.

Audrey played the voicemail from Krause.

"Where are you?" he demanded in his usual curt style, as if he had the right to demand answers. "Stuart called me. He's coming here. On his way already. Do you still want to talk to him, or shall I handle this myself?"

Instantly, Audrey's mission changed. Just like that.

Brax had sent her to connect with Fox and somehow join him in his efforts to find Liam Stuart and the drone and get the project back on track.

None of that had happened. Fox was dead. Krause was still on the team.

Yesterday, Krause said he could find Liam. "I know Liam better than anyone else. I can find him."

"How will you do that? Not even his own brother could find him," Audrey asked.

"Watch and learn, girlie," Krause sneered before he disconnected the call.

"Guess the old geezer might still be useful," she'd muttered doubtfully.

Audrey hadn't expected Krause to succeed.

Which, of course, he hadn't.

Krause didn't find Liam.

Liam had revealed himself. For reasons of his own.

All of that was totally okay. Audrey cared less about means and methods than she did about results. Brax was the same. He'd be pleased because she'd found Liam. Brax cared not how she achieved things.

The message from Krause was short and plain. And clueless. She listened again, to confirm she'd caught every word.

Audrey shook her head slowly. No wonder Brax gave the order to terminate Krause. Liam Stuart was a much better asset. Between the two, Stuart was the obvious best choice.

Krause was brilliant, sure. But he was also a problem. And getting older every day. He'd had his years in the sun. Time to shove him out of the way.

Which was just fine with her.

In Audrey's experience, difficult anti-social geniuses like Krause were a penny a dozen thanks to technology and the geeks who developed it.

Affable geniuses like Liam Stuart, on the other hand, were scarcer than zero gravity.

Audrey watched the taillights on the Ohio SUV turn at the corner and continue out of sight. Regretfully, she let the vehicle go.

She'd found the two operatives once. She could find them again.

Tonight, she had more important matters to handle. Krause first. And then Liam Stuart.

Audrey spun the wheel of the sedan all the way to the left and made a U-turn onto Queen Street.

The drive to Hamilton, Ontario, was almost fifty miles. According to the GPS, an hour of drive time, mostly along Queen Elizabeth Way, a limited access highway.

At this hour, Audrey could shave a few minutes off the drive time if she were willing to risk a traffic stop. She wasn't.

Better to stay under the radar.

Follow the rules of the road and get to Krause without unnecessary delay.

That was the plan.

When she'd entered the highway, Audrey pressed the call back button on her phone. The call rang a few times before Krause picked up.

"Hello," he mumbled like a man awakened from a sound sleep. Which he probably was.

"Krause? It's Audrey. Sorry. I got caught up in something," she said, as if his message had been friendly, or even polite. Which it wasn't. "I'm on my way. Should be there in an hour. Or less, if I'm lucky."

He didn't bother to reply. After a minute of silence, Audrey disconnected and tossed the phone onto the passenger seat.

She called Brax and left a brief and cryptic status report. She had no reason to believe her communications were being monitored. But she hadn't made it this far by taking unnecessary chances.

Audrey's fingers itched to call Morin and gloat. Fox was dead. Thus, Morin's assassin of choice had failed. She laughed.

Victory was so close she could feel it, taste it, hear it like a symphony in her head complete with the pounding of those big Japanese taiko drums she'd seen performed in Tokyo. How sweet it was.

She could almost hear the drums. Loud, snappy, rapid, spirited.

An exceptionally loud boom caught her attention and she laughed again. It was actual thunder. Clouds were gathering. A storm was headed her way.

The thunder drew her attention back to business.

But she didn't call Morin to gloat that she'd bested him once again. Not yet. She savored her pole position for a bit longer.

Morin would learn of his defeat soon enough.

She'd asked Brax to deliver the final smackdown when she was present. He'd promised, of course. He'd had no choice, given his compromising sexual position when she made the demand.

Her goal now was to find Liam Stuart and the prototype and get them back where they belonged.

She smiled again. Krause had handed Liam Stuart to her like a cake on a plate.

Audrey had suggested the possibility of sex, of course. That's all it took. No need for a quick sample to prove the worth of her offer. Krause had been going through a dry spell, she figured.

He was practically salivating.

Which was more than a little disgusting.

Hell, if she'd had sex with the old geezer, he'd probably have died in the act.

Which would have been okay. Krause was expendable. He'd be dead by Tuesday, one way or the other.

Sooner would be just fine with Audrey. The less she was required to deal with the cranky old bastard, the better.

Stuart might already be at Krause's place when Audrey arrived. Now that would be sweet.

Krause lived in a single-family home in the historic Ancaster district. She'd been there a couple of times. It was an affluent bedroom community for Hamilton, Ontario, and surrounding areas.

Krause's home was situated on a two-acre parcel outside of town, within easy driving distance of Toronto.

Close enough to Ottawa. Where they'd test the Stiletto 100.

The last couple of miles along the dark and lonely tree-lined road toward Krause's home sent a shiver down Audrey's spine. She rarely spent time in any sort of rural setting. Mother Nature gave her hives.

The GPS in the rental was as accurate as she'd expected. She reached Krause's home precisely on time, given the margin of error. The long gravel drive was surrounded by an exceptionally generous lot. At least an acre, she guessed.

Another loud thunderclap and then the rain began just as she reached the driveway.

She turned left, reduced speed, and continued toward the pleasing stone clad house perched at the end, glistening in the storm.

From this angle, the house seemed smaller than 3,500 square feet. The brief description she'd read in the real estate listing touted an updated open floorplan, heated pool, outdoor kitchen and the like.

The house was certainly too large and beyond elaborate enough for Ira Krause, a single man with no family to support. Given his prickly nature, he wasn't likely to marry any time soon, either. What woman would want him?

Audrey parked in front of the double garage doors and stepped into the cold wind. Cautiously, she approached the front steps, head down against the rain.

A bright spotlight flooded the surrounding dark cocoon. Audrey gasped. Glossy paint wet with rain reflected the light, leaving her nowhere to hide. A stealthy approach was now impossible.

"Dammit, Audrey. Be more careful," she hissed under her breath when she slipped on the slick pavers.

She took the front steps quickly, strode silently across the covered porch, and reached the decorative glass entry system. Three sections, one door and two sidelights, spanned fully one-third of the length of the porch.

Most of the door system was clear leaded glass. A wide frame held the glass in place. The frame was stained to match the gray siding. On either side of the door were full-length leaded glass sidelights matching the center door.

The system allowed light to travel inside and outside but distorted the view in both directions. Which meant the only thing Audrey could see inside the house was a weak nightlight.

"On the plus side, maybe Krause won't mistakenly shoot you in the dark," she murmured as she reached out and pressed the button.

The doorbell chimed inside.

The noise awakened the cat sleeping on a porch chair. He arched his back and hissed at her.

Audrey slapped her hand over her mouth, stifling another gasp. She hated cats. They were too independent. Always skulking around and attacking people. Nasty creatures.

This one must have felt the same about her. Smart cat.

He arched his back and hissed and spit at her several times before he jumped down and ran off the porch into the trees.

"Thank god." She didn't care where he went as long as he didn't come back.

Audrey pressed the bell again and again, keeping her finger on the button much longer than necessary each time.

"Come on, Krause. It's friggin' cold out here. Wake up and let me in, dammit!" she said aloud, as if he could hear.

After ten or twenty presses of the doorbell, she gave up.

She fished around in her pocket for the phone and pressed the redial button to slap Krause with a wakeup call. The tone rang several times before the call flipped to voice mail.

"This is stupid," she said impatiently, dropping the phone into her pocket again.

She stomped down the stairs and returned through the storm to her rental. In the trunk, she found a can of compressed air and not much else in the way of tools.

"Doesn't anybody change their own tires anymore?" she complained as she searched for a tire iron. Finding none, she slammed the trunk lid closed. "Guess not."

On the side of the driveway, which was still fully illuminated by the spotlight, she spied a fist-sized rock. She stomped swiftly to pick it up, carried it up the steps, across the porch, and hurled the rock through the door glass.

As soon as the glass pane broke, a house alarm began blaring loud enough to wake every neighbor within a two-mile range, dead or alive.

"Oh, crap!"

CHAPTER 27

Saturday, June 4
Niagara-on-the-Lake, Ontario, CA

THE CHANG AND OTTO standoff had ended by détente, opponents unharmed when Kim heard the lock click. Kim flipped her attention toward the noise, prepared to defend her turf.

The entry door opened slightly. The intruder paused.

A moment later, Russell held the door with his foot and moved inside, weapon ready, Kim's laptop case slung across his shoulder.

Chang looked straight at him, eyes wide, and grabbed her pistol. She hadn't been surprised to see Kim, but she appeared shocked when Russell showed up.

Proving Chang hadn't been conducting surveillance because she'd have discovered and identified Russell.

Which meant Chang didn't know everything about Kim's recent activities.

Question was, what did Chang know, exactly?

"Who are you?" Chang demanded.

"Stand down. This is Special Agent Travis Russell, Secret Service." Kim gestured while she established identity and lowered the tension. "Russell, this is former FBI Special Agent turned private investigator Michelle Chang."

Russell cocked his head, raising his eyebrows. He wasn't comfortable with Chang, regardless of her employment history. Not to mention her loaded weapon.

"At this point, I know two things." Kim raised two fingers in response to his unasked questions. "Her name. And she didn't shoot me when she could have."

"That so?" Russell said, turning his narrowed gaze to Chang. "And what is the source of her intel?"

"We were just getting into that," Kim replied. "What took you so long, anyway?"

"Parking," he said dryly as he shrugged the laptop case off his shoulder and, freed of restrictions, turned to face Chang. "Let me see some ID. And this place doesn't offer late night room service. I don't suppose you've got any food?"

Chang handed over her ID wallet and give him a minute to examine the contents. "There's a minibar. Help yourself."

"Thanks." Russell nodded after inspecting and returning her ID. "Where's your bathroom? I need to wash up."

Chang tilted her head in that direction. Russell ducked through and closed the door behind him.

"Why are you partnered with a Secret Service agent?" Chang asked as soon as Russell was out of earshot.

"That's your first question?" Kim replied, shaking her head as she located the minibar and studied its contents. Processed junk food. Most of it had probably been in there for years. "Russell's temporary. I'm waiting for a new partner."

"What happened to the last one?"

"Moved on." Kim grabbed an overpriced bottle of water and a bag of chocolate covered peanuts. She took everything to a chair across from Chang and settled in.

"Let's wait for Russell. So we won't need to catch him up."

Chang seemed willing to follow Kim's lead. For now.

Russell came back quickly enough. "You've got two bedrooms here. Who's using the second one?"

"Why, do you need a bed for the night? It's yours," Chang replied.

"Possibly. Let's see how this goes." Russell pulled cashews and crackers and a soda from the minibar and joined them.

"You start," Kim said to Chang after Russell was settled in.

Chang remained wary and skeptical, a vibe mirrored by Kim's churning stomach. She popped an antacid into her mouth and chewed on it while she waited.

Chang took a breath and paused another half a moment before she said, "You're right. I was expecting you. Westwood and Lucas Stuart, too. Where are they? Also *parking the car*?"

Her tone suggested that Russell had lied. Which he probably had. He owed Chang no explanations and Kim figured he'd explain why he'd been delayed when they had some privacy.

But with Chang's question, another piece of the puzzle dropped into place. The man found dead at Kim's front door was probably Lucas Stuart. The name meant nothing to her. But the name could possibly advance Gaspar's efforts, when she had a chance to pass it along.

"Both Westwood and Stuart are dead. So is the man who killed them." Kim found three images of the dead men on her phone and passed them over to Chang. "We believe the first one is Lucas Stuart. The second is Ashley Westwood."

Chang studied the photos, flipping between them a few of times. Her face blanched. "That's Westwood. I've never met Lucas Stuart, but this could be him."

"Check the third photo," Kim said.

Chang enlarged the image of the skinny guy and leaned toward the light to get a better look. She shook her head. "No. Sorry."

"There's a few more shots of the third man. Thumb through. Maybe you'll see something you recognize," Russell said while chomping a mouthful of cashews.

Chang did as he asked but shook her head and handed the phone back to Kim. "I don't think I've ever seen the skinny one before, either. Who is he?"

"We don't know. But we believe he killed both Stuart and Westwood," Kim said. "Fill us in. Maybe we can figure out who the third man is and why he targeted the others."

Russell shrugged. "Or the three men might not be related at all."

"Oh, they're related. Gotta be." Chang shook her head again. "Unless you're a believer in coincidence. And I've never met a federal agent who was. Don't tell me you're my first?"

"Not hardly," Russell grumped and stuck another fistful of cashews into his mouth. "Why did you say the first man *could be* Lucas Stuart?"

"I've seen photos of his brother. This guy looks as if he could be related. And I know Lucas was working with Westwood," Chang replied. "That's why Reacher sent us to Otto. Why we're sitting here, actually."

"Whoa!" Russell choked on the nuts and held up a palm while he coughed uncontrollably. Eventually, he wheezed some words. "Back up. Back up. What the hell do you mean? I'm just a jarhead. Break it down into tiny syllables for me."

"Some of the smartest and best men I know are jarheads. Don't let him fool you, Chang," Kim grinned. "Regardless of what Reacher says, if you want something done right? Send in the Marines."

Chang visibly relaxed. "In my experience, Army works just as hard and just as effectively."

"No way. Never happen," Russell choked out of his raw throat. "Sorry. Went down the wrong pipe."

When his coughing finally stopped, Kim asked, "Who is Lucas Stuart's brother and why do you know him?"

"His name is Liam Stuart. He's moderately well known in his field. Super genius engineer and uber tech nerd. He's gone missing," Chang explained. "The brother, Lucas, claims Liam's been kidnapped. Maybe held for ransom. Maybe killed. Lucas came to Westwood looking for help."

"Why go to Westwood? Why not the police? They're good with kidnapping and just plain missing persons, you know," Russell said sarcastically.

"It's complicated," Chang replied.

"So just give us the highlights, in case we get interrupted," Kim said. "Start with Reacher."

"Start with Reacher? Seriously?" Russell gave her an incredulous stare. "Three dead bodies. Two of them we can't even identify. And a missing scientist to boot. We've got more immediate issues than Reacher, don't you think?"

"Not at all. In my world, everything's always about Reacher," Kim said flatly. "So start there, Chang. How do you know Reacher and why is he involved in whatever this is?"

CHAPTER 28

Saturday, June 4
Ancaster, Ontario, CA

WHEN AUDREY THREW THE rock through the glass door, Krause came stumbling from the back of the house in a hurry, hair standing straight up, wearing nothing but boxer shorts.

"The police are coming! Get the hell out of here!" he yelled, rushing forward like an offensive lineman.

With one hand, he was attempting to belt a robe he must have grabbed on the way. The other hand gripped a pistol pointed down at the floor.

Audrey reached through the broken glass, twisted the deadbolt, and opened the door. She stepped inside and flipped on the lights so he could get a good look.

Krause knew her. The sooner he realized that, the smoother this thing would go.

She was soaked to the skin and none too thrilled about it.

"Krause!" she yelled over the blaring alarm. "Turn that damned noise off!"

He waved the pistol vaguely and stared as if she were a puzzling and dangerous specter. Which, of course, she wasn't. She was just cold and wet and totally pissed off.

Krause should have been expecting her. A fact he seemed to have totally forgotten.

Audrey rushed forward, knocked his pistol to the floor, and grabbed him by the arm. She dragged him to the alarm panel beside the front door and shoved him toward it, leaving a trail of wet footprints on the hardwood floors.

"Turn. This. Damned. Thing. Off," she yelled directly into his ear with considerable menace.

Krause seemed to awaken from whatever state of altered consciousness he inhabited. He pushed her away.

Then he swiveled his head, raised his hand, and punched a six-digit code into the keypad.

The alarm stopped.

Abruptly.

Audrey's brain took half a moment to recognize and process the surreal silence.

"We don't want the cops showing up here. Does this alarm trigger an automatic response from the police? Do they call you first? How does it work?" Audrey demanded, still twisting his arm painfully behind his back.

Krause shook his head sharply. "The alarm company calls me first. I tell them to stand down. Or they send someone out if I don't say everything's okay."

As soon as he finished the last word, a phone rang from the back of the house. Krause shuffled quickly in that direction. Audrey followed.

They covered the open floor much more slowly than Audrey preferred. The ringing acted like a beacon pulling Krause toward the phone.

Audrey grabbed a towel on the way through the kitchen and used it to sop the water from her face and hands. She stopped in the bedroom doorway watching as Krause found the phone on his bedside table ten feet inside the room and picked up the call.

"I'm sorry. False alarm," he said before the dispatcher had a chance to say anything at all. "My safe word is—" he glanced furtively toward Audrey, turned his back, and lowered his voice—"Stiletto 100."

The words shot through her cold, soggy body like a taser charge, setting every nerve ending on full alert.

The Stiletto 100 was a top-secret project.

Krause should not have had access to it. Not even to the name itself.

How did he know? Who had he told? What was he planning?

Krause disconnected his call and tossed the phone and his gun onto the bed. He turned to face her, eyes glaring, mouth set like an aggrieved ape.

Before he had a chance to do anything more, Audrey raised her weapon and pointed it straight toward his heart.

"Sit down in that chair next to the bed, Krause," she gestured. "Hands up."

"What the hell is wrong with you?" he demanded as he raised his hands, palm out.

He didn't move.

Krause was far from stupid.

But he was arrogant. Entitled.

Outraged.

Superior body size coupled with extreme intelligence had opened doors for him his entire life. He'd never knelt to any bully and certainly not to a female drowned rat less than half his size.

He didn't intend to do so now.

Whether she had a gun or not.

"Tell me what you know about Stiletto 100," Audrey demanded.

Krause pursed his lips and shook his head. "You don't have the proper clearance. I'll tell you nothing."

Five minutes ago, she'd hadn't expected him to know anything at all about the code name assigned to Liam Stuart's secret prototype.

Morin didn't expect him to know.

Hell, Brax didn't think Krause knew anything, either. He'd certainly have mentioned that in her briefing.

Liam Stuart had been Krause's protégé. The two men had worked together for years.

Krause got his boxers in a twist about some perceived slight and raged off the team before Stuart had even conceived of his Stiletto 100 prototype.

So how did Krause know now?

They had a leak. Someone involved in the Stiletto 100 project had told Krause. No other possibilities.

Lightning flashed outside and illuminated the bedroom through the big eye window mounted near the top of the cathedral ceiling. The lighting fragmented in the beveled leaded glass shooting brief flashes in several directions like a dancing fairy.

A moment later, the truth flashed into Audrey's head.

Had Liam Stuart been consulting with Krause all this time?

Were they sharing information and data?

Is that why Stuart called tonight?

Audrey's initial adrenaline rush had already subsided. Cold blood and icy calculation drove her now.

When Krause had uttered the project's code name, he'd transformed from annoying asset to lethal liability in a hot second.

And he didn't even seem to realize it.

But he would.

"Don't give me any baloney about clearances, Krause. My clearance level is higher than yours," she said flatly, feet set shoulder width apart, well balanced, weapon leveled.

From this short distance, she couldn't possibly miss. Which must have been obvious to Krause.

"What do you know about Stiletto 100?"

Krause sneered. "You're not gonna shoot me, little girl. We both know that. You don't have the balls. And Brax would have your pretty little ass if you even tried."

"You think so?"

"I know so. Brax needs me. He doesn't need you. Women like you are everywhere," Krause shrugged. "Where's he gonna get another prize-winning genius to develop his weapons and keep his secrets, eh?"

Audrey ignored his sloppy insults. She had no insecurities of any kind. She couldn't be baited. Better men than Ira Krause had tried.

"Seems he's already found another genius. You should know. You trained Liam Stuart. When the student became the master, you stomped off like a child," Audrey sneered, her pistol aimed directly at his chest. "But Brax never came after you. Never begged you to come back. Never gave you a second thought. He's got Liam Stuart now. He doesn't need you anymore."

Her words infuriated him because they were true and he knew it.

He was at least ten feet across the room.

He lowered his hands and charged toward her, snorting like a raging bull.

She didn't move so much as an eyelash.

He took two steps forward before he realized she would never yield.

But he was already committed. She could see the brief indecision in his gaze.

"Stop, Krause, while you still can."

Bullheaded pride won his internal debate. He took another step forward.

Audrey steadied her pistol and shot him straight and true.

Twice.

Krause fell backward near the bed. He slid down to a seated position, head against the mattress, dead eyes wide open, arms flopping at his sides.

Another loud thunderclap punctuated the death.

Krause's sloppy carcass triggered Audrey's autonomous nervous system. Her mind returned to the present. She blinked hard.

"That was stupid, Mr. Genius," she said aloud as if Krause could hear her. "Bet you're not all that pleased with yourself now, are you?"

She wasn't too thrilled about the situation, either. Not for the same reasons.

Krause had jumped on her gun before she'd acquired the intel she came for and before she could interrogate him about Stuart.

She'd driven all the way out here and had nothing to show for it. Brax would not be pleased.

Now what? Search the house?

Before she had a chance to execute any kind of search, a brief lull in the storm allowed her to hear the unmistakable sound of tires on gravel.

A vehicle out front. Approaching the house. No question.

She scanned the room quickly one last time, gaze resting on Krause's phone.

Stuart called me, Krause had said. *He's coming here. On his way.*

The call was a slim lead, to be sure. But it was better than nothing.

She stepped carefully to the side of the bed, leaned over, and snagged Krause's phone. Then she retrieved his gun and placed it near his shooting hand.

Any good cop would realize Krause hadn't fired the weapon. But the chances of getting a great cop out here in the storm at this hour were fifty-fifty. Night shift cops in a sleepy burg like this weren't likely to be the sharpest knives in the drawer. Staging the scene might buy a bit more time.

One last glance around the room. She'd done all she could. They might not search the bedroom first if they couldn't see the body through the open doorway. She closed the bedroom door, adding another few seconds' delay.

Seconds mattered. She knew from experience.

Audrey crept to the front window and peered into the darkness. A boxy SUV was coming slowly along the driveway. She didn't recognize the vehicle. Headlights blinded her temporarily. She couldn't see the driver through the downpour.

Was it Liam Stuart? Could she possibly get that lucky?

The Range Rover pulled up too close to the garage door and parked. The same motion sensor Audrey had dealt with tripped again and floodlights burst through the dark.

A few seconds later, a man emerged from the driver's side of the luxury SUV.

A man she recognized.

Nigel Morin.

Audrey grinned and whispered, "Morin, you've made it so easy."

She watched as he moved around the far side of the garage toward the back entrance. Then she quickly, silently let herself out the front door.

She fired up her sedan and backed down the driveway, lights off.

Once she'd reached a safe distance, she used a fresh burner and dialed 9-1-1. The sleepy dispatcher answered with a yawn.

"What's your emergency?"

Audrey screamed hysterically. "He's in my house! He's got a gun!"

"What's the address ma'am?" The dispatcher, fully awake now, asked exactly the right question.

Audrey recited Krause's address and then screamed. "Hurry! He gonna kill my husband!"

While the operator was still speaking, Audrey screamed again, lowered the window, and threw the burner phone into Krause's bushes. They could trace the signal and confirm the phone's location. Which would also confirm Krause's address. Sirens should show up shortly.

Audrey wondered what the response time would be.

A few minutes, at least. Time to put some distance between her and the house.

Audrey raised the window and floored the accelerator.

When they got there, they'd find the body. Morin was probably armed, and Krause's gun rested in plain sight. It would take time to process the scene and sort things out.

Time she could use to find Liam Stuart and the Stiletto 100.

Morin would be tied up with the local cops. Which would put him off the playing field for a while.

"Serves you right, jackass," she said with a righteous nod.

She wondered how he'd try to explain that he didn't shoot and kill Krause. Morin wasn't all that clever. He'd probably just keep his mouth shut and call Brax.

Brax would be livid and blame Morin for the whole fiasco.

Audrey laughed out loud.

Her mirth was short lived. Mission status returned to top of mind.

How would she complete the assignment?

Four men, each of whom might have led her to Liam Stuart, were now dead.

Which was okay. Audrey rarely felt any sort of remorse and she tried to save it for situations that mattered to her. Empathy was overrated.

But she had no idea where Liam Stuart was or what he'd done with the drone.

Krause had said he was on his way "here." But that didn't necessarily mean Krause's home. Or disclose where he was coming from. Or estimate how long it might take him to arrive.

No, she couldn't simply wait here for Stuart to show up. Assuming that had been the plan.

Even if he did try to approach the house, when he reached the driveway he wouldn't advance. Not with first responders and the chaos on the scene.

So now what?

Audrey had no idea where to start looking for Liam Stuart now that Krause was dead.

Which was definitely not okay.

Not even remotely.

But Liam had been on his way, Krause said.

That was hours ago.

Surely he was close by now.

CHAPTER 29

Saturday, June 4
Ancaster, Ontario, CA

MORIN HAD MADE THE drive from Manhattan to Ancaster with only one stop for fuel and black coffee. Alone in the Range Rover, he'd had plenty of time to sober up and refine his strategy.

While Fox and Audrey searched for the scientist and the drone, Morin planned a direct assault on Ira Krause. The goal was to get Krause back on board. Which sounded simple but would be far from easy.

The last time they'd seen each other, Morin had escorted Krause directly off the team and told him not to come back.

Krause's savage response was unprintable in a family newspaper. "Watch your back, Morin. You're an easy man to find."

Morin had been rattled by the venomous attack. He hadn't pegged Krause as a dangerous enemy. Live and learn.

Brax had called three times. Morin let the first two calls go to voicemail. Brax left no messages.

When the third call came, Morin was crossing the border into Canada.

Which was how he discovered Brax had flagged his passport. The border agent scanned the passport as a part of the entry routine. The system notified Brax electronically.

No doubt about it. Brax called again before Morin rolled through the checkpoint.

Brax had trusted him implicitly for two decades. Something had recently shaken his confidence, leading first to Audrey's deployment onto Morin's patch, and now to monitoring his movements.

Whatever made Brax wary was something Morin needed to discover and settle as soon as possible.

"Must be pretty early in Quan, isn't it?" Morin said, yawning, as if he were surprised by the call. "Man, I'm too old to stay out all night."

Driving now in weak daylight helped some, but he searched the roadside signs for a Tim Horton's. Strong black coffee and half a dozen donuts would make all the difference.

On the other end of the call, Brax demanded, "Status."

Good question. Morin had no idea what the project status was. But he couldn't say as much.

"On track," Morin replied. "Something special you're interested in that Audrey hasn't told you?"

Brax chuckled on the other side of the world. "So you've seen Audrey, then."

"Hard to avoid her. She showed up at my bar. Plopped her ass down right next to me. Nothing much I could do about it," was Morin's snide reply.

"What are you worried about?" Brax said with a smile in his tone. "Competition is good for a man. Keeps you sharp."

Morin pressed his lips together to hold his comeback in check. Audrey was a nuisance. Nothing more, nothing less. She'd be gone soon enough, one way or another.

He kept his focus on Krause.

Krause knew more about the Stiletto 100 than anyone except Liam Stuart, his missing protégé. Krause was working feverishly to design a similar weapon. The two designs, should both come to fruition, would be direct competitors.

The man who won the race would reap both acclaim and lucrative rewards for himself and his employer.

The losing project would be spiked into the waste bin of history. As it should be. There could be no second place in a high-tech weapons war. Only the winners had a chance to survive.

"You found Liam Stuart yet?" Brax demanded. "Because if you haven't, I'd say you're losing this particular arms race, wouldn't you?"

"Krause is a better option," Morin said, not for the first time.

Krause had proven himself many times over the years.

Stuart's fitness was unproven.

Liam Stuart and Krause had been close, personally and professionally. Which meant the upcoming FQT was a test of Stuart's loyalty to Brax, now that he'd become the lead developer on the project, as well as his expertise.

Nothing less than Stuart's one-hundred percent fidelity to Brax and his team was acceptable.

The question, quite simply, was Liam Stuart's reliability.

During their association, Krause had taught Stuart everything he knew about design and development of high-tech military weapons.

Brax pushed a long stream of air across the miles. "We've discussed this. Krause is done. Stuart's our man."

Eventually. Morin added in his head.

The goal had always been to replace Krause with Stuart. Timing that change of horses was the issue.

The two men fought bitterly when Stuart's star began to rise. Stuart wanted to shine but Krause wanted to keep him in his place. After the final showdown, Krause left the company and accepted a job in Canada.

Stuart, by all accounts, had been devastated when his friend and mentor announced his departure from the defense company they'd both helped to build.

The friendly competition that had always fueled their working relationship became toxic.

When Stuart completed his Stiletto 100 project far ahead of Krause's competitive design, the decision seemed to make itself.

"The timing is unfortunate. The situation in Quan and elsewhere has changed," Brax said breaking the continued silence from Morin. "We had no alternative but to decide between Stuart and Krause sooner than we intended. As you know, the choice was not obvious until recently."

"That's an understatement," Morin replied. "Stuart is young, energetic, brilliant, enthusiastic. But Krause is experienced, competent, confident."

"Exactly. Both men have their worthy qualities. Both also have issues. As you well know," Brax said coldly. "There's no need to rehash all of this, is there?"

A few weeks ago, Morin had named Krause as his final recommendation.

Brax had chosen Stuart as the final decision.

After barely half a moment's hesitation.

"We must bet on the future, Nigel, not the past. The fate of the world depends upon forward momentum. Falling behind," Brax said, "is not an option."

Just that quickly, Brax chose the younger man instead of the experienced one.

Morin held his objections. Brax didn't want to hear them.

For a while, it seemed Brax had made the right choice. Stuart had worked long hours demonstrating insight and ingenuity.

Quickly, gambling on the younger man had paid off. Stuart developed his prototype first. His Stiletto 100 was ready for FQT.

"Krause isn't far behind, though. His competing prototype, the Premium, is only a few weeks from completion," Morin continued to press tonight in the way he should have done a few weeks earlier.

His gut said Stuart wasn't ready. Unreliable. Emotional. Uncontrollable. The way he'd disappeared was just one solid example.

"Exactly," Brax snapped. "We can't have two new weapons. We've selected the Stiletto. The Premium is canceled. Effective immediately."

Morin didn't bother to ask why. The answer would be lack of funding for two weapons. But the real truth was that if two new drones became available instead of only one, Brax would lose the advantage.

One of the projects, and its inventor, had to go. Permanently.

In the end, circumstances prevailed. The Stiletto was ready. The Premium was not and, as a practical matter, might never be ready.

Bird in the hand and all that, Morin understood.

"Time to move on, Morin. We can't allow ourselves to drag our feet here." Brax had relaxed a bit. He was applying diplomacy now. "The Stiletto's design is completed. Logistics are set. The final field quality test is scheduled and the target selected."

Yes. The target was selected.

Which was where Brax had made what could prove to be a disastrous mistake.

The target made sense in the way Brax evaluated risks and benefits. But Liam Stuart obviously hadn't seen it that way.

Once the parameters of the test were settled and the target disclosed, Liam Stuart had disappeared.

Morin thought he'd developed cold feet. Planning to kill was one thing. Executing the plan was something else again. Liam Stuart had never been a killer.

Brax worried now that Stuart had taken the Stiletto to the highest bidder.

Everyone was tense.

Morin couldn't give up on Krause. Partly because he knew in his gut that he'd lost Fox over the non-payment issue. He had no confidence in Audrey's talents as a tracker. Which meant Liam Stuart might be gone forever.

But Morin couldn't say any of that to Brax, either. Not until he got Krause back on board. Not if he wanted to keep his job. Which he definitely did. Up or out. That was the rule. Always had been. Always would be.

"Look, I agreed that Stuart's Stiletto was the clear frontrunner. But that was before Stuart went missing and stole the drone," Morin said. He spied a Tim Horton's and flipped his turn indicator on. "We know now that Stuart is unreliable."

Brax snorted. "And crazy Krause is such a stalwart?"

"Compared to Stuart, Krause is as stable as a river barge. He's been a solid performer for decades. The Stiletto is done. All we need is the right guy to operate it. Krause," Morin said, repeating the arguments he'd made before. He slid into the exit lane, his nose leading to donuts and coffee. "We've got one last chance to make the right choice here. Always better to go with the devil you know."

Not that Brax would admit he'd been wrong about Stuart. Morin had never seen it happen. Not once in all the years he'd reported to Brax had the man ever owned up to a mistake.

Oh, Brax had made plenty of errors over the years. His oft repeated motto, modified from Benjamin Disraeli's famous words, was "Never complain, never explain, and never, ever ever apologize."

The stakes were some of the highest they'd ever faced. Brax wanted to give Liam Stuart one last chance to prove his loyalty by coming in, bringing the Stiletto 100, performing the FQT.

Morin understood the motivation. Loyalty was a quality Morin appreciated, too.

Loyalty up, loyalty down. Words to live by.

But two days ago, Stuart didn't show up at the meeting place Morin had arranged. He didn't return the Stiletto 100 prototype, either. Stuart's actions proved he was unreliable. For Brax, that was the last straw.

"Yes, as you guessed, things have changed in Quan. We have no time to fail." Brax had inhaled deeply and made the final decision. "Eliminate Stuart. Put Fox on it. We'll go with Krause."

Vindication. Just that easy, Stuart gone. Krause reinstated.

Morin resisted the childish urge to grin and fist pump the air.

"Liam is no fool. He'll guess our next move," Morin said.

"No excuses," Brax said. "Make it so."

Morin disconnected the call and wiped sweaty palms on his pants. He pulled into the lot at Tim Horton's and parked the Range Rover.

He rubbed his hand across the front of his neck, where an imaginary garotte seemed to extinguish his air supply. He'd withheld critical information. Which was never okay, even if he'd managed to get Brax on the right path again.

Morin had not told Brax that Liam Stuart broke his vows of loyalty and silence. Stuart was a traitor. He couldn't keep his mouth shut and he couldn't be trusted.

Liam Stuart had told both his brother and Krause about the Stiletto 100. He might also have told Lucas about the planned FQT.

Lucas had been dealt with already. Liam would be silenced soon.

Which left only Krause. Who knew how to keep his mouth shut.

Murder of a foreign national on US soil by an operative in the US government was not something Brax could publicly defend. If Lucas's murder by Fox at Morin's request became known, Brax would throw Morin under the bus in a hot New York second. Without remorse.

It had turned out that Lucas was almost as smart as his brother and twice as savvy about the ways of the world. He had realized the danger Liam had put them both in.

Then Lucas had tried to fix the danger by becoming a self-proclaimed whistleblower.

Which was when Lucas approached the journalist from the *LA Times* with the story.

"Sooner or later, they all make mistakes." Morin shook his head.

He strolled into Tim Horton's, visited the men's room, and then approached the counter to place his order. Half a dozen donuts and two large, black coffees to wash them down.

A smiling young man punched spots on the touch screen and requested the total. Morin paid cash. He stepped to one side to wait.

After Liam told his brother about the Stiletto 100, the situation had rapidly spiraled out of control. There was no way to undo the damage.

Even before the journalist got involved.

Once Lucas came into the picture, keeping the Stiletto 100 out of the public eye at any cost became Morin's primary objective.

The FQT had been planned weeks ago. Operatives were already in place. Nothing could be rescheduled.

They needed the Stiletto 100.

Krause's Premium was not ready. Would never be ready if the Stiletto proved worthy.

The Stiletto 100 prototype must be found.

The test must be completed as planned.

Which was why Morin had argued the issue one last time tonight and finally persuaded Brax to agree. They had no choice but to go with the tried-and-true performer. The lesser of two evils. Ira Krause.

Another young man behind the Tim Horton's counter called the number on Morin's receipt. He stepped up to collect his order. As he reached the exit, thunder boomed overhead and the sky opened up.

He jogged to the Range Rover and climbed inside with the soggy paper bag. By the time he was settled into his seat, the storm was raging again.

He grabbed the first donut and gobbled it in two bites. He felt the half-chewed dough soaking up the booze left over from last night like a sponge.

He stuck the second donut between his teeth and reversed the Range Rover from the parking spot.

Fifteen minutes after he'd left the highway, he was back in his lane, keeping up with traffic.

Morin needed to find Krause and persuade him to jump back on board. No easy task. Under the best of circumstances, Krause was as malleable as heavy gauge steel. Which is to say, not at all.

For a rocket scientist, Krause didn't seem to be savvy about cyber security at all. Morin had uncovered his home address in Ancaster, Ontario, with a simple internet search.

Which also made Morin uneasy. If he'd been creating a pro/con list, the cons on Krause would be overwhelming.

Maybe Brax had been right. Maybe Krause wasn't the answer.

"But dammit, what choice do we have? None. No choice at all," Morin muttered around the donut.

Even in the storm, Morin located Krause's home easily enough. The driveway wasn't gated, which meant he didn't need to mess with punch codes and security questions to reach the house.

He turned onto the gravel and pulled up close to the garage.

Through the downpour, Morin saw a dark rental sedan was already parked in front of the right garage bay.

Briefly, he wondered why the sedan was there and who it belonged to. But he'd come this far. He wouldn't turn back now. He parked next to the sedan in front of the left bay.

Morin knew Krause well enough. They'd talked many times over the years. Even though Morin's visit was out of the blue, Krause shouldn't be hostile.

But the sedan?

Krause had no living relatives and few friends. He should have been home alone at this hour. He wasn't. The small hairs raised on the back of Morin's neck.

Morin always had an alternative plan. He'd obtained a key to the back entrance, and he fished it from his pocket.

He left the Range Rover and walked through the storm, around the garage to the rear of the house. He stepped in a deep puddle, soaking his shoes and socks, stifling a stream of curses. By the time he reached the back door, he was thoroughly drenched, head to foot.

His wet fingers fumbled the key. A couple of tries and he managed to unlock the door and push it open.

Morin waited for the house alarm. He had memorized the four-digit code to shut it off before it triggered a call from the security monitoring service.

The alarm didn't sound. Which was odd and alarming in its own way.

Krause had become too comfortable here. All of his training seemed to have vanished.

During one of their many arguments, Brax had said Krause was too sloppy to depend upon. Brax wasn't wrong.

Morin shrugged, dropped the key into his pocket, let himself inside, and shut the door firmly behind him.

There were no signs of activity in the house.

A quick scan showed Krause's bedroom door was closed. It was late. Morin's unauthorized entry had not awakened the old guy. Which was more than okay.

Krause was difficult to handle under the best of circumstances. Awakened in the middle of the night and subjected to questioning, he'd be furious. Belligerent. Bordering on unstable, too.

Better to wait until daylight when there'd be a chance he'd be fully functioning.

The guest, whoever he was, must have been abed as well. The second bedroom door was also closed. Good.

Morin opened the refrigerator and grabbed a bottle of water. He drank half of it in one long swallow. He carried the bottle with him across the open room to the seating area that served as most of Krause's living space.

Morin slipped his shoes off and lay back on the sofa, listening to the thunder and the pouring rain on the metal roof. In less than a minute, exhaustion and tension overcame him. He fell into sleep, snoring softly.

Which was why he didn't hear the approaching sirens until they were already blaring loudly in the driveway.

Before he had a chance to get up off the sofa, officers had stormed the house, pounding on the front door.

CHAPTER 30

Saturday, June 4
Niagara-on-the-Lake, Ontario, CA

THE THREE INVESTIGATORS HAD fallen into a cooperative conversation lubricated by similar professional objectives. Which is not to say they trusted each other. All three were operating in the old fashioned "trust but verify" phase.

In response to the question about Reacher's motives, Chang shrugged. "Reacher's up to his thick neck in this thing for only one reason. Because he wants to be. You must understand that much about what motivates him."

"Copy that." Kim grimaced, nodding. Reacher never did anything unless he felt like it. Nothing on earth could force him to act against his will. Many had tried. All had failed. Some paid for the effort with broken bodies and others, with their lives.

"I ran into Reacher five years ago. Met Westwood around the same time," Chang said. "You know how life is. When you want someone to help with something, who do you call first? Folks you already know, right?"

"So Westwood called you because he already knows you. From five years ago. When you were involved with Reacher," Russell repeated flatly, as if the facts had to be more complicated than Chang made them sound, and he didn't believe she'd spilled the whole story.

He was probably right. On both points.

"Exactly." Chang nodded again. "Westwood is...was...a guy who got contacted by a lot of cranks. They were always aggrieved. Angry. Offended. And a little crazy."

"Why was he such a magnet for the unstable ranters?" Russell asked.

"Not because he was a *bon vivant*, if that's what you're asking. It was his job. They wanted him to blow the whistle on someone or write an expose of some sort. They were sure theirs was the story of the century." Chang shook her head. "They'd become rich and famous just for doing the right thing. You know the type."

"I do. They break the law and cause untold harm because they're so damned sure they know better than everybody else. Westwood encouraged and enticed these lawbreakers, I gather." Russell's tone was one thousand percent sarcasm. "Yeah, the world needs more *journalists* like that."

"Have some respect. The man's dead." Chang snapped in response, glaring fiercely. "Do you want to hear this or not?"

Russell didn't seem the least perturbed by her anger. He wasn't the kind of guy to cower for any reason.

Chang stopped talking for a good long while.

Kim closed her lids to rest her eyes. It had been too long since she'd last slept. She didn't have energy to devote to squabbles.

After a brief cooling off period, she inhaled deeply and prompted Chang in a reasonable tone. "So Lucas Stuart called Westwood. What did he want?"

"Said his brother, this hot shot genius scientist, had been working on a secret weapon for the DOD," Chang reported in a huffy tone. "And now the brother was missing. And so was the weapon. The implication was that the DOD had something to do with the brother's disappearance."

When Chang mentioned the DOD the scope of the problem escalated instantly, mushrooming like she'd tossed a nuke into the desert. For once, Russell had no comeback. Heavy silence overwhelmed the room.

In Kim's experience, there were no secrets anymore. The age of social media and the constant internet news cycle had pretty much eliminated *clandestine* from the modern dictionary.

Weapons weren't developed in stealth or shrouded in secrecy anymore. An active and inquisitive free press was just one reason. Leakers, whistleblowers, spies, and the like were only too anxious to share top secret details.

Social media made disseminating all sorts of secrets as simple as sharing recipes and cat videos. Any fool with a phone and an internet connection could say whatever the hell they felt like saying, true or not.

Long gone were the days when a nuclear bomb could be paid for, developed, and deployed without the knowledge of the public.

Not much stayed under wraps outside the spotlight's glare nowadays.

At least, that was the fiction deployed by governments around the world.

The idea that the DOD could be developing weapons in secret was the stuff of great fiction. But in the real world, intel about new and powerful weapons was a powerful deterrent usually deployed by governments as an effective threat to their opposition.

To get the conversation moving again, Kim said, "Lucas wanted Westwood to find his brother?"

Chang nodded. "Before the brother did something stupid. Or someone less…friendly…found him and took the weapon from him by force."

"I see," Kim said, nodding, drawing her along like leading a stubborn donkey.

"Westwood ignored Lucas's calls. He always did a thorough background check before he agreed to meet with a potential whistleblower," Chang said.

Kim nodded again.

"As I said, most of them were cranks and kooks. Meaning they were often unstable and unpredictable. Something about Lucas raised Westwood's threat meter into the red zone," Chang stopped to draw a long breath. "Westwood was super wary. Careful."

"And then?" Russell prompted.

"What do you mean?"

"Clearly something changed and Westwood decided to get involved. What was it?"

"I told you." Chang shot another glare toward him. "Reacher called Westwood. Out of the blue. After five years of no contact."

"Why?" Russell asked, brow furrowed, bewildered.

Chang shook her head. She did the thing with her hair again, drawing it back from her face with both hands and letting it fall across her shoulders like a black curtain.

"Reacher had heard rumblings about this new weapon. Said the weapon was being discussed in the wrong circles. Mentioned on the dark web by the wrong people," Chang said. "Reacher asked Westwood to check it out."

Kim cocked her head. Until this moment she'd have bet money that Reacher had never heard of the dark web and had no clue what it was.

He was tech-adverse. Guy didn't even own a cell phone, let alone a laptop.

Reacher wasn't into porn or fetishes or drugs or any of that. Why would he care about the dark web?

"What kind of *wrong circles*?" Kim asked.

"He didn't say."

"What's Reacher's interest in all this?" Russell asked.

"Don't know." Chang shook her head.

"Westwood didn't tell you?" Kim asked.

"He said Reacher didn't give him much intel, either. Just said the new weapon could be a big problem," Chang replied. "Reacher didn't like it."

"Didn't like what?" Russell asked.

"The weapon? The missing scientist? The dark web rumors?" Chang shrugged and did the thing with her hair again. Some sort of nervous habit, for sure. "I don't know. Could be all of the above."

"We'll come back to that," Kim said, head cocked, eyes narrowed, thinking things through.

She was sure Chang and Reacher had been lovers at some point.

Reacher liked strong, independent women who worked in law enforcement. It was a thing for him.

Chang was exactly Reacher's type, although she was more substantial physically than some of his exes Kim had met.

His prior relationship with Chang probably informed his decision to get her involved this time. Like she said, he knew her from before. He trusted her.

But history was not the present. Kim wanted the discussion to stay on track. "What did Westwood want you to do?"

"Good question." Chang ran her hands through her hair again, for luck maybe. Like a child rubbing a rabbit's foot.

"How was the dark web involved?" Russell's tone implied that each new piece of intel Chang offered was more preposterous than the one before.

Kim was intrigued by Chang's comments about Reacher but not totally shocked by most of it. She had been hunting Reacher long enough to know the ring of truth about him when she heard it.

In fact, Kim might know more about Reacher now than anyone else on the planet, possibly including him. He wasn't the kind of guy who spent much time navel gazing.

But Reacher involved with the dark web? Seemed like a bridge too far.

Reacher's profile was terrifying, sure. She'd been adding to the bare bones she'd received initially over the past seven months.

By now, the augmented Reacher profile should have allowed her to predict his behavior. And it did. Up to a point.

But Reacher had also proven to be unpredictable when she least expected it.

Mostly he did whatever the hell he pleased whenever the hell he felt like it. He didn't need an objectively good reason.

Reacher's rules were all that mattered.

Which was why Chang's story hung together and fit with the few facts Kim already knew.

Even if none of it made sense.

Yet.

CHAPTER 31

Saturday, June 4
Niagara-on-the-Lake, Ontario, CA

THE HOUR WAS LATE and Kim had been running on her standard triple As for too long. She needed sleep.

Adrenaline, Ambition, and Anxiety could only carry her so far.

But she wanted to get crystal clear on the situation while Chang was in a talkative mood.

"So Westwood had written a few articles on the dark web over the years. Maybe he was some sort of expert. Sounds like Reacher might have discovered that," Kim said thoughtfully, as if Chang were a colleague and they were working things through together.

Maybe they were. Chang had been FBI once, too, after all.

But Kim's gut said Chang knew more than she was telling. Which could be okay. Or not. Too early to know.

Chang nodded, "Yeah."

"That's why he contacted Westwood," Kim said, nodding as if those facts made any kind of sense. "But why did Westwood contact you?"

"He said Reacher suggested me. The three of us had worked on a dark web thing five years ago," Chang said. "I guess in Reacher's head, the idea made sense. He has a peculiar way of thinking. It's not always easy to figure out where his head's going, you know?"

"Hold up," Russell interjected, palm raised like a traffic cop. "Reacher worked *directly* with the FBI five years ago? What the hell was that about?"

"I had the impression that Reacher's worked with the FBI in the past," Chang explained with a frown. "But when I met him, I had already left the FBI. I was working as a private investigator. He helped me with one of my private cases."

"And how'd that go?" Russell seemed genuinely curious.

"About like you'd expect," Chang chuckled. "He's a one-man SWAT team. Very handy to have around. But not so great at teamwork."

Kim smiled, nodded, and filed the Reacher lore in her head. Then she tried to get the conversation back on track. "So this time? Is Reacher involved in this case?"

"Reacher thought Westwood and I could handle things on our own, I guess. Like I said, he's not easy to read." Chang shrugged and fell silent, a troubled frown marred her features.

Nope. Kim couldn't see that happening. Reacher wasn't a team player. Nor would he have handed off the ball. Chang was lying or she didn't know Jack Reacher well at all.

But Kim didn't say any of that. Her goal was to gather intel, not supply it.

Aside from Kim's intuition, Chang's guess on Reacher's motives contradicted Westwood.

He said Reacher had sent him to Kim.

If Reacher expected Chang and Westwood to handle the situation alone, he would have stopped there. He wouldn't have sent them to Kim at all.

No reason to believe Westwood had lied about Reacher's directions. She shrugged.

Not like she could ask him directly now, either.

Russell and Chang kept talking, but Kim's thoughts wandered.

What was Reacher doing? What was his goal? His motivation? What had set him off on this trail? Why did any of it involve her?

If she could figure that out, she might know what to do going forward. And she might also know where to find him.

Her mental hard drive had collected quite a bit of intel on Reacher. Sorting through it all and making the right connections was an ongoing quagmire.

Reacher as silent partner in the Stuart operation made sense. He'd played the role before.

Reacher was also freakishly strategic.

He was more than just a brawny hulk. He had brains, too.

And intellectual curiosity.

And unfathomable methods for figuring things out.

Kim's boss didn't know it, but Reacher had been helping her for a while. Usually operating in the shadows. Without benefit of any kind of briefing or backup.

Sometimes, she wasn't even sure whether he'd been there or not. Only in retrospect could she see his hand in certain events.

He had been bafflingly proactive about her assignment recently. He'd even contacted Gaspar and offered assistance. More than once.

It was as if he'd decided to subtly shift his role from target to something else, in ways she couldn't quite fathom.

She certainly hadn't figured out Reacher's game.

He knew where she was. He knew what she wanted. He knew why she wanted it. He could have come forward or walked away at any time.

But he didn't.

Instead, he went about contacting and assisting her in oblique but essential ways. This time, it seemed he'd sent Westwood and Chang.

The question was, why? To what end?

Lucas Stuart, assuming that's who he was, had died at her front door.

Surely Reacher wasn't the one who killed him?

Why would he do that?

What was all this about?

What was Reacher involved in here?

Messing around with weapons research and manufacturing didn't seem like his area. Never had been. He was more interested in using whatever weapons he found at hand instead of dreaming up new ways to kill the enemy.

And he wasn't all that interested in the DoD anymore, either.

Reacher wasn't the kind of man to suffer regrets or remorse. He moved relentlessly forward. He'd left the Army fifteen years ago and never looked back.

Since then, he'd been into busting heads and eliminating two-legged vermin when they approached him.

Reacher was a trouble magnet, for sure. But he didn't go looking for trouble.

Usually.

At least as far as Kim had discovered.

She had been told to find him because her boss wanted Reacher for some sort of classified assignment.

Could Reacher's strange behavior here have anything to do with that assignment?

Maybe Reacher had gotten wind of the plan, whatever it was.

Maybe he liked it.

Maybe he didn't.

Maybe he was exploring the idea.

Maybe he intended to volunteer.

The thought made her smile. That old army standard, the one she'd heard from her dad, came to mind.

"Never volunteer."

Advice to live by.

So what was Reacher doing and why had he involved Westwood and Chang and Kim in this deal?

Never-ending questions traveled through her head in rapid succession. She remembered all the reasons hunting Reacher was dangerous business.

Without backup from Cooper or Finlay, the assignment bordered on suicidal.

She tuned in again to Chang and Russell in conversation and opened her mouth to ask a question when another random thought popped up.

Kim had seen a small town near Oklahoma City on a map once. After a bit of searching, she'd found the origin of the town's name.

An old Arapaho word, difficult to pronounce, had been corrupted to *Mother's Rest*.

Like the town of Mother's Rest, Reacher's orbit seemed, always and forever, the place where bad things grow.

All of which meant Liam Stuart, and everyone associated with him, was in serious trouble.

CHAPTER 32

Saturday, June 4
Hamilton, Ontario, CA

FIVE MINUTES INTO THE hike, Liam realized he had underestimated how difficult this plan would be.

He'd chosen the location because it was remote enough, but not too far from Krause. He intended to demonstrate the Stiletto 100. He needed open space with no overhead wires and few, if any, people around.

The Devil's Punchbowl had seemed to fit his requirements. It was a dramatic gorge with two waterfalls in the flatlands of Ontario, between Ottawa and Ancaster.

On the maps, the distance between the cabin and the gorge looked short enough to cover quickly. Reality was much worse than the map.

The old cabin was downhill and about a mile west from Devil's Punchbowl. A large, wooded area covered most of the uneven ground between. Liam wasn't much of an athlete. But he jogged a few miles now and then.

A one-mile hike, even uphill and through the woods while carrying the drone, wasn't that far. He was in reasonably good shape. If Krause could do it, Liam could do it.

He hadn't planned for a storm. He'd brought no rain gear for himself or for the Stiletto.

When the lightning finally stopped, he had struggled through the mud, pushing against strong winds. Long before he reached the flat grassy area near the observation point along the rim of the Devil's Punchbowl, he was cold and soaked to the skin.

The Stiletto's weight seemed to increase with every step he took. The muscles in his arms and legs began to ache.

He intended to test the Stiletto 100 under field weather conditions similar to what he'd face during the Ottawa parade tomorrow. He hadn't expected to carry the drone so far. He'd planned to fly it after he cleared the trees. But the high winds and rain interfered.

As he approached the launch site, Liam squinted to see the parking lot off to his left where he would meet Krause later.

Between Liam and the ridge road straight ahead at the top of the bluff was the gaping maw of the Punchbowl. Almost a two-hundred-foot drop. Two waterfalls. A creek at the bottom. The rocky pathways along the gorge were slippery and dangerous.

The Stiletto would have enough open space to maneuver above the Devil's Punchbowl. It was a perfect spot. The drone was functionally invisible to the naked eye of a casual observer, unlikely to be spotted.

Liam imagined he felt the stare of another early morning hiker piercing his back, but he shook it off. Not likely. The area was too dark, the terrain too rough for anyone else to be out here now, given the weather.

He looked at the ground. A wrong step and he might find himself more than a hundred feet down, splayed at the bottom of the ravine, bones broken, limbs akimbo, and no longer breathing.

When he'd cleared the trees, he chose a location to set up the Stiletto for launch. He watched the Stiletto lift into the air like a magnificent bird.

He felt better already. Krause would be astonished. Liam grinned.

Operating the drone soothed his agitation better than anything else.

The Stiletto performed perfectly even in bad weather. He'd expected nothing less. Still, the perfection of this baby impressed him like nothing he'd created before.

At the break of dawn, even with the heavy cloud cover, allowing the drone to fly was a calculated risk. Testing was necessary, but so was secrecy. Stiletto 100 was constructed of stealth materials which made it much less visible than other commercial and military drones.

But Brax wouldn't like exposure to any unnecessary risk. Keeping the Stiletto 100 out of the public eye was essential. Not only for the test at the parade in Ottawa, but any deployment anywhere.

Until Krause perfected his competitor, or some other weapons engineer stumbled onto Liam's proprietary and revolutionary technology, the Stiletto 100 must remain hidden under the tightest security.

In addition its technologically advanced target identification software, the Stiletto 100 was also a two-part system. It had a larger drone with range and power.

Stiletto 100 could spear the target with either a bullet or a bomb and make a clean escape.

Or the larger drone could deploy a smaller one to fly closer to the target and emit a deadly poison within a few inches of his nose. Or send a fatal dart into his jugular.

Both methods of attack would only be viable until the enemy learned Stiletto 100 existed.

Once discovered, the Stiletto 100 would inevitably be disclosed and its usefulness diminished or destroyed.

Which meant the Stiletto must stay out of sight as long as possible. Months at least. Years if possible.

Two bright halogen headlights turned off the north road into the nearby parking lot. Liam couldn't be seen from the parking lot, but if the driver left his car he might see something he shouldn't.

Liam's morning solitude was over.

The Devil's Punchbowl was a popular hiking destination. Early morning hikers were to be expected, he supposed.

Liam shrugged and recalled the Stiletto 100. He stayed in the shadows as the drone returned to base.

He collected the Stiletto and trudged toward the cabin. Krause would be here soon enough.

Liam was a little surprised to find himself anticipating the meeting with his old friend. They'd not spoken since Krause stomped off in a huff.

At the time, Liam hadn't been concerned. He knew he didn't have many friends other than Krause, of course.

He shrugged. Turned out Krause was his only friend.

He didn't count his brother, Lucas, among his friends. They were brothers. Which was fundamentally different.

The cabin was a long mile away, along a trail overgrown with brambles and weeds. Trees blocked what little early morning light there was, casting the rough trail in darkness.

Liam trudged carefully, one foot placed firmly in front of the other. The last thing he needed was a twisted ankle.

He couldn't risk a flashlight beam which might be noticed from a distance. Both hands were occupied with carrying the increasingly heavy drone, anyway.

In full daylight and good weather, with his hands free, Liam could have covered the distance in a brisk twenty minutes or less. Not that he had a hot date or anything.

But he was excited to see Krause. And hungry. He hadn't eaten in a good long time.

Around the last bend, peering into the shadows, he was relieved to see the decrepit cabin ahead. His SUV was still parked in the drive where he'd left it.

Liam smiled. Briefly. Until he saw another vehicle approaching.

The headlights were traveling along the rutted, overgrown path that led to the cabin from the road.

He was expecting no one other than Krause. They were meeting in the parking lot at the Devil's Punchbowl, not here at the cabin. And Krause wasn't due until later.

Liam stopped abruptly. Watching. Waiting.

Gooseflesh rose on his arms.

Had his subconscious picked up an actual watcher in the parking lot earlier? What had the watcher seen?

His body shivered involuntarily attempting to shake off the foreboding.

Liam climbed deeper into the woods, hiding both himself and the Stiletto 100 as best he could while still allowing him to see the path to the cabin.

The approaching vehicle was a sedan. Probably a rental. No one who owned a sedan would drive it along that path. For one thing, the paint would be scratched all to hell. And the abandoned trail was barely navigable, even in a larger vehicle with more ground clearance.

The sedan pulled to a stop six feet behind his SUV.

Liam waited for him to turn the engine off and step out of the car.

He hoped the driver had made a mistake. Perhaps the guy would go back where he came from.

That slim hope was dashed when the driver slid the sedan's transmission to park and turned off the engine. He left the headlights on to illuminate the weedy path to the cabin's only entrance.

The door opened and the driver stepped out, putting both booted feet firmly on the ground.

Liam gasped under his breath and clamped his lips shut immediately. His pounding heart picked up its pace.

Two things surprised him.

First, the driver was not a man.

Second, the woman held a pistol gripped in her right hand. She carried the weapon as if she'd had a great deal of experience with guns.

None of this was good.

Not the sedan, the headlights, the woman.

Or the gun.

Liam's thoughts had jumbled together and he sorted quickly through the few options he could think of given the pressure building in his head.

The Stiletto 100 was very heavy now. He couldn't set it safely on the ground amid the underbrush.

So he stood there making both himself and the drone as invisible as possible, trembling with the effort.

What would the woman do?

What would he do?

Answers to both questions were beyond him.

With no alternatives popping into his mind, Liam continued to watch her from afar. She raised her weapon, holding it at the ready. Liam had no doubt she could shoot and hit her bullseye.

First, she walked around his SUV peering into each window.

Of course, she saw nothing remarkable inside. The SUV was a rental, too. He'd left no personal possessions inside.

Morin had instructed him to pick up a vehicle in Toronto in preparation for the Ottawa parade.

Of course, those instructions were not applicable. But Liam thought they made sense. So he'd followed the protocol.

He'd left his personal SUV in the airport parking lot.

And now he was glad he'd been especially careful. Because this woman with her gun would find nothing in that rental to identify him or the Stiletto 100.

The drone was small but awkward. Thinking about the drone reminded him that he'd been holding it for a long while.

He struggled with the weight.

He couldn't set it down here in the woods. The ground was rough, uneven, littered with debris of all sorts.

If the Stiletto 100 prototype were damaged, Morin would have his head. Rightfully so. The FQT could not be compromised under any circumstances. Damage to the Stiletto was not an option.

The woman finished her inspection of Liam's rental and prepared to breach the cabin. Or whatever she'd have called breaking into the place.

She held her gun as if she meant business.

She stepped carefully toward the warped plank door, swiveling her head to and fro as if she expected to be ambushed or something.

Which might have been amusing under different circumstances, he supposed.

Exactly what did she plan to do next?

CHAPTER 33

Saturday, June 4
Hamilton, Ontario, CA

FROM BEHIND THE TREES fifty feet from the cabin, Liam's view of the woman was obstructed by three things.

The distance between them.

The two vehicles in the driveway.

And the way she carried herself, straight up but sideways, which made her an even thinner target, he assumed.

She approached the door obliquely. Not as a friendly visitor would. More like a stealthy hunter closing in on a drug den or a sleeping bear. Or whatever.

Which made him wonder if she might be law enforcement. No uniform, though.

Since she was alone, maybe she'd been trained in law enforcement but wasn't on duty now. Liam hadn't interacted with cops much. But he had the impression they worked in groups of two or more, usually. Maybe not a cop, then.

Liam hoped she wouldn't damage the door. She didn't need to blast the lock or anything. If she tried the knob, the door would open easily. She could go inside, look around, do whatever she'd come to do, and leave.

But how long would that take? He noticed himself shivering now, from the cold, but also from holding the drone's weight. The muscles in his arms were fatigued and his legs weren't feeling all that sturdy either.

The wind had picked up again and another batch of low clouds blocked what little sunlight penetrated the dense tree cover.

Liam could barely make out the woman's silhouette in the distance.

She didn't shout or flash any lights or even pound on the door.

He squeezed his tired eyes closed for a second to clear his vision.

When he opened his eyes again, she was gone.

"Crap!" he muttered under his breath.

A moment later, he realized she must have opened the door fast and ducked inside when he wasn't watching.

Which was exactly the best thing she could have done, given the alternatives.

She'd find nothing of interest and leave. But while she was inside, he swept his gaze around the immediate area, hoping to locate a better vantage spot.

He moved to a tree with a large and sturdy trunk and leaned against it, resting his elbows and the weight of the drone. Which was a marginally better position.

He grimaced. By the time she gave up altogether, his arms might fall off from supporting the weight of the Stiletto 100.

Which was a good thing to know.

When they prepared to use the drone in the field, they'd need a method for carrying it. Something he hadn't thought of before. Also a problem he'd need to solve quickly for the FQT.

He waited ten minutes. Then he waited another five. The woman didn't come outside.

Liam frowned. The little cabin could have been investigated thoroughly in a single glance.

"What the hell is she doing in there?" he mumbled.

But then he remembered.

He'd left a small bag with a few things on the table inside. She'd found it. She'd rummaged through the contents.

Which was okay. There was nothing in the bag that would help her.

But now she knew the cabin was being used. By a man.

Which was not okay.

Not even remotely.

Because now she wasn't simply looking inside. She was waiting. For the man to return. She didn't seem like the type who would give up without whatever it was she came to collect.

If he hadn't seen her with the gun, he might have simply walked over there.

As it was, she might be planning to kill him.

At the very least, she'd try to force him to do something he didn't want to do.

He needed to get rid of her. Before Krause arrived at the parking lot.

And she couldn't see the Stiletto 100. Not even a glimpse.

The drone had grown so heavy that the muscles in his arms quivered steadily with the strain.

He struggled mentally and physically.

Worried about Krause and Lucas.

Concerned about the killer inside his cabin.

He didn't know what to do. He couldn't think clearly.

The only thing he knew for sure was that he needed to return the Stiletto 100 and rest while he still could. The drone was the most important element in this equation. Even if it wasn't, he couldn't possibly deal with the woman unless his hands were free.

She was inside.

The cabin had no windows offering a view in his direction.

He could cross the distance without being discovered, as long as she didn't come out and catch him in the process.

Which was a risk he was willing to take.

Mainly because his arms might give out if he didn't act now. And he could not, under any circumstances, drop the drone.

Quickly, he calculated the distance to his SUV and the speed with which he could cover it. If she came outside before he reached the SUV, he'd be screwed.

He pushed that thought aside.

Every minute he waited was a minute she might rush out.

The clouds brought more rain. Sprinkles for now, but he saw lightning in the distance and smelled the returning storm in the wind.

The prototype Stiletto 100 absolutely could not get wet. Not even a few drops. The final version would be weatherproofed. But the protype had been rushed. He'd had no time to weather test yet.

He had to go now. While he still could.

Liam took a deep breath and sprinted across the divide before he came up with five dozen reasons why he shouldn't.

A moment before he reached the SUV, the sky opened like a firehose. He was drenched all the way to his skin and shivering like a scared puppy.

He dashed around to the back of the SUV, opened the hatch, and carefully placed the Stiletto in the cargo area. The drone was at least as wet as Liam, but he had no time to worry about the issues that might cause.

He closed the hatch, fished the key fob from his pocket and pressed to lock the vehicle.

Once the Stiletto 100 was as secure as he could make it in the moment, Liam had two options.

Go inside or jump behind the wheel and make a run for it.

As soon as she heard the SUV start up, she'd be out of the cabin and after him. He wouldn't be able to outrun her. Not with the Stiletto unsecured in the back of the vehicle. She was unpredictable. Who knew what she might do? What if she shot out the windows or door locks and took the drone.

He could not allow anything like that to happen.

He tossed the key fob into the bushes on the left side of the cabin. When she searched him, she wouldn't find the fob.

Which might keep the Stiletto 100 from her clutches long enough.

Long enough for what, exactly?

He shrugged and then squared his shoulders and approached the cabin door, moving like a condemned man climbing the steps to the guillotine.

The rain came down hard and fast, puddling in the low-lying areas. Liam was completely soaked now. Even his underwear and socks were wet.

"Time to face the music," he muttered as he reached out, turned the knob, and pushed the door open.

His eyes had adjusted to the dim outdoor light. Inside, the woman had lit a candle on the small table in the center of the room, which improved visibility.

She was seated in the only chair. Her posture was relaxed, even as she held the gun pointed directly toward him.

"Come in out of the rain. It's cold out there," she said in a fabulously sexy voice. The kind of voice any man notices, whether he's interested or not.

Liam didn't bother to feign surprise. She'd see through it if he tried any sort of subterfuge.

What did she want?

CHAPTER 34

Saturday, June 4
Niagara-on-the-Lake, Ontario

CHANG GLANCED AT HER high-tech watch and seemed surprised to notice the time. "I've got to run. Sorry. Gotta see a man about a horse. We can talk more later."

Kim cocked her head and narrowed her eyes. "My dad used to say that when he didn't want to tell us where he was going."

"Smart man, your father," Chang grinned. She holstered her gun, gathered her bag, and shrugged into a distressed brown leather bomber jacket.

Kim asked. "What if we need to find you?"

On her way to the door Chang replied, "Make yourselves comfortable. Catch some sleep. Stay as long as you like. The room's rented for three more days."

"You're planning to be around that long?" Russell asked, frowning.

She shrugged again and kept moving.

Kim replied, "Leave me a contact number."

Chang reached into her pocket and pulled out a business card. She tossed it on the table near the door.

She flipped the deadbolt and opened the door wide enough to slip through. A moment later she was gone.

Russell shook his head as the door closed solidly behind her. "What a load of crap."

"Which part?"

"All of it, probably." He stood and stretched like a tiger cramped too long in too small a cage. "Genius scientist in cahoots with the DOD gets kidnapped? Crusading journalist seeking to expose the government's illegal weapons for the good of all mankind? Mercenaries hired via the dark web? Reacher involved in all of it? Sounds more than a little insane to me."

"Oh, come on. You work for Finlay. Every bit of what she said, and a lot of other stuff that might sound even more crazy, is completely feasible. It's already happened. More than once," Kim replied steadily. "Your boss and mine have been right in the thick of it, too. So yeah, I think she's telling the truth as she knows it. Or some of it anyway. What motive would she have to lie to us?"

Before Russell had a chance to reply, Kim heard the sound of gunshots close by followed by return fire.

"What the hell?" she said, jumping up.

As she moved, she drew her weapon.

Russell did the same, following close behind.

When she reached the door, she heard more distant gunfire. The shooters were moving away from the hotel.

"You think that's Chang?" Russell said.

"Who else would it be? We have to go." Kim scanned the room. "We can't come back here. Take my laptop and pick up the SUV. I'll follow Chang. Make sure she's okay. Meet you outside."

Russell nodded. "The SUV's half a block down. It'll take me a minute to pull up."

"Yeah, what happened with parking earlier? Can't be that hard to park in this neighborhood at this hour."

"Just meet me around the corner instead of out front."

"Got it," Kim replied as she grabbed Chang's card off the table and stuffed it into her pocket. "This place will be crawling with local law enforcement shortly. We need to be gone before they arrive."

"Copy that," Russell said as he moved toward the stairs.

Kim hurried along with him scanning for cover.

At the main floor, Russell hustled toward the back exit and Kim scurried toward the front, guessing that Chang had traveled in the same direction.

She crossed the hotel lobby, gaze sweeping the room as she moved. Todd the desk clerk was talking on the phone, probably to the police. Chang was nowhere in sight.

Kim dashed out the front door and down the steps to the sidewalk. She scanned the immediate vicinity and saw nothing out of the ordinary.

No Chang. No shooters.

A moment later, halfway down the block, a dark sedan started up and sped away, traveling northeast.

Kim couldn't see the license plate from her viewing angle, but she saw two adult shadows in the front seat. One could have been Chang. The other one was much bigger.

No other vehicles started up to follow the sedan, either. If anyone had been hit during the gunfire exchange, the injured were not left behind.

Kim turned and jogged toward the corner, continuing to scan for threats as she moved. She rounded the corner to the side of the hotel. Russell was already there with the SUV running.

She opened the passenger door and jumped inside.

"Did you see Chang?" she asked.

"No. You?"

Kim shrugged. "A sedan sped away just as I came outside. Older model. Maybe a full-sized Lincoln or Ford. Two adults in the front seat. Could have been Chang and Reacher, maybe. Impossible to tell."

Russell scowled. "Could the two in the front have snatched Chang? Put her in the back on the bench seat?"

"Maybe. Hell, they could have forced her into the trunk." Kim shrugged again. "They had enough time."

"Should we go after them?"

Sirens pierced the quiet, heading toward the hotel from the east. At least two vehicles, Kim guessed. Maybe more.

"We need to move. We don't want to get stuck here. In addition to everything else, unlicensed guns are a serious problem here," Kim deadpanned.

"Solid thinking." Russell nodded, moved the transmission into drive, and punched the accelerator.

He took the corner too fast. The SUV fishtailed until he righted it on the main street. Then he pressed the accelerator again, speeding toward the sedan's taillights growing ever smaller in the distance.

"Where are we going?" Russell asked.

"We're driving along the southwest side of Lake Ontario. The next big town along this route is Hamilton. Which is about an hour away," Kim said, looking at the map on the navigation system.

Russell kept his eyes on the road. "I think that sedan might have been watching us. Following us from Niagara Falls."

Kim gave him a stare. "What?"

"That's why it took me longer to park before I came up to Chang's room. After you went into the hotel lobby, a dark sedan drove by. Slowly. The windows were tinted and it was dark on the street, so I couldn't see who was driving or how many were inside."

"Lots of slow-moving cars in a town like that. Speed limit was only twenty-five. What made you suspicious?"

"Just a feeling. The way it passed. Like they wanted a good look at me. I waited awhile but the sedan didn't come back."

"And no one else showed up. But they may have identified our SUV. So they might have been watching you."

"Could have been car thieves, I guess," Russell nodded. "Took me a while to find a gated lot, which might have slowed them down a little."

Kim nodded, keeping her eyes on the taillights ahead. "You didn't notice the sedan until we pulled up to the hotel?"

"I wasn't watching as carefully as I should have been." Russell shook his head, disgusted with his sloppy work.

"Yeah, and maybe they didn't follow us. They could have been following Chang. Or someone else. It's also possible that Chang had a lookout posted," Kim replied, talking it through. "She seemed okay to me, though."

"You mean okay until she jumped up and ran out and we heard gunfire right afterward?" Russell arched his eyebrows just in case she didn't catch the sarcasm.

"If the sedan dudes are part of Chang's crew, why would they be shooting at her?" Kim said.

"What makes you say they were shooting at her? Could be she was shooting at them," he replied.

"Which makes even less sense," Kim said slowly, turning things over in her head.

"So there's a third option. What is it?" Russell asked. "Someone else came along and coincidentally started a beef with the guys in the sedan just as Chang came outside and *they* took both the new dude and Chang?"

Kim didn't say what she was thinking. But that sounded exactly like something Reacher would do.

Only thing was, if Reacher had a beef with the guys in the sedan, they wouldn't be in any shape to drive away. More likely, Reacher had stuffed them both in the trunk and then drove off with Chang.

Kim reached into her pocket for the burner cell phone that connected her directly to Gaspar. He'd had plenty of time to work things out. Maybe he'd found useful intel by now.

Because she was floundering here and she knew it. What began as a desire to learn the identity of the man who had died on her doorstep had become something altogether different. She didn't understand what was going on or why.

Her gut said Reacher was involved. She could be wrong. Not likely.

Russell was a solid partner. He'd been doing a good job.

But he wasn't Gaspar. He didn't have Gaspar's knowledge of the Reacher case.

Beyond that, she'd tied both of Russell's hands behind his back by insisting that he not contact Finlay.

Without Finlay or Cooper, Gaspar was the only resource she had. No reason not to utilize him.

She pressed the call button and Gaspar picked up promptly.

"Where the hell have you been, Suzy Wong?" he said, as if he'd been genuinely worried. He probably had. Gaspar was like a mother hen in some ways and Kim loved him for it. She imagined his four kids might chafe a bit under his heavy hand, though.

She smiled in the darkness of the SUV's cabin. "Oh, you know, Cheech. Late night parties, dancing in the streets, skinny dipping in the Great Lakes with Aquaman. The usual."

She imagined she could see Gaspar's scowling face when he deadpanned, "Very funny."

Kim laughed. Gaspar could always make her feel like they'd be okay. Eventually.

He was infuriating sometimes. But she felt better simply knowing he was on the other end of the call. If she died tonight, at least someone would know where to find her body.

At the moment, Gaspar was deeply concerned, and he had reason to be.

He had accepted that she would never give up the hunt for Reacher until she'd accomplished her mission. He didn't bother to argue the point anymore.

She'd set out to find Reacher and that's what she planned to do.

No matter what.

But she didn't ignore the danger, either. She was tenacious, not stupid.

"Have you heard from Reacher?" Kim asked, playing a hunch.

Gaspar chuckled. "How did you guess?"

Reacher had called Gaspar several times recently. He could have called her directly. But he didn't. She had no clue why. She only knew that Reacher had his reasons, whether she agreed with them or not.

CHAPTER 35

Saturday, June 4
Hamilton, Ontario, CA

LIAM'S ENTIRE FOCUS WAS pointed like a laser at the woman. He had never seen her before. Not even a glimpse on a city street. He would have remembered. She was stunning. The exact opposite of forgettable.

She pointed the gun straight at him as if she'd had plenty of experience to back it up. What she didn't know was that Liam was a reasonably good shot as well. When he had a weapon. Which, at the moment, he did not.

"Who are you and what do you want?" Liam demanded. He expected she'd respond effectively. Which she did.

"You imagine that I don't know your name or what you've been working on. So let's clear that up right now, shall we?" she held the gun steady as if it were an extension of her arm.

Her words sent a shiver of fear up his spine. Liam had been conducting his work in solitary confinement for months. Since Kraus left, actually. Liam only had one friend and after Krause was gone, there had been no one else to talk to.

Thus, Liam had confided in no one except his immediate superiors. There were no women among them. Certainly not this woman or anyone remotely like her.

So again, who was she and why was she here? His mind kept coming back to that, like a hole he needed to fill before he could move forward.

"You are Liam Stewart. Your occupation is weapons engineer." Her words took Liam's breath away. The woman continued talking. "You've been working on the top-secret Stiletto 100 project."

Liam felt lightheaded. How could she possibly know these things? He backed up to the chair and put a hand on the solid wood to ground himself in the real world.

She continued, "You have perfected a prototype of the Stiletto 100 and you are scheduled to test it in a live environment tomorrow in Ottawa."

She arched her eyebrows, observing him for any sort of response. She must have recognized her words had induced something like a state of shock. Because she smiled. One of those canary-eating smiles bullies always used when they knew they'd made him knuckle under.

"Shall I continue?" she asked, with a broad smirk that twisted her beautiful face into an ugly sneer.

Liam nodded because he was still too astonished to speak. No matter. She kept filling the silence without any need for his participation.

She said, "You have the Stiletto 100 prototype with you. You were hoping to demonstrate it to your friend Krause who was planning to meet you here, but he has been permanently delayed."

Liam's eyes widened and his mouth fell open into a round "O" almost without his volition. He shook his head, unsure which of her outlandish statements he should rebut first.

He focused on Krause because his friend had been top of mind before he came upon this dangerous watcher. And because Krause was a real person in the real world and Liam could rely on Krause. He knew for sure.

The woman kept talking. Making demands. Ordering Liam around. It seemed like she would never shut up.

And then she came to the end of her soliloquy. "Krause is not coming. You have a job to do tomorrow in Ottawa. We need to get going. Where is the Stiletto 100?"

"Where is Krause? What have you done with him? How do you know he's not coming?" Liam demanded in rapid-fire succession, mocking her style.

"Krause is dead. You will never see him again." She paused to smile like a demented clown. "Unless you want to join him in whatever afterlife exists?"

She cocked her head as if she'd posed an actual question to which she was expecting a serious answer.

"Why would I believe you? I don't know you. I have no idea who you are or where you came from or what you're doing here. I spoke to Krause he told me he's coming I will wait here until he shows up." Liam said with all the belligerence and determination and anger he felt welling in his chest.

If he had the chance, he would take that gun away from her and shoot her in the friggin' head. She should know that too.

But he felt no need to say so. Surely she could divine his intentions since she was so damn smart.

"Where's the Stiletto, Liam? Get it. Pick up your stuff and let's go."

"Not until you answer my questions. Who are you and why are you here and how do you know these things?" Liam said.

She sighed as if she'd finally resigned herself to his irrational and stubborn behavior.

"My name is Audrey Ruston. Nigel Morin sent me. That should be enough for you to know now. I'll answer more questions later," she promised. "We have a lot to do before tomorrow's parade. We'll take your suburban. I assume that's where the Stiletto is. I'm parked behind you. You move my car and I'll drive yours."

She stood facing Liam and the door beyond him, still holding the pistol. "Let's go."

"Not until you tell me what happened to Krause," Liam said, planting both feet firmly on the floor and bracing for a physical confrontation.

He was in pretty good shape. He could probably take her. Maybe.

Ruston sighed. "Home invasion, apparently."

Liam stared. "Home invasion? In *Ancaster*?"

"Right? Hard to believe, but apparently true," Audrey shrugged. "Speculation is that Krause made a move on the guy, maybe thinking to subdue him, and the scumbag had a gun."

"Why would Krause attack a man with a gun? That makes no sense," Liam said, dumbfounded.

"Look, I don't know. I'm just passing along the information. You can ask Morin when you see him. Now let's go before you get us both in more trouble than you already are," Audrey said again.

Liam shrugged. He had intended to move on to Ottawa to prepare for tomorrow anyway. He'd just wanted to show the Stiletto 100 to Krause first and make amends with his mentor.

Liam was leaving the country tomorrow after the Ottawa parade. Today was his last chance to make things right with Krause or live with the regret for ever.

But his last chance to say goodbye to his old friend was already gone. Krause was dead. Aside from Liam's desire to resist Audrey Ruston, there was no reason to stay here in this cabin anymore.

CHAPTER 36

Saturday, June 4
Ancaster, Ontario, CA

AFTER MORIN FINALLY EXTRICATED himself from Krause's murder scene, he contacted the pair of operatives he'd tasked to keep track of Audrey Ruston.

"Report target status," he demanded as he backed his Range Rover along the driveway away from the house. What was the guy's name? Morin couldn't recall.

The skies were dark and heavy with rain clouds. He flipped on the intermittent windshield wipers and the automatic headlights illuminated. As he gained speed, the wind battered his vehicle, requiring two hands on the wheel to stay in his lane.

"We spotted Ruston's vehicle at one of the hotels in Niagara Falls. Followed her to another hotel in a small town about half an hour north," the operative stated flatly.

"And?" Morin asked, squinting into the rain.

"She stayed in the vehicle. Watched the hotel entrance. Drove past, turned around, and drove out of town," the guy said. "That's it."

"Why'd she stop at that hotel?" Morin cocked his head. Audrey was many things, including great at her job. She never took a side trip for no reason. So why'd she do it?

"Can't say. Something about the place caught her interest, but she didn't even go inside once she arrived."

"Nobody came out? She didn't talk to anyone?"

"Nope."

"Text me the name and address of the hotel," Morin said, figuring to send two more operatives there when he finished this call. He'd have six men in the field. How would he explain that to Brax? "Then what?"

"Followed her about an hour northwest from that hotel to a house in Ancaster. She drove to the house, went inside, stayed a while, and came out. Still alone."

"No one following her besides you?"

"Not that we've seen."

Morin swiped a palm across his face. "Where'd she go from Ancaster?"

"Well, see, that's the curious thing. She drove around the Hamilton area for a while. Seemed like she might be looking for something."

"Like what?" Morin asked, not expecting an answer.

"Dunno. We thought maybe she'd made us and was looking for a way to ditch her tail. But she never tried anything. Finally turned into a narrow drive leading into a wooded area near the Devil's Punchbowl."

"The what?"

"The Devil's Punchbowl. Big hole in the ground, I guess. It's inside a conservation area on the escarpment."

"The what?" Morin parroted.

"You know, escarpment. Bluff. Ridge. Whatever. Hell, we don't know. We just read the sign. Anyway, we lost sight of her in the woods," he said.

"You lost her? What the hell?"

"Not lost, exactly. But lost sight of her. We couldn't follow her down that path. She'd have seen us," he said. "The two-track is a dead end. Nowhere else for her to go. She'll turn around and come out and we'll pick her up again when she does."

Morin punched the Devil's Punchbowl into his GPS. A brief description, along with a few images and a map, promptly displayed on the screen.

He scanned the description. The area was an uninhabited nature attraction. Activities like hiking were popular. A deep cliff, a couple of smaller waterfalls than it's Niagara cousin. Some tourist attractions nearby.

Nothing special about the place, as far as he could tell.

What the hell was Audrey doing there? Meeting someone. There could be no other logical explanation.

"Text me the location of the path she turned into," he demanded. "Let me know immediately if she leaves. Don't lose her."

"Copy that."

Morin terminated the call. The text came in half a moment later. He opened his map to pinpoint Ruston's exact location.

Satellite imagery of the wooded area around the path was obstructed by cloud cover. He tried several different angles before he gave up.

Morin couldn't confirm Audrey was there, but he had no reason to doubt that she went in, just as the operative reported. She'd found something. Or she was waiting for someone. She knew something.

Time to find out exactly what that something or someone was.

He punched the coordinates into the GPS and headed toward Devil's Punchbowl.

Driving with his left hand, he opened the laptop with his right and picked up the trace signal he'd assigned to her vehicle.

The blue dot pulsed near the location of the path in the woods. Not exactly confirmation of the operative's report, but probably not that far off, either.

Morin made a quick call to deploy two operatives to shadow Krause's murder investigation. He had no suitable personnel active inside Canada that he could repurpose for the task.

By the time the covert team arrived from New York, anything remotely useful at Krause's residence would probably have been removed by the local law enforcement team.

Morin shrugged. Better late than never. He hoped.

"Audrey Ruston, what the hell are you up to?" Morin swore under his breath, puzzling through the options aloud. "Why kill Krause? Makes no sense. Even if you've found Liam Stuart, you've eliminated our backup. Stuart could fail. Then where will we be? Dumb thing to do. Totally stupid."

Ruston's hubris was almost as limitless as her ambition. It was one of the reasons he had ended their affair years ago.

In his business, confidence was essential but only when tempered by experience. There was always a better shot, a stronger fighter, a smarter tactician. Hubris, in short, could get you killed.

Audrey never seemed to learn the right lessons from the failures of her colleagues. She took their failures as a challenge instead of a chance to do better.

"Okay. So you've found Stuart. And you're with him now." Morin shrugged, talking it through as if Ruston was in the passenger seat. "It's not enough to recover the drone. We also need an operator. How will you persuade Stuart to complete the FQT tomorrow?"

He imagined her sultry smirk in reply.

Audrey's secret weapon was sex. She used sex to get what she wanted. And she was masterful at that game.

One of the best.

Morin and Brax could so testify from personal knowledge.

"But Stuart isn't the same as other men, Ruston. His singular focus is his work. Your considerable sexual expertise won't work on him."

Morin had been so engrossed in his analysis that he'd lost all sense of time. When the GPS system announced his turn was five miles ahead, the robotic voice startled him back to the present.

He squinted at the small screen display and located the turn.

The GPS guided Morin to pull off the main road onto the entrance to the Devil's Punchbowl conservation area. Casting his gaze from the poorly illuminated road to the map, he slowed to a crawl and lowered the window.

He stuck his head out, peering amid the trees for the two-track.

The tree canopy concealed, and the underbrush camouflaged the narrow trail well. The rain and wind pelted his face.

But a few feet farther up the road, his diligence was rewarded. He found it. The path was so well hidden that he'd have driven past if he hadn't been told it was there.

Which meant Audrey had been told exactly where to look, too. Not for the first time, Morin wondered who was feeding intel to her. Brax? Fox? Someone else?

He turned onto the dirt two-track and squelched his headlights, peering into the shadows as he moved cautiously along. If Audrey Ruston was back in here somewhere, she had a good reason. And Ruston's reasons were good enough for Morin.

His gut led him toward her like a moth to flame, knowing full well she could and would burn him to ashes without a moment's remorse.

Unless he burned her first. Which was his plan.

The path narrowed further and twisted a few times as he inched ahead, bouncing along the ruts and potholes. The tree canopy and low storm clouds conspired together to snuff ninety percent of the natural light.

He couldn't see much out there. He flipped his parking lights on, but they didn't help at all.

After another fifty feet, a sharp turn came up fast. He yanked the steering wheel to the right and lifted his foot off the gas. Rounded the turn much faster than he should have. The Range Rover performed as it was intended to do. Which meant the vehicle didn't flip. It bounced a few times and finally settled into forward motion, still traveling too fast for conditions.

At the last second, he saw the red reflectors.

Taillights, on the back of a dark colored sedan, parked in the center of the two-track, straight ahead.

He slammed the brakes, bouncing over the rutted ground, and came to a stop less than two feet behind the car.

His engine stalled.

Which was fine because he could go no farther.

He squelched his parking lights. He looked around the immediate vicinity seeking anything at all remarkable.

Morin's phone pinged.

The operative had sent two pictures of the sedan Audrey Ruston drove away from Niagara Falls. He compared the images to the license plate on the vehicle blocking his path. An exact match.

Audrey was here. As expected.

Which was more than okay. Finally, a break.

But he recognized the sedan, too. Independently of the photos. His breathing quickened, keeping pace with his pounding pulse.

This was the sedan he'd seen parked in front of Krause's garage when he arrived at the Ancaster house a few hours ago.

Which meant Ruston had been at Krause's place before he died.

Not much of a leap to conclude that Ruston had killed Krause.

Which was the opposite of okay. It was infuriating.

Morin slapped his palm hard on the steering wheel. A low growl rumbled in his throat. He inhaled deeply to suppress the rage Ruston could still ignite without half trying.

Audrey Ruston was trouble. Simple as that. The sooner she was off the board, the better for everyone concerned.

He'd only intended to find her. Wring information from her. Shove her out of the way.

But that was not enough. Ruston was impossibly tenacious. She'd never give up until one of them was defeated.

What the hell was she doing out here? If he found her hunkered down inside that car, he might kill her here and now.

Brax would be outraged, but Morin no longer cared.

Morin swore a blue streak using words no self-respecting gangbanger would utter in a bar fight. His tantrum was fueling his rage instead of squelching it.

Ruston was one infuriating woman.

He took several deep breaths to control himself.

He sent a quick text to the operatives. "Block this path. Let NO ONE enter or leave."

A fast thumbs-up pinged his phone. Satisfied that Audrey couldn't escape this time, he dropped the phone into his pocket.

Morin slid the Range Rover's transmission into park, pressed the stop button, and left the vehicle as quietly as possible. He stood with his left hand in his pocket and his right hand holding his pistol which he held down by his side concealed in the folds of his coat.

He walked carefully toward the sedan, half expecting Ruston to jump out at him from a hiding place in the trees.

He hoped she would.

He'd put two slugs in her skull without a second's hesitation.

As he approached her vehicle, he could now see why the sedan was parked where it was.

A full-sized Chevy Suburban SUV with a New York license plate was parked directly in front of Ruston's car, completely blocking travel farther along the two-track.

A quick glance established that thick trees lined the path on both sides of the Suburban and the sedan.

No room to move.

No way out.

The only way to get any vehicle out of here was to reverse all the way to the road. Visibility was close to zero. Driving backward between the trees effectively wearing a blindfold. At least two miles back.

Since the Range Rover was the last vehicle in the line, Morin held the advantage. Neither the Suburban nor the sedan could bash through the Range Rover to escape. Ruston, and whoever was with her, were both boxed in.

Morin glanced into the windows of the sedan to confirm it was unoccupied. He felt the hood. The engine hadn't cooled. She could still be nearby.

Once again, where was she?

And who did she meet here?

And why?

And where were they now?

All good questions without answers.

Morin examined the exterior of the Suburban and tried to peer inside. The windows were heavily tinted. He could engage the dome light, but that would be like flashing a beacon.

He carried a flashlight in his pocket. Turning on the beam now would also make him an easy target.

So he left the light where it was, satisfied for the moment that the Suburban was also unoccupied and boxed in.

Two vehicles. No drivers. No passengers.

Which meant there were at least two people somewhere nearby.

Friends or enemies? Odds were fifty-fifty, he figured. Could be one of each.

Wind whipped through the treetops, rustling leaves and shaking cold raindrops onto Morin's head that dribbled down his collar and onto his back. He barely noticed.

He stared into the darkness, swiveling his body in all directions, not sure what he was looking for exactly.

Ruston might have fought her last battle here. She could be injured or worse. Her body could have been dumped somewhere nearby. Hell, he might trip over her on the forest floor.

Morin took a few steps forward, swiveling his head, gaze sweeping one-hundred-eighty degrees, back and forth, as he moved along.

Twenty feet from the Suburban, he saw a square shape in silhouette ahead, off the trail on the right.

A small one-room cabin. Maybe eight feet by ten feet.

Probably no indoor plumbing. Maybe no electricity. No windows. No outdoor illumination.

Weak and dim light that might have come from a camping lantern filtered out through the cabin's cracked wood siding and along the sides of the warped plank door.

Morin stepped carefully and quietly forward, weapon ready in one hand and flashlight in the other, all senses on full alert. At the door, he leaned forward to listen to the voices.

"Morin is counting on you, Liam," Ruston said as if scolding a child. "You're the only one who can operate the Stiletto 100 in Ottawa. The success of the whole program depends on you. What the hell were you thinking?"

"We both know you're not going to shoot me. Put that gun away and tell me what you've done with Krause. He should be here by now," Stuart replied.

"He's not coming. I told you that already," Ruston snapped.

"You're lying. I talked to him. He is coming. He's on his way now," Stuart replied angrily. "He's excited about the Stiletto. He wants to see it. Nothing could keep him away."

Morin smirked. Now he had no doubts. Ruston had killed Krause. Stuart wouldn't be thrilled about that at all.

Morin felt Ruston's defeat envelop him like a warm blanket. Ruston was done. Which was more than okay.

The feeling lasted only a moment because Morin recognized the danger now.

Once Stuart learned Ruston had killed Krause, Stuart might strike out somehow. If he did, Ruston would react surely, swiftly, and with extreme prejudice.

Stuart was no match for her. Stuart would die as quickly as Krause had died.

Which was unacceptable.

Stuart absolutely must be able to complete the FQT tomorrow in Ottawa. Stuart's expertise with the Stiletto could not be replaced. Brax had made that crystal clear.

The argument inside the cabin escalated to shouting. Ruston raised her voice to be heard over Stuart's booming anger.

If Stuart tried to harm Ruston, she'd kill him as quickly as she'd killed Krause. She'd call it self-defense. Brax would blame Morin because crap like that always landed on Morin's shoulders.

He had to act now.

Morin raised his pistol, flattened his back against the cabin's rough exterior planks and kicked the flimsy door wide open. The rickety wood panel banged loudly against the wall boards instantly halting all discussion.

"Ruston! Hold your fire!" Morin yelled half a moment before he slipped inside, sweeping his gaze across an unarmed Stuart before aiming his weapon, fully prepared to kill her.

CHAPTER 37

Saturday, June 4
Ontario, CA

GASPAR SAID, "I'D RATHER not repeat all of this. Can Russell hear?"

Kim held the phone between them and put the call on speaker. "He can now."

Gaspar's report was brief and succinct. "Reacher called me because he's pissed. Feels like he got Westwood killed. Lucas Stuart, too."

Russell snorted. "Reacher's got some sort of conscience now?"

"More like a god complex. He put things in motion for which he feels responsible," Gaspar replied with humor. "It doesn't matter why. Just understand he's decided to deal with the situation himself. Otto, he says you need to stay out of the way."

"Last time I checked, I don't take orders from Reacher," Kim replied.

Gaspar chuckled, "I told him you'd say that."

Russell gave her a hard look. "What's he gonna deal with? And how, exactly, does he plan to handle the situation?"

"Reacher wanted Westwood to expose the new weapon Liam Stuart designed. Reacher doesn't like how they planned to use it," Gaspar said. "He thought the exposure would be enough to kill the project. He didn't expect them to kill two civilians to cover up. The murders were a bridge too far, he said."

"I have no idea what you're talking about," Kim said.

"Did Reacher whisk Chang out of the hotel back there?" Russell asked.

"Probably," Gaspar replied.

"Where are they going?" Kim asked.

"He didn't say. I think he needs Chang to help him figure that out. Which means he's with her, wherever she is," Gaspar replied. "Maybe you should ask him yourself."

Tiny beads of sweat popped out on Kim's upper lip and her stomach increased the churning. Nerves. Anxiety. The usual.

She had been hunting Reacher for months. Every time she got close to him, he managed to evade her.

This time felt different. A little crazier than usual, maybe. But more immediate, too.

Reacher was here. Close by. He'd told Gaspar and there was no reason for either of them to lie about that.

She didn't have Cooper to rely on.

She didn't even have an FBI partner with her.

This whole mission was illegal, but so much worse now in so many ways.

What the hell was she doing?

First things first. She needed cover, and lots of it.

"I have to call Cooper," Kim said.

"Finally." Russell sighed. "That's the first thing you've said that makes sense. I'll call Finlay. He'll be faster."

"Because he doesn't ask as many questions, you mean?" Kim said shaking her head. "Forget it. I'm not handing Reacher over to Finlay. No chance. Cooper is angry with me now. I can't even imagine how livid he'd be if I did that. My career at the FBI would be over. I'd be lucky to avoid prison. You, too, for that matter."

"Cooper has no control over me or my career," Russell replied huffily.

"Yeah, you keep thinking that," Kim replied with a decisive nod. "See how that works out for you."

"Kids, stop squabbling. You've got a narrow window of opportunity here. You don't have time for either Cooper or Finlay to intervene," Gaspar interrupted. "You're in Canada. Without official permission or approval, for starters. You have no jurisdiction of any kind. If you call Cooper, he'll tell you to stand down until he gets all the intel and makes his own plan. You'll miss Reacher. Again. Is that what you want?"

A long silence settled over them.

This was Kim's decision to make. She'd be the one to take the heat, too. They'd follow her lead.

Indecision twisted her belly into knots.

She pulled another antacid out of her pocket and plopped it into her mouth, stalling. Not that the situation would get any better with less stomach acid.

"Gaspar, check this plate." Russell sped up to get closer to the sedan and read the number aloud. "Looks like a late model rental. Should have trackable tech installed. Can you locate it?"

"I see it. I've got you, too," Gaspar replied. "Looks like you're headed to Hamilton, Ontario. I gather you're following that sedan because you think Reacher and Chang are traveling in it."

"But is he? In the sedan?" Kim asked.

"How the hell would I know?" Gaspar replied.

"Use one of the cameras in the sedan and take a look around," Kim said flatly.

"Already tried. Interior cameras are disabled. Microphones, too. We can't see them or hear them talking. The whole vehicle seems to be blacked out." Gaspar inhaled deeply. "You think Reacher is savvy enough to have done that?"

She knew what he meant. Reacher was more tech-phobic than any man she'd met in the twenty-first century. He barely used a cell phone. Disabling tracking devices in a vehicle was well beyond his wheelhouse. If he'd wanted to take everything offline, he'd have simply destroyed the sedan.

"Reacher couldn't do it. But I guess Chang could," Kim replied.

"Or she's got help from somewhere," Gaspar said. "Another partner. Maybe even Westwood before he died. He seemed to be tech sophisticated."

"What's in Hamilton that caught Reacher's interest?" Russell muttered. "It's a sleepy place. Once a manufacturing town, if I recall correctly. But isn't it mostly a bedroom community now?"

"Pretty much," Gaspar said, clacking computer keys as he researched Hamilton. "Not too far from Toronto. And a little farther from Ottawa. Which, as you know, is the seat of Canadian government."

"Are Chang and Reacher headed there?" Kim wondered aloud.

"There's a big parade in Ottawa tomorrow," Gaspar replied as if he were reading the screen. "Celebration of local business and industry. The Prime Minister is expected to make a speech. Several bigwigs from government and private businesses are slated to attend."

"Reacher say anything about that when you talked to him?" Russell asked.

"Not specifically, no."

Kim cocked her head. "What is this thing Liam Stuart has developed that Reacher's so worried about?"

"A new drone. Reacher got wind of it somehow."

Russell snorted. "There's lots of drones out there and every engineer interested in weapons thinks they have a better idea."

"Yeah, well, it seems like Liam Stuart did actually have a better idea. And on top of that, his design apparently works," Gaspar said. "Reacher says this one's a game changer. And he's a guy who knows weapons."

"Maybe Stuart's planning to demonstrate the drone live in Ottawa tomorrow," Kim mused.

"Demonstrate what, exactly?" Russell asked.

"Probably not how well the drone captures video," Gaspar replied with sarcasm.

Kim noticed the sedan had slowed. "Russell. Heads up."

He lifted his foot from the accelerator.

"Where's he going, Gaspar?" Kim asked. "Is there a side road up ahead?"

"Not on the maps I've got here," he replied. "You're driving through farmland. Vineyards and wineries, mostly. Approaching an area outside of Hamilton called Devil's Punchbowl."

"What is that?" Russell asked, gaze firmly focused on the sedan still slowing ahead.

"Looks like a nature park. There's a road that runs along one edge. The driver might be searching for the turnoff," Gaspar said.

"Can you see the road from your satellite?" Kim asked, leaning forward in the seat.

"Too much cloud cover. But I can pull up an image from another day," he said, amid more keyboard clacking. "Okay. Got it."

"What's out there?"

"Not much. Some rough terrain. Looks like a few hiking trails. A big gorge. two waterfalls. Maybe some interesting rock formations," Gaspar said, as if he were reading the images like a magazine. "A giant cross that lights up on the overlook."

"Nothing specific to interest Reacher or Chang at this particular moment, then," Kim said slowly.

Without using a turn signal, the sedan veered off the roadway up ahead.

"If they've turned onto an actual road, it's not showing on the maps," Gaspar said.

"What do we do, Otto?" Russell asked. "Turn or not? If we follow now, they'll notice and evade."

"If Reacher's in the vehicle, we might be able to stop him," Kim said.

"Yeah, but he won't like it. Which will create a new batch of tough problems," Russell replied. "This is your show. What's the play here?"

"Pull him over," Kim said, tightening her seatbelt, ignoring the taste of bile that rose in her throat.

Sooner or later, she'd come face-to-face with Reacher. The idea would never get any less terrifying.

"Copy that." Russell pressed the accelerator to the floor.

CHAPTER 38

Saturday, June 4
Ontario, CA

RUSSELL'S LEAD FOOT ON the gas rapidly closed the gap between the SUV and the sedan along the unpaved two-lane road. Loose gravel flew up behind the tires landing fast and furiously on the SUV's steel.

The sedan was several car lengths ahead, throwing a dusty cloud in its wake. Briefly, Kim wondered how the ground could be so dry when it had been raining here.

Regardless, the thick dust was there and she couldn't see through it. Neither could Russell.

The sedan driver sped up and engaged textbook evasive maneuvers like he'd been exceptionally well trained. In the back of her reptilian brain, Kim viscerally understood the driver wasn't Reacher. His driving skills were weak at best. This guy was a pro.

Kim pulled her weapon and kept her gaze laser focused, peering into the dust. She could barely make out the red taillights weaving across the lanes, gaining distance faster than Russell could close the gap.

"Russell. Where did they go?" She leaned forward and blinked a few times to clear her vision.

She wasn't wrong.

The red taillights had disappeared.

Russell pulled the switch to turn on the SUV's bright lights. The dust cloud was like driving in grainy fog. The brights made visibility worse, not better.

Still driving at speed, Russell punched down to fog lights. Didn't help.

He rounded the next curve along the two-lane. The dust cloud had begun to settle. Fog lights cut through the moonless night.

Kim slammed her hand onto the dash. "Russell! Look out!"

Straight ahead, the sedan was stopped sideways across the road.

Russell stomped on the brakes to slow the SUV. He swiveled his head, looking across the fields on either side of the gravel.

He grabbed the steering wheel with both hands and turned. The front of the SUV responded immediately.

The front end traveled left of the roadblock and the SUV moved off the road into the field of grape vines.

They traveled another twenty feet before Russell was able to bring the SUV to a jerky stop.

All four wheels were embedded in the mud.

Grapevines blocked the SUV's doors and the front end of the vehicle.

"Are you okay?" Russell asked, glancing across the cabin as the SUV rocked to a stop.

Kim was pinned to her seat by the seatbelt. The alligator clamp she'd installed at the retractor when she got into the vehicle had functioned exactly as expected. When the seatbelt engaged, the clamp flew off and the belt tightened to hold her securely away from the windshield.

"You're bleeding," Russell said, handing her a napkin from one of the side pockets in his door.

The sharp edges of the belt's webbing had cut the skin of her neck. She wiped away the blood trickling along her skin toward her collar.

She hadn't been beheaded.

Kim unlatched her seatbelt and turned to stare at the sedan. The driver and passenger were no longer inside. Where did they go?

"The only way out of here is to reverse all the way until we reach the road again," Russell said. "This field's muddy and the grapevines are thick, with posts close together. We've got all-wheel drive in this SUV, so we can get out. But the paint's gonna be ruined and the SUV will look like hell when we get there."

Kim shrugged. "You're thinking we might get plucked out of here by the hand of God or something? When there's only one choice…"

She let her voice drift off.

Rain began to fall again. Which would keep the dust down. But soon the irrigated grape field would be too muddy for any sort of traction.

"Right." Russell slid the SUV into all-wheel drive and the transmission into reverse. He applied slow, steady pressure to the accelerator until the wheels grabbed. The SUV began to move.

Russell accelerated and braked, jerked, and stopped, used all of the mirrors and engaged the backup camera until he'd maneuvered across the field. When the SUV reached the gravel road, Russell straightened the wheels. The sedan was straight ahead, still across the road, blocking the only way forward.

"Okay," Russell said, relaxing his white knuckled grip. "Now what?"

Before she had a chance to say anything, the first bullet hit the windshield. Glass shards were pushed into the seat near Russell's head.

A second gunshot hit high and closer to Kim.

The SUV's engine block was the only hope they had to escape gunshots fired directly into the cabin.

"Get down!" Kim yelled, punching the release button on her seatbelt and sliding into the wheel well.

Russell was much larger than Kim. He tilted the steering wheel up and crouched as low as he could get. But at least half his body was still visible and in the line of fire.

"Why is Reacher trying to kill us?" Russell demanded.

"He's not."

"Why do you say that?"

"Because if Reacher wanted to kill us, we'd be dead. These two lack Reachers skill set."

"Not to mention his cold-blooded nature. He'd have marched right out into the field and killed us with his bare hands," Russell said flatly.

A long shiver convulsed Kim's body, confirming Russell's assessment. "So who are these guys and why are they trying to kill us?"

Another bullet penetrated the windshield near the driver's seat. If Russell had still been sitting there, he'd no longer be talking.

"We have to get out of here," Russell said, weapon already in hand. "The shooters have taken cover behind the sedan. We're sitting ducks. If they fire through the SUV's side doors, we'll be done."

"They may have night vision, too. We don't," Kim replied.

Another bullet slammed the windshield, hit the middle of Kim's seat, and embedded into the backseat.

"We have to go," Russell said again.

Kim nodded. "Open the front doors simultaneously and roll out onto the road. Head into the vineyard. We'll draw their fire in two places. Have a chance to hold them off."

"Okay. Ready?" Russell asked.

"Now," she replied.

Like a choreographed dance, they reached up, pulled the door handles, and pushed the doors open at the same time.

Before their feet hit the ground, more bullets pierced both doors.

They hurried out of the SUV, crouched low, through the rain.

They ran to opposite sides of the road and flattened into the muddy vineyard.

The exercise proved two things.

There were two shooters.

One was positioned behind the front wheel and the other behind the rear wheel of the sedan.

The engine block would stop bullets in the front of the sedan. The gas tank in the back would not.

Unless the sedan was armored, the guy behind the rear wheel was vulnerable.

Kim crouched low and advanced toward the sedan, using the rain and darkness and silence to conceal her movements.

If the shooter had night vision, he'd be able to see her. In which case, he'd shoot again. Which would reveal his location and she'd return fire.

Otherwise, she could get eyes on him first.

Either way, moving in was the only real chance she had to disable him.

The storm had intensified. Thunder, rain, and wind were loud enough to cover any noises she might have made. The only lightning was in the distance, too far away to reveal her position.

She imagined the shooter's mental state. He'd lost sight of her. Was he worried? Concerned? How much patience did he have? Would he try to outlast her?

Kim was only a few feet from the sedan now.

An exceptionally loud thunderclap blasted through the quiet. Followed by a round of gunfire from the vineyard where Russell was dealing with the second shooter.

She hit the ground between two rows of grape vines half a moment before the lightning bolt brightened the entire area like a circus spotlight.

Briefly.

Kim had focused on the sedan and the area around it while the lightning flashed. She'd seen the shooter.

His back was flattened against the car. Feet near the rear tires. The rest of his body concealed by the rear pillar.

Kim stood, aimed, fired, while she still had a clear image of his position. He left his cover, pivoted on his right foot and planted his left foot eighteen inches away.

Assuming a shooter's stance ingrained by law enforcement training everywhere, he aimed to fire.

Kim shot first. Three times. Center mass.

The lightning flash ended.

She was once again blinded by the dark.

Kim fell to the ground and crawled away, moving in an oblique direction from where she'd stood to aim.

She waited for the shooter to try again.

She heard nothing but silence at first.

And then four rounds of gunfire toward and from the front of the sedan.

Followed by sounds of the pouring rain, howling wind, and Russell calling her name.

"Otto? Two down. Nice work. You okay?" He shouted over the storm as he trotted across the road toward her.

She climbed out of the mud and stood in the rain to let it wash off the worst of the grime. They met up near the sedan.

Kim pulled her phone out of her pocket and turned on the flashlight as they walked around to the back of the sedan to check the victims.

Both were dead.

"Do you know these guys?" Kim asked, head cocked.

Russell shook his head. "They look like they could be law enforcement, though."

Kim knelt to pat down the one she'd hit. She found a wallet in his breast pocket. When she pulled it out and flipped it open, she found his US State Department ID.

"Not law enforcement, but you're in the right ballpark."

"Crap. Just what we need." Russell swiped a palm across his face and over his close-cropped hair.

He searched the second shooter and came away with a similar wallet, the same ID type.

"We can't leave these two here. At the very least, if they're found here, it will cause some sort of international incident," Russell said, reaching for his phone. "We've got to get them extracted. I'm calling Finlay."

"Let's put them in the sedan and find a place to conceal them until we finish this."

"Too risky."

"Wait another twelve hours," Kim said. "Reacher's close. We know that. Give me a chance to find him before you call."

Russell said nothing, but he didn't make the call.

"Twelve hours. Finlay's still out of the country. He won't be back until tomorrow, anyway," Kim argued. "These guys shouldn't be here, either. They were firing on two federal agents. They're dirty as hell. We both know that. There's no harm in waiting awhile longer before we give them up."

Russell still said nothing.

"Finlay will be fine with all of this if we find Reacher. No harm, no foul," Kim pointed out reasonably. "Otherwise, we're both in a world of trouble. Cooper will have our scalps."

Russell slipped his phone into his pocket, shook his head, and mumbled, "Let's get these two in the trunk and move the vehicles out of here before someone comes along."

CHAPTER 39

Saturday, June 4
Devil's Punchbowl, Ontario, CA

LIAM HAD JUMPED, STARTLED, when the plank door flew open, slamming against the cabin wall. Gusty wind blew inside carrying cold rain along with it. Everything inside already felt damp and chilled. He was more than ready to go.

Before he had a chance to move, Morin lunged through the open door. He held a steady pistol in his right hand, like he meant business.

"Stay where you are," Morin demanded, scanning the room, gaze resting first on Liam and then focused intently on Audrey. He nodded in her direction. "Put your weapon away."

She smirked. "You first."

A deep crease etched Morin's brow. "I could shoot you now and solve all my problems."

"Right back atcha," she replied evenly, as if she meant every word of her threat as much as Morin did.

Fortune favors the bold popped into Liam's head. His brother always said that just before they engaged in some crazy activity like helicopter skiing or base jumping. Lucas had always been the bold one. Liam was the follower.

Until now.

While Morin and Ruston argued, totally engrossed in their own business, Liam snuck out the open door, pulse racing, heart pounding.

How far could he get before they came after him?

More importantly, where would he go?

After he cleared the open doorway, he veered to the left, putting distance between them and obstacles in the line of sight.

He rushed to the back of his SUV and grabbed the Stiletto. He closed the door quietly and hoofed it as quickly as possible toward the road on the other side of the Devil's Punchbowl gorge.

Maybe he could flag down a vehicle and get away.

He held the Stiletto 100 away from his torso and maneuvered awkwardly around the trees as he traversed the woods. He ignored the cold rain and the wind gusts that chilled him to the bone.

Adrenaline fueled his body. His fatigued muscles ignored the pain as he ran. Breathing hard. Long strides up the incline toward the road.

Every few seconds, he glanced over his shoulder. Were they following him? Liam could see only a few feet around him in any direction. The woods were too dense and the foggy weather compounded the gloom.

If Morin and Ruston gave chase, they concealed themselves well enough.

Liam was panting now. He landed awkwardly in a hole made by some burrowing animal, twisting his ankle. But he kept going. He ignored the sharp pain shooting through his ankle and into his foot with every step up the hill.

"Not much further. Almost there," he wheezed to keep himself going.

The Stiletto 100 was unbearably heavy now. Several times, his arms dipped closer to the ground. Liam jerked up, keeping the drone from harm's way. But he felt his pace slowing and his labored breath sounded too loud in his ears.

He'd lost his bearings. He paused and looked skyward. The leafy tree canopy overhead blocked his view of the sky. He swiveled his head. Tree trunks in all directions. Underbrush, decaying leaves, fallen twigs and branches littered the ground.

Liam wasn't sure he was running toward the overlook and then the road on the other side. He couldn't carry the drone safely much longer, either. Blinding rain washed down his face.

He closed his eyes to visualize the open area he'd used to fly the Stiletto earlier. Where was that space now? From there, he could deploy the drone. Unencumbered by its weight, he could move faster. Collect the drone once he reached the overlook.

The risk was standing in the open. Morin and Ruston could spot him easily. But with the drone in flight, Liam could deploy its weapons. An advantage Morin and Ruston could not defend.

As he was peering through the tree trunks, he heard Audrey Ruston scream. Immediately after she screamed, he heard two gunshots.

The noise came from behind and to the left of Liam's current position. Which meant he was off course. He'd wandered too far north of the overlook and farther from the clearing where he'd deployed the Stiletto before.

"Fortune favors the brave," he murmured.

He took a deep breath, secured his grip on the drone, and rushed toward the clearing.

CHAPTER 40

Saturday, June 4
Devil's Punchbowl, Ontario, CA

AUDREY HAD BARELY MOVED. Her entire body was as stiff as a pole. She'd instinctively aimed her weapon at the cabin's open maw when the flimsy plank door slammed wide and weather stormed in. Bringing Nigel Morin along with it.

From the moment Morin breached the cabin shouting, "Ruston! Hold your fire!" Audrey had focused intently on the shooter.

Her thoughts ran down a list of recent mistakes.

She'd made a tactical error when she'd taunted Morin back in New York. She shouldn't have triggered his insecurity.

She should have fired instantly as soon as she had the chance before he could kill her first.

She should have left with Liam Stuart immediately instead of hanging around until Morin found them.

Too late now to indulge in second guessing.

"Neither of us is likely to miss at this range, Nigel," she said sardonically. "Comes down to a test of reflexes. After I shoot you, can you return the favor before you die?"

"Mutual kill by reciprocal firearms is a myth, Audrey. Theoretically possible, but no documented cases on the books," he replied flatly. "I'll shoot you first and that's it. You want me to do it because you're done."

She cocked her head, "Why haven't you already fired?"

He scowled. "Why did you kill Krause?"

"That's what's bothering you?" she asked, mocking him. "Krause came at me. Self-defense. What was I supposed to do?"

"Yeah, well Brax is pissed off. Go back to Quan and back to his bed if you like." Morin's tone was hard. "Your career is over."

Audrey felt a stab of doubt followed by hot anger. "You told Brax about Krause?"

"Why wouldn't I?" Morin said. "You know what they say. If you shoot at the king, you'd better not miss."

She smirked. "You think of yourself as the king, do you?"

He glared. "You're done in the field. Forever. You'll be lucky to avoid prison."

She was quiet for a couple of seconds, considering. "I don't believe you. You didn't tell Brax about Krause. Brax wouldn't allow you to kill me."

"You think not?" Morin quickly raised his arm and fired off a round. The bullet passed her head and exited the rotted planks two inches from her left ear.

The deafening noise, even partially contained in the open cabin, reverberated like an explosion blasting inside a wooden box.

She imagined sound waves washing over her, loosening her teeth, drowning her hearing. Forever.

Even as she wondered why he'd deliberately missed her head.

Morin had aimed wide of her skull. If he'd wanted to hit her, he would have. He was baiting her. He wanted her to fire back, to give him a reason to kill her.

Which meant he'd been bluffing about Brax.

Morin had not told Brax about Krause. Her career wasn't over. Not yet.

But both she and her career would be done if she aimed her weapon at Nigel Morin. He wouldn't miss a second time.

She glanced away from Morin briefly to check on Liam Stuart.

The space he'd occupied since he arrived was empty.

She scanned the room as quickly as she dared. Every move of her head produced a swimming feeling, as if she were physically under water instead of metaphorically.

The scientist was no longer inside the cabin.

"Where's Stuart?" Audrey asked at normal volume, although she couldn't hear her own words. "He's gone. Stuart is gone."

Morin kept his gun aimed at Audrey while he, too, looked around the small cabin. Stuart was not there.

"We have to find him," Audrey said, standing on wobbly legs, ignoring the nausea. "Brax will have both our heads if we lose Stuart again."

She staggered across the room and out through the open doorway, assuming Morin wouldn't shoot her in the back. Which would be impossible to explain.

He followed her outside. She hurried toward Stuart's SUV.

"He can't escape that way. Your sedan is parked behind him and mine is behind yours," Morin said.

"The drone is in his SUV. He won't go anywhere without it," Audrey said, regaining strength and stamina with every stride. "We can catch up with him."

Morin followed, pulling out his phone on the way. When the call connected to one of his operatives, he said, "Stuart is on the run. Where can he go on foot from here?"

Audrey realized he must have backup in the area. Maybe waiting at the end of the path just in case she and Stuart had tried to get away.

"Okay. You two head over to the parking lot at the overlook. We'll move in that direction on foot. We can box him in. Subdue him, but don't harm him. We need Stuart fully functional. Stay in touch," Morin said before he disconnected and dropped the phone into his pocket.

When Audrey rounded the last curve, she saw all three vehicles parked close together along the path. The back door on Stuart's SUV was open. He was nowhere in sight.

"He can't have gone far," Audrey said. "These woods are thick. Lots of tree cover. Where is he headed?"

"There's a gorge between here and the road. Devil's Punchbowl, they call it," Morin replied, already moving eastward. "There's a parking lot up there and light traffic traveling toward Hamilton. He's probably thinking he can get up there and hitch a ride."

Audrey hurried to catch up, her ears still ringing, slightly breathless. "The Stiletto is about the size of a turkey platter. Probably weighs less than ten pounds. But it's awkward. He won't have an easy time carrying it uphill through these woods."

"So he'll try to find a place where he can launch it. He can fly the drone toward the road and retrieve it there," Morin picked up the pace. "We've got to make time if we're going to catch up."

Audrey lengthened her stride. Her fashion boots were not meant for hiking in the forest. The heels were too high and the fine leather uppers too fragile. She was already wet and cold after less than ten minutes. Her teeth were chattering.

Morin moved faster. He was at least ten yards ahead and widening the gap between them. Where was Stuart? Which way to the overlook? Where was the road?

She couldn't see Stuart and soon, she would lose sight of Morin, too. The forest was too thick. Gray foggy skies limited visibility. Her damaged hearing and wobbly balance induced nausea.

Audrey holstered her weapon. She wasn't planning to shoot and holding the gun was just one more struggle.

She reached up to wipe the rain away from her eyes. While her hand blocked her view, she missed a small branch lying across the ground in front of her.

On the next step, she tripped.

Her weight shifted awkwardly.

Her left ankle bent sideways.

She went down on all fours.

Audrey called out. "Morin! Wait!"

He paused, turned, saw her crumpled on the ground.

For a moment, she thought he'd leave her there. She struggled to stand, but her injured ankle would not support her weight. She bit her lip to avoid crying out.

Morin tromped back within hearing distance. "What's the problem?"

"My ankle," she said, clenching her teeth to hold back an involuntary whimper when the pain rolled through. She made her way to a tree stump and sat. "I can't keep going. Call one of your guys to come back and help me."

"If you were a horse, I'd just shoot you and be done." Morin shook his head, a disgusted look on his face. He found his phone and made the call. "They're too close to the parking lot already. Wait here. We'll come back for you after we get Stuart. Shouldn't take long."

Her teeth had begun to chatter. Probably due to the cold. Maybe shock. Her ankle throbbed. She said nothing in reply because Morin had already moved on.

Audrey watched him through the trees until he was out of sight in the fog. She wrapped her arms around her body in a futile effort to control the shivering.

"You can't just sit here. You'll freeze to death," she said aloud. "Get up. Get moving."

She struggled to stand on her damaged ankle. She hobbled toward the path where she'd seen Morin's Range Rover.

Each step sent shooting pain up her leg.

Her ankle was on fire.

But she kept going.

Audrey almost wept when she saw the three vehicles lined up along the two-track. She hobbled forward too quickly and fell flat on her belly.

Her face hit the ground. She bit her lip.

Sharp sticks scratched her skin. A trickle of blood ran down her cheek and another down her chin. She used the back of her hand to wipe the blood away.

Audrey pushed herself upright onto her knees. Holding onto the thick trunk of a tree, she pulled herself onto her feet.

With most of her weight on her right foot and managing as well as possible with the left one, she limped all the way to the Range Rover, making slow but steady progress.

The pain in her ankle was constant now, but she blocked it from her mind. Compartmentalize, Brax's voice admonished in her head.

When she reached the driver's door of the Range Rover, she managed to open it and fall onto the driver's seat. Panting, she struggled to pull both legs into the vehicle and close the door.

Audrey stared at the push button start for a horrified moment.

If Morin had taken the key fob, she'd be stuck here. Her painful trek back all for naught.

But he didn't like to carry things in his pockets and those fobs were bulky.

"Stop thinking about it. Push the starter," she said.

She fastened her seatbelt and pushed the button. The engine fired up instantly.

Morin had sent his backup detail to the parking lot near the road at the Devil's Punchbowl gorge.

Audrey pushed a few buttons on the navigation system until she found a route that would take her there. Less than ten minutes travel time.

She pulled her weapon and placed it close enough to grab when she needed it.

Then she flipped on the heat, put the transmission in reverse, and used the backup camera to back slowly and carefully out of the two-track and onto the road.

CHAPTER 41

Saturday, June 4
Devil's Punchbowl, Ontario, CA

KIM DROVE THE SUV along the road toward Hamilton and Russell followed in the sedan. She turned into a busy strip mall with a grocery store and drove around back to the loading dock.

Russell pulled the sedan deep into the lot behind the trash dumpsters and locked it. He tossed the keys into one of the dumpsters. He hoofed to the SUV and plopped into the passenger seat.

"Everything okay back there?" Kim said as she drove out of the lot.

"Yeah. Nobody around." Russell pulled off his gloves and stuffed them under the seat. "Might be a few days before they find the car and a couple more before they find the bodies."

"We'll finish this up and call in before that happens," Kim replied.

"Finish up what? Chang has disappeared. We have zero leads to figure out whatever the hell *this* is." Russell paused and added,

"Let's find a hotel. I need a shower, clean clothes, a meal, and a few hours' sleep. We can attack it again afterward if you want."

Kim reached over and turned the navigation system on again. "If you had a secret drone, some new kind of weapon, and you wanted to make sure it was ready, what kind of place would you look for to run a few tests?"

"Hell, I don't know. Somewhere it wasn't likely to be noticed." Russell scowled. "Open spaces. No people. No power lines. No CCTV cameras."

Kim nodded. She touched the screen to zoom in on the map, pointing. "The blue dot is us right now. Hamilton is north of our current position. Between here and there, what do you see?"

Russell looked at the image. "Yeah. A big hole in the ground. What did Gaspar call it? The Devil's Punchbowl. No wires, no people, no CCTV."

"Exactly," Kim replied, handing her cell phone across the console as she drove along the county road. "Gaspar sent the satellite images shot thirty minutes ago. See the parking lot at Devil's Punchbowl? No cars there."

"So what are you saying? Stuart isn't there? Or he is? Or?" Russell asked, handing the phone back. She didn't accept it.

Kim touched the navigation system again, zooming a bit wider than before. "Here's the place where that sedan turned off the road into the vineyard. What if they turned there intentionally? See how that farm road comes out at another road on the west side of the Devil's Punchbowl? What if the sedan was headed there?"

"Panicked when we turned off behind them and improvised themselves into a no-win situation, you mean?" Russell moved the maps and the images around on the navigation system for a couple of seconds. "Yeah. There's a road that approaches the visitor parking lot from the west."

Kim nodded. "I asked Gaspar to pull satellite images all around that area. He found a cabin deep in the woods about a mile west of the gorge. Thumb through those shots on my phone. You can't see the cabin now because the trees are leafed out. But in the winter, images show the place clearly."

"You're thinking the cabin is a rendezvous point?" Russell asked, handing the phone back. "Can Gaspar see anyone at that cabin now?"

She shook her head, pulled up another image on her phone and passed it to Russell. "Earlier today, a man was flying a drone in the clearing between the cabin and the gorge."

Russell adjusted and enlarged the image. "Not possible to identify the guy based on these photos. But the location looks perfect for clandestine test flights. Depending on the cloud ceiling, which has been low the past couple of days."

"Meaning someone could have seen him flying the drone because he's been flying low. Except this drone is allegedly close to invisible," Kim reminded him. "Less visible than a stealth bomber. More powerful radar or closer range radar will detect it."

Russell shook his head. "I don't get why Reacher would be angry about all of this. He's an army guy. He understands weapons. Knows why a drone like Stuart's could be a game changer. What's his beef?"

Kim sped up to pass a slow moving mini-van and returned to her lane. "Chang said Reacher was not happy about how the drone will be used."

"It's a war weapon. It'll be used to kill. Or to deter attacks by others. Same thing all weapons are used for," Russell replied. "Reacher knows all of that. Hell, he was a soldier for thirteen years. Served in combat. From all accounts, still enjoys knocking heads and eliminating enemies. So again, where's the beef?"

Kim shrugged and slowed the SUV. She turned left onto a smaller county road. Following the navigation system's route around the north side of the cabin in the woods.

"Gaspar sent images of the Devil's Punchbowl, too. You can pull them up on my phone. See what we'll be dealing with once we get there," Kim instructed.

Russell thumbed the images, talking as he flipped through. "Two running waterfalls. A big drop from the rim. More than a hundred feet down. Rocky at the bottom. The pool beneath the waterfall isn't deep enough. You fall in there, you're dead."

"The road's on the east side. The parking lot is a few hundred feet from the gorge along a paved trail. And that big lighted cross at the edge is used as a marker of some sort," Kim said.

As they traveled along the narrow road, the woods became thicker and the area darker. Kim tried the high beams, which helped to illuminate the thick tree cover. She imagined wildlife living here and slowed the SUV to a speed that would allow her to stop well short before hitting a deer or a bear.

The road curved and twisted through the trees, growing narrower as they traveled closer to the cabin.

"This road eventually comes out at the parking lot near the rim of the gorge. There are hiking trails along here, too," she said.

"What are we looking for?" Russell asked, peering into the gloom.

"A small two-track on the right side. It runs about three hundred feet into the woods and stops near the cabin," she replied. "Gaspar says infrared shows at least three people in the cabin."

"Three?"

"One's probably Stuart," Kim said.

Russell swiped a palm over his face. "Let me guess. You think the other two are Chang and Reacher."

"More likely these three are the ones Reacher's after," Kim replied. "One was probably the guy flying the drone earlier today. Probably Liam Stuart. Makes sense that he'd have a team."

She slowed to turn into the tunnel of dense trees. The winding path was little more than two rutted tracks where heavy vehicles had recently traveled. She slowed the SUV to a crawl as it bounced over tree limbs and dipped into holes along the way.

When she rounded a curve, she saw two parked vehicles. A sedan behind an SUV. Both vehicles were unoccupied and not running.

Kim stopped the vehicle and slid the transmission into park. "There's a flashlight in the glove box."

"You think they're still here?" Russell said after he located the flashlight.

"I guess we'll see." Kim drew her weapon before she opened the door and stepped outside.

CHAPTER 42

Saturday, June 4
Devil's Punchbowl, Ontario, CA

MORIN MOVED QUICKLY THROUGH the woods, careful to
avoid treacherous natural traps covered by dead leaves and debris
on the ground. There were few poisonous snakes in this area, but
any kind of animal encounter would slow him down.

Time had become Morin's enemy.

Stuart had at least a ten-minute head start. Maybe more. It
was also possible that Stuart was not alone or had already hitched
a ride.

Morin carried his pistol in his right hand and scanned the
woods as he traveled. Left to right and back again.

Looking for movement among the stationary tree trunks.

Listening for gasping to breathe, grunting with exertion, or
sharp cries when confronted with unexpected hazards.

Morin was neither a hunter nor a tracker by nature or training.
He lacked the skills as well as the grit for the job.

He was vicious by nature, but his enemies wore suits and ties and sat across long oval tables in skyscrapers in big cities around the world.

He slayed his opponents with treachery and cunning.

Stalking Liam Stuart was another thing entirely.

Aware that he was failing this test, Morin's pride pushed him harder and faster toward the Devil's Punchbowl. He felt confident he'd find Liam near the road, seeking to hitch a ride to take him out of shooting range or friendly fire.

Morin drew gulps of air into his parched throat. He was sweaty and cold and perspiring. Mucus ran from his nose and he wiped it away with the back of his free hand.

Twice, he'd stepped awkwardly and tumbled a few feet before righting himself and scrambling forward.

The plan was to put Stuart between Morin and his two operatives.

The three of them would round Stuart up, collect his drone, and move on to Ottawa for tomorrow's test.

Morin would go back for Audrey, but only to control what she told Brax.

Once the FQT was completed tomorrow, and Quan's ambassador to Canada was as good as dead, Morin would have plenty of time to take credit.

Brax would cut Audrey loose or find another hobby for his lover and Morin's team could return to normal.

Cold, stinging sweat dripped from Morin's brow into his eyes. His vision blurred and his eyes burned. He closed his eyes tightly, pausing to catch his breath.

When he opened his eyes again, he saw a vague image ahead on his right. Could that be Stuart? Who else would it be?

Stuart was standing with his weight balanced on both feet, holding a large elliptical object outward, away from his body.

He pulled a rectangular box about the size of a large tablet from his pocket.

He held the tablet in his right hand while he balanced the disk in his left palm. He held his left arm up and away from his body.

Using his right thumb, he tapped the screen of the tablet and the drone rose into the air.

The pewter-colored drone was difficult to see in the gray and foggy atmosphere.

As the drone rose higher, Stuart was unencumbered by its weight and free to run forward at a faster pace.

Faster than Morin could comfortably follow.

The distance between Morin and Stuart widened.

Morin retrieved his phone and called his operatives. "He's in the clearing just west of the big cross. He's launched the drone. It could be armed. Stay alert."

"You're saying he could kill us with that thing?" the operative replied incredulously.

"And you wouldn't even know he'd fired," Morin said flatly. "The weapon has sophisticated software to locate and lock onto the target. It carries a variable payload. Shoots bombs, bullets, darts, or poison. If he chooses bullets, you'll be dead before I can reach you."

The operative paused to absorb the intel. "We can't get the car down the hill to his present location. What do you want us to do?"

"Keep track of him. If I'm right about his intentions, he'll come up to the overlook. Don't let him reach the road. Failing that, don't let him hitch a ride."

"So you're saying we should terminate him instead of letting him get away?"

"Certainly not." Morin's frustration had been building with every moment. He might actually explode. "I want him alive. Unharmed. And don't damage the damned drone!"

Morin slammed the phone into his pocket and began to run toward Stuart.

He kept the drone in sight.

He watched the ground for traps.

He never lost sight of Stuart.

But he was breathing heavily, raggedly. Losing speed.

The distance between him and Stuart and the drone continued to widen.

He couldn't win this contest.

Stuart was younger, fitter, and knew where the hell he was going.

Morin stopped running, breathing hard, and glanced around wildly for a better alternative.

Which was when he saw headlights approaching from the south. A car coming along the ridge road on the east side of the gorge. Headed toward Hamilton.

Between Morin's position and the ridge road was the gaping deep gorge.

On the north side of the gorge a retaining rail ran alongside a paved walkway.

The walkway snaked along the ridge maybe five feet from the edge. From the ridge road side of the gorge and the far side of the lookout point where the tall lighted cross perched.

The drone was flying across the open air above the gorge, headed toward the ridge road.

Liam was running along the west side of the deep slope.

The approaching car stopped on the road, across the gorge from Liam's position.

A woman was driving. Morin couldn't see her clearly in the distance.

A big man, almost a giant, climbed out of the passenger side and slammed the door behind him.

He took a few long strides to cross the road, stepped over the guard rail, and approached the east edge of the gorge.

Morin realized he had run off course. He was too close to the gorge. Too far south of the parking lot.

Liam Stuart had made it almost to the base of the lookout.

The drone was already up there. Hovering. Waiting to be recalled to Stuart's arms, like a falcon returning to perch on its master's glove.

Morin stared incredulously upward.

Stuart was getting away. The drone would be gone.

Unacceptable.

Morin corrected his course and began to run again faster than before, but still too slow.

Just as a blast of gusty cold wind swooped in from the lake, Morin lifted his weapon and fired a warning shot toward Stuart.

Stuart stopped and turned, losing his focused attention on the Stiletto.

The wind gust caught the Stiletto and lifted it higher into the atmosphere.

A moment later, the downdraft plunged the drone down into the gorge.

"Stuart! Wait!" Morin yelled into the wind.

He moved toward Stuart's position, failing to keep his eye on the ground.

Morin stumbled, weapon still pointed in Stuart's direction. His finger twitched, firing off another shot toward Stuart.

The car sped along the road toward the parking lot where Morin's operatives waited to capture Stuart and the Stiletto.

The big man started down the side of the gorge, as if he intended to climb all the way down and back up the opposite side to reach Stuart and Morin.

Which would be a stupid thing to do.

Maybe he wanted the drone.

Morin's mouth fell open as he watched. The gorge was deep and steep and dangerous. No way the guy could make it before Stuart escaped. He'd be lucky not to tumble to his death.

The drone continued to drift downward, pushed by the wind.

Stuart furiously worked the controls on his tablet, but the wind gusts were too strong and the drone too light to overcome them.

Morin had lost control of the situation. Too many threats coming at him all at once.

A second vehicle entered the parking lot from the opposite direction.

Three vehicles up there now.

And one, Morin realized with amazement, was his Range Rover. "What the hell?"

CHAPTER 43

Saturday, June 4
Devil's Punchbowl, Ontario, CA

KIM HEARD THE DISTANT gunshot through the fog almost as soon as she'd parked the SUV. "Where'd that come from?"

"Over there." Russell pointed toward the Devil's Punchbowl. "I'll check the cabin to be sure they left no one injured or restrained or anything."

"Copy that," Kim replied, already moving eastward.

Russell headed in the opposite direction, calling over his shoulder, "I'll be right behind you."

Kim hustled through the woods, careful where she stepped. She'd been a Girl Scout. Hiked in the Michigan forests all her life. She knew the hazards to watch for.

She called Gaspar on the way. He picked up instantly. "Can you see what's going on over at Devil's Punchbowl? We heard a gunshot."

Just as she uttered the words, a second gunshot rang out. She increased her speed as much as she dared.

"Still too much cloud cover for the satellites I can access," he said. "But heat signatures suggest six humans in the vicinity."

"Where are they?"

"One inside the gorge on the east side, moving down from the rim. Four in the parking lot. Two down below the lookout point. One of those two is perilously close to the west edge of the gorge," Gaspar recited as he checked his screens reporting the facts without embellishment.

"Anything else you can tell about them? Males, females, armed?"

"I'd guess maybe four males and two females." He paused. "Yeah, two females and two males in the parking lot. One man heading down into the east side of the gorge. He seems to be stumbling and fumbling. Two down below close to the lower rim."

"And the drone?"

"Can't see it," Gaspar said slowly, as if he was searching hard.

Kim's physical conditioning served her well. She ran quickly through the woods and came out into the clearing below the overlook.

She glanced to her left, upward toward the parking lot. Her sight line was blocked by the solid wall of rock between her position and the pavement above.

Another gunshot rang out on her right. She swiveled her head toward the blast.

The entire tableau revealed itself slowly through the fog as she came closer.

The first thing she noticed was the big man going down the far side of the gorge. From this distance, she couldn't see how he managed what should have been a free fall with a disastrous landing on the rocky bottom.

But he wasn't tumbling headfirst, which seemed to defy gravity.

The other odd thing was the drone. It wasn't invisible at all. She could see it plainly flying over the open gorge.

But the drone was in trouble. It dipped and rose in the wind more like a kite than a remotely controlled plane.

The man with a tablet near the overlook, furiously attempting to get the drone under control, must be Liam Stuart.

The other man, the one with the gun in his hand, was much too close to the edge of the gorge. He was running toward Stuart, holding the weapon with the kind of hard-won expertise that suggested both training and experience.

He stumbled a couple of times along the way. Once he tripped and fell and scrambled to his feet again.

The next gunshot came from the overlook. Kim looked up to see a man with a gun at the railing. He was aiming toward the huge man running down the gorge on the east side.

The overlook gunman wasn't watching his six and he seemed to have no backup.

A luxury sedan came up behind him, moving at least two tons of weight much too fast.

The sedan driver honked the horn.

The gunman jumped and turned around. He fired his weapon into the windshield of the car. One, two, three rounds as the sedan failed to slow.

The sedan kept coming until the front bumper hit the shooter squarely with overwhelming speed and weight.

His body flew up in the air and landed on the sedan's hood.

The gun flew out of his hand.

The sedan's driver stomped the brakes hard and fast.

The body flew off the hood into the deep gorge, landing on the rushing waterfall and tumbling along with the water all the way to the bottom.

The sedan backed up again, reversing away from the retaining rail. The vehicle completed a sharp three-point turn and retreated away from the edge of the gorge.

A second man came running around the sedan on foot, shooting into the side of the vehicle repeatedly. He must have hit the sedan's driver because the sedan finally stopped moving.

The second gunman ran past the sedan and slipped under the guard rail and ran flat out toward Liam Stuart.

The man running in the clearing near the west edge of the gorge had watched the sedan and the body, wide-eyed. Like he knew the dead gunman. And the second gunman who shot the sedan all to hell.

Which he probably did.

He shouted, "Stuart! Stop!"

Stuart ignored the orders, continuing to struggle with controlling the drone. He was loping up the hill now, toward the overlook, encouraging the drone to follow like a child leading a puppy.

Which seemed stupid until Kim realized Stuart's effort was working.

Stuart had harnessed something about the drafts and the gusts and the drone's controls to lift the drone out of the ravine and toward the overlook.

The second gunman was closer now. He waved his gun toward Stuart probably demanding that Stuart stop and retrieve the drone.

Stuart ignored him.

The second gunman pointed his pistol toward Stuart and yelled something else Kim couldn't hear.

Stuart continued to ignore the threat.

The second gunman raised his gun to fire, aiming directly at Stuart.

Which was when the man below in the clearing, running alongside the western edge of the gorge, fired his weapon with accuracy and precision. He'd aimed at the second gunman.

Two shots, both solid hits.

The second gunman fell forward, momentum carrying him over the edge of the gorge.

Stuart lost control over the drone when it hit the down draft again. He stopped, furiously pounding the tablet, attempting to maneuver the drone up and away from danger.

This time, his efforts failed.

The drone became caught in the wind current again. Which pushed the drone down into the gorge.

Stuart sprinted the rest of the distance up the hill and ducked under the guard rails to stand at the overlook and make one last attempt to retrieve the drone. Nothing he tried seemed to reverse the drone this time.

A Range Rover rushed up next to him. Kim couldn't see the driver.

The driver must have said something to Stuart to persuade him to give up his effort to retrieve the drone. He jumped into the Range Rover and the SUV sped away.

The third gunman, the one in the clearing alongside the gorge, cursed furiously. Outraged, he turned his attention to the big man still heading down into the gorge from the other side, possibly trying to intercept the drone before it crashed.

The two dead gunmen must have been working with this third gunman.

Why did they want Stuart dead?

The third gunman peered into the gorge until he located the big man. He aimed and fired. Twice.

What a fool. Not even Reacher could kill with a handgun from that distance and trajectory. And Reacher had won medals against the best shots in the world.

He'd never hit the guy from that angle. Unless he got incredibly lucky.

Kim called out. "Police! Hold your fire!"

The gunman turned toward her and fired off a shot in her direction. But the bullet went wide. Too wide to take the shooter seriously.

Kim called out again. He ignored her and shot again.

This time, she fired back.

Kim's bullet caught him in the belly.

The force of her shot was enough to knock him off stride.

Amid the brushy undergrowth, he was closer to the edge than he'd realized.

He lost his footing and struggled to stay upright.

Kim ran forward to help, but he was too far away.

He glanced over his shoulder as he ran.

His arms flailed like a windmill as he swayed and tried to avoid falling.

A moment later, he lost the battle.

He went over the edge of the gorge, one long, earsplitting scream pierced the air on his way down.

The screaming stopped long before he hit the bottom.

CHAPTER 44

Saturday, June 4
Devil's Punchbowl, Ontario, CA

KIM RAN TOWARD THE edge of the gorge and looked down. She didn't suffer from vertigo. But the steepness and depth of the gorge made her woozy.

The big man running down the other side had made it all the way to the bottom. He was running south along the creek bed, still chasing the erratic drone as it dipped and soared and dipped again.

She cocked her head to watch as he moved farther away along the creek bed. The wind current seemed to hold the drone just out of his reach. He seemed determined to catch the drone at his first available opportunity.

Kim tried to put the pieces of this bizarre puzzle together. Who were the three gunmen? Why were they trying to kill Liam Stuart? What was really going on here?

She shook her head. None of it made sense to her yet. Too many missing pieces.

The third gunman's body lay crumpled at the base of the gorge near where he'd fallen, face up. Kim used the zoom feature on her phone's camera to take a few snaps of the man's mangled body.

Gaspar might be able to do something with the photos. If she got lucky.

She snapped a few more shots of the gorge, just to get a better look when she zoomed into the images.

The first gunman had landed in the pool of icy snow melt at the bottom of the larger waterfall.

The water came in from the top of the gorge and fell more than a hundred feet into the icy pool below.

Kim imagined a pile of bodies at the bottom of that pool. Briefly she wondered about the tales those silent witnesses could tell. Suicides, homicides, vertigo-caused accidental deaths.

Gaspar probably knew how many had been found there over the years. She made a mental note to ask him.

The wind gusts had picked up again and so had the cold rain. She shook off her macabre imaginings and stretched her neck northward looking for the second gunman.

She couldn't see him from her location. His body might have snagged on the way down the gorge or something.

Nothing she could do for any of them except call a rescue service to haul the bodies out and notify next of kin.

She switched her phone from camera mode and called Russell first. He didn't pick up after several rings.

"Where are you?" she asked, as if he had answered her call.

"Great. Now what?" Kim considered running all the way back to the cabin to search for him.

She heard three short blasts of a car horn from the overlook above.

Liam Stuart had sped away in the gray Range Rover, so he wasn't trying to signal anyone now. Who else was up there?

The car horn sounded three longer blasts, followed by three short beeps again.

Unmistakable.

SOS.

Someone up there was in trouble.

Kim dropped the phone into her pocket, holstered her weapon, and ran through the pelting rain and gusting wind up the sloped hill toward the overlook.

When she reached the top, she saw a luxury sedan shot up by bullets. Russell had the driver's door open and was attempting to render aid.

Kim trotted closer toward the scene. When she was close enough she could see a woman slumped over the steering wheel. Unconscious. Bleeding.

Michelle Chang.

Russell was pressing each of Chang's neck and shoulder wounds with his hands in an effort to stop the bleeding. The blood still pumped, which meant her heart was still functioning.

"Otto, call an ambulance," he said when she hustled close enough to hear him.

She grabbed her phone and made the call, relayed the relevant facts succinctly, and disconnected without giving any names. "The dispatcher says they're on the way. Ten minutes out."

Russell shook his head. "Hope she can hang on that long."

"Me, too," Kim said quietly.

"A stunning woman drove up and swooped Liam Stuart out of here," Russell said. Probably reporting to pass the time as much as to pass information. "Range Rover. New York State Department plate."

Kim widened her eyes. "Same as those two guys who ambushed us? The two we left in the trunk of that sedan?"

"And maybe those three shooters lying at the bottom of the gorge, too," Russell said, nodding. "You get any photos?"

Kim shook her head. "No chance. But they'll be identified when the bodies are located."

Russell nodded again. "Will they find any bullets from your weapon when they do the autopsies?"

"Self-defense. He shot at me first," Kim replied quietly.

"How are you planning to prove that?" Russell asked.

After a moment, she said, "I'll leave that issue to Cooper."

The ambulance siren sounded in the distance, coming closer.

"Good. It's long past time to put Cooper in the picture. But we also need to go," Russell said. "Our SUV's over there. I can't remove the pressure I'm applying to Chang's wounds until the ambulance gets here. But let's be ready to move. They won't need us. We don't know anything about Chang's medical history, anyway."

"If they don't see us, they won't know we were here?" Kim offered a wry smile.

"Something like that," Russell replied.

"We could be back in the US before they figure out who we are. It'll take them a while to identify everybody," Kim said, warming to the realities. "They might never find the gun that put a bullet in that third gunman, data bases being what they are."

"Exactly," Russell nodded.

"Okay. I have to check something. You wait here for the ambulance. I'll come back to pick you up," Kim said, heading toward the SUV.

"Where are you going?" Russell called to her. When she didn't reply, he yelled, "Don't be late."

Kim was already seated behind the wheel of the SUV. She pulled the seat up and didn't bother to adjust the mirrors.

She turned the SUV around and pointed the nose toward the cabin. She'd seen a side road on the navigation system earlier. It led to the base of the gorge, where the creek ran out into the woods and eventually ended at the Niagara River.

Hikers could enter the Devil's Punchbowl from there.

The big man had probably ended up there. She might even catch him along the access road.

On some level, she knew hers was a fool's errand. But Chang had been the driver behind the wheel of that sedan. So where was Reacher?

He had to be the guy who jumped out of Chang's vehicle and scrabbled down into the gorge. Didn't he?

Who else could it have been? Everyone else working with Chang on this drone situation was already dead.

Which meant Reacher could be down there along the creek bed now.

She could find him. Finally.

CHAPTER 45

Saturday, June 4
Devil's Punchbowl, Ontario, CA

KIM DROVE ALONG THE dirt road until she found the turnoff to the lower gorge trail. She pulled the SUV into the unpaved parking lot and shut down the engine.

She heard the sound of running water from the creek bed. Following the sounds and the signs, she found the trailhead.

The ground sloped gently upward along the creek bed. Kim hiked over the rocky path, slipping on the wet stones occasionally. She watched for evidence that the area had been disturbed recently, just in case the big man had already passed through.

He might have reached this point and moved on to help Chang.

He was big and his stride was much longer than hers. But he'd have had to cover a lot of ground a lot faster than Kim thought likely.

She kept walking up the trail, alongside the creek. She passed the places where old moonshiners sold their wares from hastily built moonshine stands, because the trail was not very accessible to the sheriffs back then.

When she turned a corner, she heard the ambulance siren in the distance, coming closer. She couldn't leave Russell out there while she chased a ghost.

But she knew Reacher was here. Somewhere. She felt it in her gut. The one reliable instinct that never let her down.

Reacher was here. Or he had been here, anyway.

Kim made it to the open gorge and scanned the area from top to bottom and along all sides. The drone was no longer dancing in the wind. Reacher, if he'd been the guy chasing the drone, wasn't there now.

The sound of the ambulance siren traveled across the open air of the gorge. It was very close now. But for the trees blocking her view where she stood by the creek bed, she might have seen the ambulance arriving at the overlook.

Indecision stalled her progress. She was close to Reacher. Perhaps closer than she'd ever been. She might find him here if she kept looking.

Which would mean failing Russell. Could she do that?

Russell had come to extract her and the dead Lucas Stuart when she'd needed him back in Detroit. He'd been a reliable partner throughout this thing, sticking with her through thick and thin, even though he wasn't required to do so. Finding Reacher was not his assignment, after all.

No, she couldn't possibly leave Russell to face the consequences alone.

She kept hiking along the creek a few more yards. But when the ambulance siren stopped, indicating it had reached its destination, she knew she'd run out of time.

Kim paused and swiveled her head in all directions, rotating her entire body three-hundred-sixty degrees. She peered deep into the woods and listened intently. She inhaled the scents of rain and old leaves and maybe a rank animal or two.

But she didn't see the big man. Or anyone else. Or the drone, for that matter.

"Kim. You've got to go. Now. Russell is depending on you." She scolded herself as she searched a few minutes more. Finally, she turned and ran back to the SUV.

She kept scanning the area around the trail as she ran. When she reached the parking lot, she noticed a set of fresh tire tracks.

Another vehicle had been parked here.

When?

Had the tracks been there when she arrived?

Or had the vehicle come and gone while she was searching?

Where was it now?

She jumped into the SUV and hurried back to the overlook.

She spied the big luxury sedan with the bullet holes in the doors and the destroyed windows.

Chang had been lucky. A few centimeters one way or another with those bullets might have made all the difference.

The ambulance had arrived. Four paramedics on scene. Two were loading Chang onto a back board and then to a gurney.

Russell was standing near the driveway. Kim pulled up alongside of him. He took the passenger seat and slammed the door after himself.

"Let's go," he said.

"Copy that," Kim replied as she pressed the accelerator and headed away from the Devil's Punchbowl.

After a while, Russell said, "Did you find Reacher?"

Kim shook her head. "Not this time."

She didn't mention the second vehicle. No reason to bring it up with Russell.

"You think he ran down into that gorge. Seems like a crazy thing to do, even for him," Russell said.

"It does." She nodded. "But when he ran down, the drone was headed down into the gorge. He might have been concerned that the drone would be destroyed."

"Since he didn't like the damned thing in the first place, why would he care about it being destroyed?"

Kim shrugged. "I don't know. Maybe the drone is traceable. Maybe he thinks someone can reverse engineer it to make another one unless he destroyed it personally. Maybe he wanted a toy for his kids. How the hell should I know?"

She reached for her phone and found the photos she'd taken of the third gunman. The one who had her bullet in his back. She passed the photo over to Russell.

"That's the one who tried to kill me," she said. "Do you recognize him?"

Russell looked carefully at the images. To be fair, the man's body was mangled and pretty far away from the camera. But Russell seemed totally engrossed in the images.

"So you do recognize him." Kim said flatly.

"It's hard to be certain. He looks really beat up. The guy I'm thinking of isn't a field agent. Can't imagine why he'd be out here," Russell handed the phone back. "They say we all have a doppelganger or two in the world. Maybe the dead dude isn't the guy."

Kim nodded. "Okay. So who do you think it is?"

Russell shook his head. "I'd rather not say until I'm sure."

"Why?"

"Because this situation is bad enough already. And if I'm right, we're in a lot more trouble," Russell said quietly.

"What kind of trouble?"

"The kind even Cooper can't get us out of."

"I can't even imagine what kind of trouble that might be," Kim deadpanned.

Russell frowned but said nothing more.

CHAPTER 46

Saturday, June 4
Ontario, CA

AFTER A WHILE, KIM asked, "What do you think is going on with that drone? Why does Reacher care about how they plan to use it?"

"Who knows," Russell shrugged. "There's the rest of us, and then there's Reacher. He makes his own rules."

Kim nodded. Russell was right.

But Reacher wasn't against weapons or killing or war. Why did this one weapon matter to him?

She added this to her very long list of unanswered Reacher questions.

After a while, Kim pulled into a gas station and filled up the SUV while Russell made a coffee run. They were back on the road in short order.

Several things were bothering her, now that she'd started composing her internal report. The one she'd upload to her secure server as soon as she had the chance.

Paying her insurance premium, she called it. Contemporaneous reports could save her ass when the hunt for Reacher went even further south than it already had.

This was normally the point in a case where she'd hash things out with Gaspar. If she'd been alone in the SUV, she'd have called him now.

But she didn't have the same level of rapport with Russell. His ass wasn't on the line like hers was. His depth of knowledge on Reacher was shallow.

What could he add that she didn't already know?

And Russell was Secret Service. His job was to protect Finlay. Which meant he'd be duty bound to read Finlay into the case and Kim wasn't ready for that.

She couldn't ask Russell to keep Finlay in the dark, but she hoped he would.

Her instinct was to play the situation much closer than Russell would agree to do. Which meant she should bring Cooper up to speed and she'd be smart to do it before Russell briefed Finlay.

But what would she say, exactly?

An unidentified dead man had been dropped at her front door, so she went looking for his identity and the man who killed him.

Cooper would want a full report. He'd ask whether she'd found the killer.

She could say yes in good conscience. The skinny dude from the Niagara Falls hotel had killed Lucas Stuart. She felt confident of that, even if she couldn't prove it.

None of the events she discovered during the rest of the case was, strictly speaking, relevant.

But she should report the Reacher connection for self-preservation reasons. Cooper would find out anyway. And when he did, he'd have her head.

Russell and Kim rode a few dozen miles in silence until he finally asked, "Where are we going?"

"Where this whole mess started. Back to my place," she said cheekily.

Russell scowled and said no more.

Kim used her phone to send images to Gaspar. Photos of the drone as well as the gunman she'd shot in the back. Maybe Gaspar could do something with them.

She also sent an encrypted text asking Gaspar to find the Range Rover with the US State Department plates. He could hack into traffic cams and find it, surely.

Finally, she asked him for more thorough research on Liam Stuart. Whatever Stuart was involved in with the US State Department, Reacher didn't like it.

Which meant Kim needed to know what it was.

She'd missed Reacher again. But she felt closer to finding him now than she'd been before.

And she had acquired enough intel to suggest a way forward. All of which was progress. Of a sort.

That's what she'd say in her official report, anyway.

The drive to Port Huron, across the Blue Water Bridge, and back to Detroit consumed a few hours. When they'd stopped for gas, they'd switched drivers.

Russell dropped her off in front of her apartment building.

She climbed out and collected her bags from the back. Before she left, she said, "See you when I see you."

"Same." He nodded and replied, "I'll take care of the SUV."

"Okay." She didn't ask him what he planned to do with it.

Given the amount of trace evidence all over the damned thing, she assumed Russell would destroy the vehicle.

Don't ask, don't tell, was as good a motto for these situations as any.

CHAPTER 47

Sunday, June 5
Detroit, Michigan

BY THE TIME SHE trudged up to her apartment, took a long hot shower and wolfed down a frozen burrito, she was too tired to care.

She was also too wired to sleep well. She tossed and turned for half an hour and then gave up the effort.

Kim padded into the kitchen to pour a glass of wine, planning to work on her report for a while before sleep. As she recorked the bottle of Brunello, she heard a muffled noise at her front entrance. Something like a light knock, which should never happen under any circumstances.

Her apartment building was one of the most secure in Detroit. There was an armed security guard at the front entrance. CCTV cameras everywhere. Elevator access to her floor required a key.

In short, there should be no one outside her apartment unless she'd granted permission in advance. Theoretically, anyway.

A foreboding sense of déjà vu overwhelmed her.

She sipped the wine and waited for follow up sounds. Shuffling feet or even a hard fist pounding on the door.

She heard nothing like that at all.

Kim checked the CCTV, knowing she'd find nothing there, either. "Just like the last time," she mumbled. When Lucas Stuart had died on her threshold.

It was late. But Gaspar wouldn't be sleeping. He rarely slept more than a couple of hours at once. He'd told her to call any time, but she tried not to abuse the privilege.

Surely she could open the door to her own apartment without a lifeline tethering her to Gaspar. What the hell could he do from Miami anyway?

She inhaled deeply to stiffen her spine, set the wine glass on the table, and strode to the door. She retrieved her gun from the entry table and leaned forward to peer through the peep hole.

No one was standing within viewing range.

Kim glanced down to see a sealed envelope had been slipped under the door. Not the usual padded manila envelopes she received from Cooper at the start of a new Reacher project.

This envelope was four by six, heavy stock, cream colored. The flap was sealed with a self-sticking gold circle.

It had not been delivered by the postal service. It contained only her name printed on the front. No address, no return address, no postage.

She pulled a pair of surgical gloves from the entry table and gloved up before she retrieved the envelope.

Kim returned the gun and carried the envelope to the kitchen.

Before she opened it, she took several snaps with her phone and sent them to her secure server. She used a kitchen knife to slit the flap of the envelope and pulled out a postcard.

On one side were several images of the Tunnel at the Niagara Parks Power Station. The brief printed description said: "Travel deep below this restored power station and explore the 2200-foot-long tailrace *tunnel* built more than a century ago leading to a never-before-seen view of *Niagara Falls*."

The suggestion made Kim shiver. "No thanks. Been there. Seen all I need to see for a while."

She picked up her wine glass with a shaky hand to sip the warm, red liquid courage. As the wine's warmth settled into her body, she flipped the postcard over.

Taped to the back of the postcard was the unmistakable image of Liam Stuart's drone.

The photo must have been taken at the bottom of the Devil's Punchbowl. Kim recognized the creek bed and the walking trail beside it.

Below the photo was a hand-printed note.

Tonight. 8:51 p.m.

And the words "Come Alone. R."

Kim took a bigger sip of the wine and flipped the postcard over to take a closer look at the professional images of the tunnel again. A red circle had been drawn around the center image. She held the card under a brighter light.

The tunnel photos refreshed the nightmare of Westwood's death.

These professional photos were taken during daylight. They were meant to be enticing to tourists.

Her nighttime experiences on that very spot were hellish. She had no desire to repeat them.

But this message came from someone who'd been there and knew she'd been there, too.

Reacher. He'd contacted her directly. He wanted her to come.

With a grimace of regret, she poured the Brunello down the sink and rinsed her glass.

Only one choice. Kim had to go back.

First, she called Gaspar.

CHAPTER 48

Sunday, June 5
Detroit, Michigan

KIM TRAVELED LIGHT THIS time. No bags. No laptop. A new gun. One she'd never used before and could not be traced back to her.

No passport. No credit cards. Only Canadian money in her pockets.

She expected to be gone for a few hours.

She'd meet with Reacher. Discover what he wanted. Come home.

That's as far as she was prepared to go for now. A simple plan.

"I don't like this, Suzy Wong," Gaspar had said, just as she'd expected.

"I have to go. I can't refuse. I've been hunting Reacher for more than seven months. He wants to talk. I'm going," she declared, brooking no argument. "Will you help me get there and back or not?"

"What did Cooper say?"

"You know I didn't tell him. And I'm not going to tell him. Not until I know what's going on," Kim replied.

"Wait a couple of days. Flint is out of the country. When he comes back, he'll go with you. Be your wing man."

"No."

"Then let me come along. I'm not helpless, you know."

"No."

The discussion had continued like that for a while, but in the end, Gaspar gave in. He had arranged transportation in exchange for her promise that he could notify Russell if this thing went south.

She refused to concede more.

The ride from the helipad atop her apartment building in Detroit to the casino helipad in Niagara Falls was faster and much more nerve-racking than driving again. They'd traveled the faster route across the lake and through Canada.

The helo would pick her up in Niagara Falls when she was finished and fly her home.

Kim had had plenty of time to work things out during the flight, which kept her mind off her queasy gut and her brain from running through the thousands of things that could go wrong.

When the helo landed, she removed her headset, opened the door, and stepped down onto the concrete helipad.

She gave her pilot a single thumbs-up, stooped below the rotor wash, and hoofed it to the casino's exit.

Kim took the elevator down fifty-three flights and exited on the street side of the casino resort. The sun was already low in the sky. No time to waste.

Reacher had scheduled the meeting shortly after sunset. Presumably because the popular tourist spot would be less crowded, Kim assumed.

She had dozens of concerns, yet she was strangely calm about them. Foolishly, Gaspar claimed, she believed she would be perfectly safe meeting Reacher in a public place.

If Reacher had wanted to harm her, he'd have chosen a more secluded location, surely.

But what did he want?

Reacher and Cooper knew each other. He could have called Cooper directly if he'd wanted to volunteer for the classified assignment Cooper was considering him for.

The suggestion brought a smile to her face. Reacher was army, through and through. He'd never volunteer for anything.

Kim turned left at the exit, striding casually toward the tunnel's entrance.

Foot traffic was light along the sidewalks at dusk. The fireworks would start a couple of hours later. Tourists were having dinner or napping or whatever tourists did between the sights they planned to see.

At the corner, the traffic light stopped Kim amid a group of kids corralled by a teacher and a couple of moms. All were engaged with each other and speaking a mix of French and English like a mischief of magpies.

When the light turned green, the tribe of magpies moved as one, like a flock, cackling and shouting, excited to be there.

The magpies moved into the roadway just as a flashy yellow convertible took the closest corner on two wheels and sped toward the intersection.

The bouncing, laughing, skipping children filled the street between the sidewalks.

Perhaps because she was not much taller than the children themselves, Kim saw the yellow car before the teacher or the moms.

The convertible noticed the group too late.

The driver stomped hard on the brakes and the convertible went into a long skid like a slow-motion film.

Horrified pedestrians began to shout as Kim darted into the intersection, arms wide, moving the kids toward each other and away from the careening vehicle.

A split second later, the teacher and the moms realized the danger and joined in Kim's efforts to move the kids to safety.

They were screaming and crying and creating earsplitting noises so overwhelming that no chaperones could possibly think clearly.

At the last possible minute, the convertible's driver turned the steering wheel away from the group.

The driver screamed as the car's tires hit the median with a glancing blow that flipped the car over like a child's toy.

The convertible landed on its top, the open space where the roof should have been.

The driver had not been wearing a seat belt.

When the car flipped, she was thrown from the driver's seat onto the pavement. The jaunty yellow convertible landed on top of her.

Only one glance was required to know the driver had not survived.

Almost instantly, pedestrians pulled out their phones and began taking video and photos. Several rushed up to Kim to thank her for her quick action.

Kim tried to shield her face from view. She brushed off the grateful survivors and hurried along to a side street where she found a quiet alcove to catch her breath.

She glanced back to the scene. The intersection was now filled with first responders, kids, teachers, pedestrians, and gawkers. Several sirens were approaching from afar.

Because of the crash and its aftermath, the casino's entrance was thoroughly blocked. She sent a quick text to the helo pilot to change their departure location.

Kim wouldn't be able to return to the casino for a good long while after she met with Reacher. Assuming the incident didn't prevent him from showing up at all.

Kim checked her watch. She was already late.

She straightened her clothes and hurried along the alley to the next street, seeking an unobstructed path to the meetup location.

Sensing she was being followed, she glanced back several times. She didn't see anyone. "Fatigue is making you paranoid, Otto," she murmured under her breath.

Kim finally spotted a sign pointing the way to the tunnel and trotted quickly in the right direction.

Too late.

When she arrived at the building, the front entrance was already closed.

The attraction had closed five minutes ago. But surely there were still tourists inside. They had to come out somewhere.

She'd familiarized herself with the building using their promotional materials online while she was enroute. She scanned for an open entrance.

The three main doors were solidly secure. But Kim finally found a side exit and waited around until a group of four came out.

She ran up to grab the door and slipped inside.

Reacher's meeting spot was on the lower level near the falls viewing area. He'd circled the location on the postcard.

She'd examined it so many times she would recognize the exact bench even in total darkness.

People were now leaving the exhibit in droves. Kim pushed her way against the crowd like a salmon heading to spawn upstream.

Wet and shivering tourists had been drenched by the falls. Their yellow slickers dripped water onto the concrete floors, making them dangerous to cross.

Kim finally made her way to the curved entrance to the tunnel. She imagined she could see the circle around the specific location Reacher had chosen for their meeting.

From twenty feet away, she caught brief glimpses of the bench in the gaps between tourists.

The unoccupied bench.

Reacher was not there. Her shoulders slumped.

But Kim couldn't give up.

She wasn't that late.

Twenty minutes, tops.

He might still be in the area.

Watching for her.

Surely he had that much patience. He'd been an expert sniper once. Those guys were required to wait and watch, sometimes for very long periods.

Sure, Reacher could definitely wait.

But would he have waited for her?

Kim made her way through the throng to the concrete bench. She climbed up on the cold slab and peered over the heads of the crowd, looking for a giant.

One she would recognize with nothing more than a brief glimpse.

She scanned the open area, peering in every direction. She spotted a couple of big men and a few tall men.

No Reacher.

The interior lights were flashing to indicate the exhibit was closed.

Announcements were made.

Two security guards approached five minutes apart and asked Kim to leave.

Still, she waited.

Even as she knew, somehow, that Reacher wasn't there.

Finally, when the exiting crowd had thinned to a trickle, another security guard came by gesturing toward the exits.

"Ma'am, we're closed. We need you to leave now. We'll reopen tomorrow."

"Yeah, okay,"

Kim climbed down off the bench, prepared to give up, even as she kept scanning the cavernous room.

Distracted, she made one last turn, murmured, "Time to give up. Just for now."

Her foot slipped on a puddle on the concrete floor. She lost her balance and went down hard, both palms flat and holding her torso off the grimy wet surface.

Which was when she glanced under the bench.

A sturdy brown cardboard box was stuffed into the corner.

She reached to pull it out into the open where she could lift it onto the bench.

The box was sealed with clear packing tape.

On the tape, written with a black felt tip pen, was block printing she recognized. She'd seen it on Reacher's postcard.

Four words.

For Your Eyes Only.

The security guards had moved on. There was no one else in the room at the moment.

Kim lifted the box and strode to the closest exit, hurrying outside and away from prying spies.

She found a low, sturdy retaining wall with a flat top. She set the box down and pulled it open.

Inside was a damaged matte silver drone.

One she'd seen before.

Flying over the Devil's Punchbowl.

Kim grinned as she resealed the box and carried it away toward the waiting helo.

"Nicely played, Reacher."

CHAPTER 49

Monday, June 6
Detroit, Michigan

HOLDING A MUG OF steaming hot coffee, Kim sat staring at the distressed cardboard box occupying her tabletop. She listened with half an ear to the television news that played in the background. The main story was, once again, the island nation, Quan.

Quan's ambassador to Canada had collapsed suddenly at the parade in Ottawa late on Sunday afternoon and died a few hours later. Deputy Secretary of State Derrick Braxton's controversial trip abroad to the island country of Quan was interrupted to allow him to extend deepest condolences to the ambassador's brother, the Emperor of Quan.

The deceased brother had been first in line to the throne. Now, the line of succession was snarled beyond simple explanation.

Braxton's diplomatic mission to Quan had been pushing aside more interesting news for more than a week. The country was always in a state of distress, often on the verge of war. And especially so now.

Kim and quite a few news pundits and world leaders speculated endlessly again. Why had Braxton made the trip to Quan?

The entire diplomatic mission had raised tensions in the region to the breaking point. The death of Quan's only royal heir fanned the flames.

Many feared open rebellion or a peremptory coup fueled by anti-democracy influences.

The story went to commercial break without supplying answers to even the most serious of questions. Kim tuned out the sales pitch for laundry soap and returned her full attention to the cardboard box.

Before she moved it into the helo in Niagara Falls and several times since, she'd searched the box thoroughly. She'd confirmed that the only thing inside was the drone.

No weapons. No tracking devices. No thumb drives or keys or postcards from Reacher or anything else.

No remote-control devices, either.

Which meant she couldn't operate the drone, even if she wanted to.

Before turning the problem over to Gaspar, she had scoured the internet for news of Liam Stuart. Or the drone. Or Reacher.

She found nothing.

Which was odd. But not the only odd thing.

Kim had been looking over her shoulder both literally and electronically for months, wary of Cooper and Finlay and Reacher. They'd been keeping constant surveillance on her activities, one way or another, each for their own suspicious reasons.

Yet, she'd heard nothing from Cooper since Lucas Stuart fell dead on her doorstep.

Finlay had stepped aside shortly after she'd called him about the dead man.

And Reacher. He'd involved her in the case, lured her to Niagara Falls to collect the drone, and ghosted her once she found it.

"Now what?" Kim said aloud, sipping the scalding hot coffee, watching the box as if a snake might slither out.

Didn't happen.

Gaspar called on a fresh encrypted burner. Again, she flipped on the sophisticated anti-surveillance devices she'd installed to block surveillance inside her home and picked up. "What's happening?"

"Too much."

"Such as?"

"A US State Department operative was found murdered inside an abandoned hunting cabin near Devil's Punchbowl in Ontario early this morning. Female. Audrey Ruston," Gaspar said. "She must have been quite a looker. Even her corpse was attractive."

"Who killed her?"

"Who knows?" Gaspar added dryly, "The list of enemies one acquires in her line of work must be endless."

"How?"

"Neck snapped. Probably just one quick twist. Pretty neck, too."

Kim frowned, even though Gaspar couldn't see her. "State Department? Are you sure?"

"Yep. Just like those two guys who ambushed you in the vineyard. And three more were retrieved at the Punchbowl," Gaspar replied. "One of the punchbowl guys was Nigel Morin. Right hand man to none other than Assistant Secretary of State Derrick Braxton."

"Wow," Kim said slowly.

"One wonders how they'll manage to field a team, given the number of hands they lost on this operation. State usually runs a bit thinner than the CIA or the other three-letter agencies," Gaspar said as if he were preoccupied by something else.

"Any news on Liam Stuart?"

"Not yet. Still searching."

"He's probably been whisked out of the country by now," Kim mused.

"Or maybe buried somewhere like the others. He'll turn up. Eventually."

Kim moved to the kitchen to refill her coffee and make toast. She'd forgotten to eat for way too long. "Any news on Reacher?"

Gaspar snorted. "Yep. Found the Abominable Snowman. Nessie, too. Amelia Earhart. Jimmy Hoffa. Found them all."

"Ha ha ha," Kim deadpanned. "You're hysterical, you know that?"

"Oh, and D.B. Cooper. We're having a party. Everyone's coming around for cocktails at seven. Wanna join?"

"So we have no idea where Reacher is. Again," Kim said sourly, buttering the toast and refilling her coffee.

"Sarcasm doesn't become you, Sunshine," Gaspar replied.

"What about the drone?" Kim said, taking her toast and coffee back to her seat where she could stare at the box while he talked.

"Nothing you don't already know. Liam Stuart and Ira Krause were engaged in their own little arms race to build the drone of their dreams. Krause is definitely dead. And Liam Stuart probably is, too. And you have the busted prototype. Case closed, I'd say. Wouldn't you?"

Kim swallowed the toast with a swig of coffee so hot it scalded her tongue. Just the way she liked it. "And I keep meaning to ask about Michelle Chang?"

"She was taken to a hospital in Hamilton," Gaspar said, warming to his subject. "I hacked into the CCTV at the hospital. She was banged up, but not critical. Admitted, treated, and released."

"Huh."

"You haven't heard the best part," Gaspar said. "They rolled her to the exit in a wheelchair where she was picked up after a few minutes wait. A fair-haired man driving an old Lincoln Town Car was behind the wheel."

Kim nearly choked on her toast. "Reacher?"

"Possibly."

"Where's the Town Car now?"

"Great question."

Kim sighed. Gaspar wasn't being deliberately obtuse. Her questions, and many more simply had no available answers. Not now. Maybe not ever.

"What should we do with the drone? It can be reverse engineered if it falls into the wrong hands," Kim said. "We need a secure place to store it. At least until I find Reacher or figure out why he gave it to me."

"Or find another use for it."

"Right," she nodded. "I can't just stuff it under the bed. The box is too big, for one thing."

"Turn it over to Cooper. He'll demand it as soon as he finds out anyway. You could win some points if you offer it up first." Gaspar suggested a final option before he disconnected. "Do some good for your career for a change."

Kim had considered and rejected his suggestion already.

If Reacher wanted Cooper to have the drone, he'd have given it to him. He didn't. 'Nuff said.

Her gut said Reacher's desire to keep the drone from Cooper while entrusting it to her was important.

Although she didn't know precisely why.

Which was one more reason to keep the drone hidden for as long as possible. But where could she hide it?

Somewhere close to enable her to retrieve it easily.

A place where Cooper and Finlay's prying eyes couldn't or wouldn't see.

Where security and surveillance technology didn't routinely penetrate.

Which meant not a bank vault, or a locker at the bus station, or the long-term parking lot at the airport, or buried at a landfill.

Ruling out the usual hiding places, one by one, left her with few options.

Where could she hide the drone?

CHAPTER 50

Monday, June 6
Detroit, Michigan

GASPAR'S QUIP ABOUT FINDING Jimmy Hoffa had given her the answer.

Kim emptied a plastic storage bin and put the drone inside. She stashed the empty cardboard box in the bottom of her closet. She covered the box with some old clothes she planned to donate to charity.

The box was an early warning device of sorts. If a thief attempted to steal the box, she'd know they were actively searching for the drone.

After sunset but before full dark, with the drone inside the plastic bin resting in the trunk of her neighbor's sedan, Kim drove away from downtown Detroit. She was not followed.

About twenty minutes later, she turned into the place that was a magnificent monument to more than a century of Detroit history.

Since the late 1800s, Mt. Olivet Cemetery had been the final resting place for the famous and infamous, including reputed

Mafia bosses, prohibition bootleggers, and Titanic survivors. The cemetery covered more than three hundred acres of manicured lawns, colorful gardens, and valuable statuary.

Dozens of private family mausoleums were scattered about the property. The one Kim sought was near the northeast corner of the grounds and housed the crypt reserved for the family of one of her closest childhood friends.

No one had died in the family for at least two decades, but the grandmother's estate paid for perpetual care, so the place didn't seem abandoned.

Kim parked near the granite mausoleum and carried the plastic container to the entrance. Unlike the cemetery grounds surrounding it, the old building itself had received little attention over the years. It looked old and weathered and boring. Perfect.

After a brief struggle, the key Kim had retrieved from her bedroom gun safe slipped into the lock.

Using all of her body weight, she pushed the heavy wood door inward and then moved the drone inside. The crypts were contained in a vault below ground.

Kim carried the drone in its plastic bin down the musty cold granite steps into the vault.

The empty crypt she'd chosen was on the bottom row in the back. The area was secluded and dark. Even with a flashlight, it would be difficult to see.

Kim wacked away the rust on the hinges with her shoe and opened the door.

She slid the drone inside and shoved the door closed again.

Kim stood back to inspect her work. Satisfied that no one would notice the crypt had been opened and closed again, she left the vault and locked up outside.

Back home once more, writing her reports with a large glass of Brunello beside her on the kitchen table, Kim ran through the entire operation again. She uploaded her report to her secure server and then stashed the key to the mausoleum in her gun safe.

As she headed off to bed, she was well aware that there were lose ends and open questions. But she'd settled on a sanitized version of events to report to Cooper that should prevent his head from exploding.

Which was the best she could do.

Until she found Reacher.

The other big news is Diane Capri—a friend of mine—wrote a book revisiting the events of KILLING FLOOR in Margrave, Georgia. She imagines an FBI team tasked to trace Reacher's current-day whereabouts. They begin by interviewing people who knew him—starting out with Roscoe and Finlay. Check out this review: "Oh heck yes! I am in love with this book. I'm a huge Jack Reacher fan. If you don't know Jack (pun intended!) then get thee to the bookstore/wherever you buy your fix and pick up one of the many Jack Reacher books by Lee Child. Heck, pick up all of them. In particular, read Killing Floor. Then come back and read Don't Know Jack. This story picks up the other from the point of view of Kim and Gaspar, FBI agents assigned to build a file on Jack Reacher. The problem is, as anyone who knows Reacher can attest, he lives completely off the grid. No cell phone, no house, no car…he's not tied down. A pretty daunting task, then, wouldn't you say?

First lines: "Just the facts. And not many of them, either. Jack Reacher's file was too stale and too thin to be credible. No human could be as invisible as Reacher appeared to be, whether he was currently above the ground or under it. Either the file had been sanitized, or Reacher was the most off-the-grid paranoid Kim Otto had ever heard of." Right away, I'm sensing who Kim Otto is and I'm delighted that I know something she doesn't. You see, I DO know Jack. And I know he's not paranoid. Not really. I know why he lives as he does, and I know what kind of man he is. I loved having that over Kim and Gaspar. If you haven't read any Reacher novels, then this will feel like a good, solid story in its own right. If you have…oh if you have, then you, too, will feel like you have a one-up on the FBI. It's a fun feeling!

"Kim and Gaspar are sent to Margrave by a mysterious boss who reminds me of Charlie, in Charlie's Angels. You never see him…you hear him. He never gives them all the facts. So they are left with a big pile of nothing. They end up embroiled in a murder case that seems connected to Reacher somehow, but they can't see how. Suffice to say the efforts to find the murderer and Reacher, and not lose their own heads in the process, makes for an entertaining read.

"I love the way the author handled the entire story. The pacing is dead on (okay another pun intended), the story is full of twists and turns like a Reacher novel would be, but it's another viewpoint of a Reacher story. It's an outside-in approach to Reacher.

"You might be asking, do they find him? Do they finally meet the infamous Jack Reacher?

"Go…read…now…find out!"

Sounds great, right? Check out "Don't Know Jack," and let me know what you think.

So that's it for now…again, thanks for reading THE AFFAIR, and I hope you'll like A WANTED MAN just as much in September.

Lee Child

ABOUT THE AUTHOR

Diane Capri is an award-winning *New York Times, USA Today,* and worldwide bestselling author. She's a recovering lawyer and snowbird who divides her time between Florida and Michigan. An active member of Mystery Writers of America, Author's Guild, International Thriller Writers, Alliance of Independent Authors, Novelists, Inc., and Sisters in Crime, she loves to hear from readers. She is hard at work on her next novel.

Please connect with her online:
http://www.DianeCapri.com
Twitter: http://twitter.com/@DianeCapri
Facebook: http://www.facebook.com/Diane.Capri1
http://www.facebook.com/DianeCapriBooks